✗ "B"

D1487602

JUL 1 8 2000

∿

Dead Man's Bay

Also by Darryl Wimberley

A Rock and a Hard Place

Dead Man's Bay

DARRYL WIMBERLEY

Thomas Dunne Books
St. Martin's Minotaur
New York

THOMAS DUNNE BOOKS.
An imprint of St. Martin's Press.

DEAD MAN'S BAY. Copyright © 2000 by Darryl Wimberley.
All rights reserved. Printed in the United States of
America. No part of this book may be used or
reproduced in any manner whatsoever without written
permission except in the case of brief quotations
embodied in critical articles or reviews. For information,
address St. Martin's Press, 175 Fifth Avenue, New York,
N.Y. 10010.

www.minotaurbooks.com

Library of Congress Cataloging-in-Publication Data

Wimberley, Darryl.
    Dead Man's Bay / Darryl Wimberley.—1st ed.
        p. cm.
    ISBN 0-312-25218-8
    1. Afro-American police—Fiction. I. Title.

PS3573.I47844 D43 2000
813'.54—dc21

                                                00-025729

First Edition: July 2000

10   9   8   7   6   5   4   3   2   1

Acknowledgements

I especially enjoy thanking the many folks who work hard to bring my books to press. Thanks go first to Ruth Cavin, a gracious and unflagging editor. Her assistant, Julie Sullivan, has been equally generous. Add Elizabeth Shipley to that list for her efforts in publicity and marketing. As for the writing of these books—I am always indebted to Russell Mobley, my friend and retired lawman, for his experience and knowledge. I owe a similar debt to command pilots Randy Hethrington and Bob Livingston, my classmates and living libraries for any information related to aircraft or outdoor activities.

Many thanks go to my best fans, Doris and Morgan and Jack. Thanks as well to "P.J." and Lucy! And thanks, finally and always, to my readers.

Dead Man's Bay

1.

Spring Break

It was early morning but already a rusted Ford Escort gathered lazy johns across the street from a downtown bar. Spanish moss hung limp as a washrag from the magnificent live oaks which routinely buckled Tallahassee's sidewalks into uneven surfaces, like ice floes jammed in a fjord. The trees here, towering as they did, still failed to shade either the Ford or the No-Tell Bar & Grille which simmered across the way in what locals called Frenchtown, a district segregated *de facto* if not *de jure*, shoeboxed into a strip mall with a bicycle shop, a greasy spoon and a 7-Eleven.

COME IN a neon sign buzzed like an outsized mosquito. IT'S KOOL INSIDE.

"God."

A black man slouched at a plywood counter next to the bar's plate glass window. Rode hard and put away wet, you might say, a can of Budweiser sweating inside his fist like a whore in church.

"Damn, it's sticky."

He was generally known to regulars as the Bear. He was heavy in the shoulders, like a bear. Big humps above the neck, like a grizzly. And heavy slabs of muscle still hung from a large-boned skeleton over a gut that, with recent habits of nutrition, was actually wasting.

But the sobriquet which followed Barrett Raines probably came from his early morning habit, the one you could see him at, now, as he abandoned his beer to spoon gobs of honey from a mason jar into a mug of scalding coffee that steamed alongside.

"Good morning, Tallahassee!" A deejay cackled like a magpie from a radio Bear guessed had been salvaged from the French Resistance. "It's seven forty-five for those of you confused about yer watch. And we've got sunshine in the Sunshine State!"

Did they ever. The heat and humidity index for north Florida began its inexorable climb to misery every year just about this time, a fact joyfully chronicled by meterologists who apparently never spent a day outside.

"A beautiful day here in the Capital City," the deejay chattered on breezily. "Humid, though. Ninety-seven percent at the moment. And not a smidgeon of breeze showing . . ."

"Not a smidgeon," Bear agreed.

He reached for breakfast. An alligator-sized pickle waddled with a boiled egg on a plastic plate.

". . . and if you notice the streets look a little empty," the deejay chirped on, "guess what? It's spring break! Yeah! All those frat boys and coeds out of town! Daytona! Pensacola! Wherever! Gotta tell you, though, it's fine by me. A break in the traffic!"

The deejay's chatter segued to Vince Gill—"When I Call Your Name." Something about a guy coming home to find his wife's left him.

"Would you cut that shit off, Shark?"

"Click," a black man with a tonsure wreathed in silver killed the bar's radio.

Barrett could not help but notice that the Shark

showed not a bead of perspiration whereas he, twenty years younger and propped beneath the bar's single and massive window unit, was sweating like a June bride in a feather bed. Bear just shook his head. Some things were imponderable.

"Cigarettes, Shark?"

Shark Snyder banged a roll of quarters into the register. He owned and ran the No-Tell and was not pleased with the tab Bear had amassed since separating from his wife.

But Shark would not deny a man his smokes. The Marlboros were supplied with the grace of a true Southerner, something Barrett Raines could appreciate. The Bear, after all, was originally from Deacon Beach, a small town on the Gulf. (What the hell did "originally" mean in that context, anyway? Could you originate from more than one place?! Wasn't that redundant, or tautological or some shit?) There were nothing but fishermen on Deacon Beach. Shrimpers, mostly. Sunburned men, angry and white, who owned *everything.*

Barrett zipped off the Marlboro's ribbon like the string from a Band-Aid, tapped a smoke free. He couldn't understand how he'd wound up in this place. He'd done all the right things. Had always managed to make his mark.

But something always tarnished the trophy. Take school—Barrett graduated valedictorian from a high school where most black kids didn't even finish. Didn't mean shit to the shrimpers of Deacon Beach. There were no scholarships waiting. No eager inquiries from colleges or universities.

The young Raines immediately enlisted in the army because *there,* he knew, was a way off the Beach. And that went all right. Bear took his G.I. bennies and a hitch in the reserves to a small, liberal university in Texas. He discovered literature and pursued a double major, was respected by his profs and popular with students eager to champion social justice and tolerance and the like.

But at the tail end of his senior year, Iraqi tanks rolled into Kuwait. Barrett's artillery unit was activated, and the Bear went to war. Students and faculty seemed cool upon his return. The black man familiar to them, the earnest student notorious among his classmates for actually *enjoying* Aeschylus and Euripides, did not sit well with the returned soldier who without apology killed tanks and infantry in a terrible, desert storm.

"One day I'm Koom-Bye-Yah with the white boys." Barrett shared that thought with Shark on a previous occasion. "Next day they're treating me like a house nigger."

"Ain't nuthin' new in that." Shark's grunted rejoinder was short on sympathy.

Then Bear married his hometown's homecoming queen. Girl of his dreams. Any man's dreams. They'd made nine, almost nine and a half years. Couldn't say without a hitch, who could? But nine good—*damn* good years. With two boys. Twins! And now, looked like, that was all going down the drain, too.

The beer chugged down Bear's throat like molasses. Hell of a thing, being separated from your wife. Your family.

But at least he had the work, his calling, his gift. The work had been wonderful, at first, had sustained the Bear and justified him righteously. That was then. But now, scarcely a year after coming to this unfamiliar place, Barrett Raines slouched in a bar at eight o'clock in the steaming morning, nearer to forty years than thirty, in debt and in danger of losing along with his job the only woman he'd ever loved in his life.

Bear fumbled open a book of matches. A hot draught of tobacco and tar coiled into overtaxed lungs.

"Thought you was quittin'," Shark interrupted the Bear's rumination.

"I am. Sometime."

Barrett told himself, and Shark, that nicotine kept his weight down. Raines was lucky to have a coffin's worth of height and a rawboned physique to carry his weight. It was a chassis that held the strength and tone more tenaciously than most. Even against cigarettes.

"Killed John Wayne," Shark reminded Barrett mournfully. "Kill him, it'll sure as hell kill you."

"Not if I eat well."

Time for the morning ritual: Down with the pickle, the egg and then the beer to chase.

"Go Seminoles!" Barrett belched, and then to Shark, " 'Nother one."

"Pickle? Or aig?"

"Very witty," Barrett twisted a clip-on tie from his frayed and ringed Arrow collar.

"You owe me forty-eight dollars and fifty cents," Shark reminded his sole customer of the morning. "That's a lot of Bud."

"No cash." Barrett pulled out his pockets to prove it. "State's got our paychecks held up."

"Since when do state workers miss a check?"

"The budgets stalled, all right? The governor's constipated. What am I supposed to do?"

"Vote democrat. Take Ex-Lax."

But Shark slid a Budweiser down his marine-ply bar. Barrett caught it just in time to hear the door tinkle open. A new prospect for the morning? Spiked heels. Tank top. Ambitious breasts. Celia stretched beneath the air conditioner like it was a shower. "It's hotter than four hundred hells melted and poured in a tin thimble."

"Have a seat, Ceal." Barrett pulled one out for her.

"My meter's running."

"I'm down to a stroll myself," Barrett smiled broadly. "But you're welcome to a seat."

"How 'bout a smoke?"

"All right." Barrett tapped the pack for two when brakes locked to draw his attention outside.

"Shee-it," Shark paused at the register.

A trio of teenagers spilled from a rusted van onto the sidewalk across the street. Gang members. Shirts and shoelaces. A jack slammed beneath the Ford.

Barrett turned to Shark, "Your car?"

"Naw."

Only a couple of seconds to raise the car. Hubcaps spilled to the sidewalk like nickels on a plate. Celia was already bored.

"How 'bout we start the day off with a bang." She slid a finger inside Barrett's collar.

"Sorry. No can do."

A power wrench hammered at lug bolts outside.

"Tired?" Celia swung into Raines's lap.

"Well, yeah, but mostly broke."

"We can go on credit."

"I'm in debt."

"So's the government." She stretched like a cat. "Doesn't stop them."

"Good point," Barrett nodded, though whether he was talking about the government or her tits would be hard to determine.

Wham! The Ford collapsed to its axles. The van inhaled its hoodlums, burned rubber out to the street. And then a siren wailed.

"Here come de cavalry." Celia sucked her Marlboro.

The cavalry had come. But not for the teenage hoods. An unmarked Crown Vic glided smoothly to a halt beside the compact Ford. The driver heaved out, a boulder-sized redhead with a leather bulge beneath his shoulder. He strolled, this man, from the Crown Victoria to the No-Tell's entrance, tapped the door open—

"Raines."

What was that accent? Wisconsin? Minnesota? Some-place, for sure, where they ate a lot of cheese.

"Cricket," Barrett greeted the newcomer. "Good mawnin'."

"Time to travel, Bear."

Barrett heaved a huge sigh, finished the last slug of his Bud, ground out his butt. Only after he fetched a jacket from the floor would anyone see the badge and the gun which clued the work that once had made the Bear a proud man.

Only then would you know that Barrett Raines was a cop.

2.

The Summer Means Fun

Takes more than a gun and badge to do this job!"
That was about all Barrett had been able to drag out
of his partner since they'd crawled into the car. They were
on Phillip's Road now, three or four miles northeast of
downtown. Suburbia petered out quickly here to allow
patches of open land, pine trees, even some livestock.

"How late are we?" Barrett shook his watch.

"Captain was at the governor's mansion at seven,"
Cricket kept dead on 55.

"I'm sorry, Cricket. Look—"

"Look, my ass!"

You miss a meeting at the mansion and it was a *big* fuck-
up, Barrett knew that. And this morning, of all mornings,
to screw the pooch! The department, always kissing the
legislature's rotund ass, sometimes brought field agents to
do a dog and pony show with the latest state representa-
tive or chairman or citizen who showed the least inclina-
tion to give a shit about the FDLE's affairs.

This morning (how could he have forgotten?!) Barrett
and his partner had been tapped to accompany their boss
for a powwow with Governor B. and his pet representatives.

"You're looking like a goddamn fool," Cricket grated.

And Captain Henry Altmiller did not tolerate fools lightly.

Barrett kept silent as Cricket cursed Tallahassee's famously unsynchronized traffic lights. It had been nearly two years since the homicide of a politically connected white woman brought Bear to the attention of the capital city and FDLE. The state legislature years earlier established the Florida Department of Law Enforcement. That innocuous-sounding title established, in fact, a kind of instate FBI with broad jurisdiction and the best investigative talent in the southeast. Originally organized as part of the war on drugs, the agency expanded its scope to include white collar and violent crime. Facilities expanded, too, so that now counties too poor to afford forensics and specialized equipment could call on Tallahassee and the FDLE for help. Every sheriff in each of Florida's sixty-seven counties used the department on a regular basis. Most of Florida's citizens didn't even know it existed.

It was a real honor to be selected as an investigator for FDLE. Barrett was one of only four black men who even got an interview. Cricket Bonet hadn't been happy to be assigned to the newcomer.

"I don't intend to be partnered with a token," Cricket made his feelings clear to Altmiller with Barrett standing not two feet away.

"Give it a chance," Altmiller said without even a hint of censuring Cricket's prejudice.

Barrett learned soon enough that Bonet migrated to the States while still a boy from Quebec. He learned that the Crazy Canuk earned his stripes in Chicago, one of the most dangerous beats around. And Cricket went undercover for the DEA in Minneapolis, too, before finally coming to the Sunshine State. Barrett would have to earn this man's respect. Luckily, he'd been partnered with Cricket less than a month when they broke their first case.

It was a spectacular initiation so far as law enforcement officials were concerned. Would have been a yawner for TV, though. No sexy informers, no corruption in high places. And no violence. A slain prostitute found on the interstate had a check in her purse made out to a dry cleaner in Live Oak. A released felon was recently employed at that business. He was a Caucasian man with two previous convictions, both drug related. Lived in a trailer park.

Barrett got the idea to search the man's trash can. Took an extra warrant but it paid off. The druggie's mess gave Barrett and Cricket receipts from a Wal-Mart. Nothing unusual about shopping at Wal-Mart except that this particular store was four or five hundred miles south in Fort Lauderdale. That's a long way to go for towels and wall putty. A month's surveillance established that the Fort Lauderdale store was, in fact, a rendezvous for traffickers from all over the state. Big-time pushers from Pensacola and Key West cut deals for coke in a warehouse stacked with CDs and diapers. The druggie's impulse purchases led Barrett and Cricket to the heart of a massive operation; the "Trash Can Caper" broke one of the most sophisticated drug cartels in the state. Cricket had partnered with Barrett ever since.

Cricket was a fiercely proud, fiercely competitive man. He'd saved Barrett's ass both literally and figuratively on a couple of occasions since that trash can bust. And Barrett had once saved Cricket's life. A multiple murder had brought the FDLE to Gasden County. Barrett and Cricket had cleared signals with the local sheriff, were interviewing some folks at an apartment complex. At the time nobody had a clue who'd committed the murders. But the killer, living at the apartment, didn't know that. He thought the cops had come to pick him up. Cricket found himself ambushed by a thirteen-year-old boy with a twelve-gauge shotgun. Barrett spotted the boy. Had to kill him. Happened not two months into the job. It was an occasion neither Barrett nor Cricket wanted to remember.

Still, all in all, the work was great. That first year he was getting good cases; he was busting bad guys. And most importantly he was tight with Cricket. "The Dynamic Duo" they were called then, "Shit on a Stick". But everything good at work got matched with escalating problems at home to the point that Spring Break found the Bear separated from his family.

A depressing situation. Normally, come spring, Barrett Raines would take Laura Anne and the boys to Fort Walton. They'd drive "the wreck" as the boys with stubborn loyalty described Barrett's partially restored Malibu. They'd check into a Holiday Inn like a tribe of Nubians, feast on fruit plates and Grand Slams. Barrett would find some excuse to hustle his sons onto the beach so that he and Laura Anne, remaining behind, could make love on the sly like teenagers.

But Barrett was separated from Laura Anne and the children for over three months. With his family returned to Deacon Beach, the Bear now found himself alone and slipping—at work. With colleagues. *Colleagues* might be stretching it. Bear was the only African American in the Second District field office; he wasn't sure in what regard he was held by the Caucasians who were nominally his peers and associates.

Raines vacillated in his new isolation between an empty house and the No-Tell jughouse in cycles which a year ago would not have seemed possible. Without Laura Anne and distant from his boys, Barrett Raines was a man without anchor. He just quit caring and when you quit caring, you quit working. It's okay, in the law enforcement canon, to piss away your own career. But you never, ever, piss on a partner. Especially a man as good as Cricket Bonet.

"A dozen folks get their ass up early," Cricket was saying. "Important people. Department heads. Legislators. Not to mention our goddamn *boss*. Even the governor of the steaming, fucking *state* gets up with the roosters 'cause he wants to see the Supercops, right? Batman & Robin! But where were we, Bear? Huh?"

"You're getting really steamed, Cricket."

"*Where were we?*"

Barrett knew when to shut up.

"Pumping pickles and prostitutes."

"I owe you one," Barrett said quietly.

"One? Tell you what, partner, it's gettin' where if you don't cornhole me at least once a week my ass gets sore!"

Cricket hit the turn signal so hard Barrett thought it'd rip off. Work lay just ahead in what used to be an open field. Three quadrangles, three stories each of brand-spanking new brick and glass housed the Florida Department of Law Enforcement. Years earlier an abandoned TB hospital stood a stone's throw away. The state locked and fumigated that building, insisting it was not a source of contagion or sickness or death. Sunnyland now stood on the spot, a facility which treated persons with severe mental handicaps. FDLE employees liked to say that most of their supervisors resided in Sunnyland.

Barrett and Cricket were assigned, unless fired in the next few minutes, to the Division of Criminal Investigation. Like most employees they parked beneath DCI's quad. Security came with a plain white card, no photograph. An identification number appeared on the back but the real security became obvious once you left your car and approached a transparent cage whose bullet-proof glass enclosed an elevator.

It had taken Barrett a couple of months to get used to that elevator. At first Cricket thought his partner was some kind of freak who liked stairs. It was a while before Barrett admitted to a touch, well maybe more than a touch, of claustrophobia. It was a fear that Barrett carefully hid, figuring, probably correctly, that if claustrophobia showed up on his medical file it would kill his career at FDLE.

Cricket ripped his card through a magnetically-keyed slot as if he were gutting a mackerel. Barrett had to hurry to join his partner inside the bullet-proof foyer. The waiting elevator launched silently from its pad. Up two floors they passed the appropriately dubbed "Putrid Room." You wanted to get rid of somebody quick you just took 'em to "The Puke." A variety of body parts from all over the state and in various states of decomposition were stored in that room waiting to be examined for identification purposes, usually, or other forensic analysis.

Barrett's favorite and permanent exhibit was "The Hand In The Jar." Seems some well-meaning coroner from downstate was brought to a John Doe rotting in a roadside ditch. Body was too far gone to send whole so the coroner cuts the hand off, pops it in a dill pickle jar filled with formaldehyde, and sends 'er on up to Tallahassee for fingerprinting. Well, by the time Identification gets the specimen the skin is pickled hard as ivory. But, ever resourceful, an FDLE sleuth scapels the skin off the severed hand's forefinger, wraps that skin around his own finger, and rolls that palimpset for a print. It worked. The dead man's fingerprint was on file. The body was identified.

It was routine, now, and cheaper to send hands instead of bodies for identification to the FDLE.

One more floor. Full stop. The elevator doors hissed open like a turbolift to deposit Cricket and Barrett before a set of secured doors which opened to DCI's version of Miss Moneypenny. Except that this was Miz Rawlings. Amanda Rawlings rose with the grace of a gazelle, even at fifty years, to warn Barrett and Cricket—"He's on his third cup of coffee and fifth DiGel." She opened the Director's door, "Agents Bonet and Raines, sir."

"Let them in, Amanda. No calls, please."

Anyone with military experience would feel at home in Henry Altmiller's office. A handful of cheaply framed commendations and a couple of plaques graced otherwise bare walls. The director's hightop chair and laminated desk looked over an industrial-weave carpet to a conference table which offered genuine wood contrast to an otherwise lime-green interior. The Florida State flag took its place with Old Glory beside a single houseplant which begged for water and Miracle-Gro. The view was nice, though. Large windows looked into a quadrangle dominated by live oaks and squirrels. The director had even been accused of feeding the squirrels, the only defect ever discerned in his character.

Altmiller rose in an old suit, rigidly pressed and starched. A meticulously wrought double-Windsor latched a tie out of season to a neck thick from past labors and present fury.

"We had an appointment, gentlemen. I was there. The governor was there. You weren't. Why?"

"Ah, problem on Live Oak, sir." Cricket, as was usual, beat Barrett to the punch.

"What kind of problem?" Altmiller hadn't asked them to sit.

"Couple of hoods," Barrett supplied. "Stripping a car."

"Detective Bonet?" Altmiller was asking Cricket for confirmation.

"Yes, sir." Cricket supplied it.

Altmiller's neck bulged at the cords. "I thought this meeting meant something to you, Cricket!"

"It did, sir. Does."

"Means something to the governor, I can tell you! Especially in the middle of a a session where he's looking at my *budget*!"

"I'm responsible for our missing the meeting, sir." Barrett tried to help out.

"Of course you were. You think I'm an idiot?" Altmiller returned to Cricket. "And then you cover for him?"

"There was an incident, sir."

"Don't piss on my leg and then tell me it's raining." Altmiller let them both stew a moment. Then to Cricket, "I'm tired of you covering for this piece of shit you're calling a partner."

"Is this official, Captain?" Barrett felt his own neck go red.

"You're a jack-off, Raines." Altmiller didn't budge. "You know it. I know it. And your partner's paying the bill."

"Captain—" Cricket started again.

"Save it." Altmiller was turning for his desk. "I'm reassigning you two out of Investigation."

That was bad. That was really bad. But the worst was yet to come.

"And I'm splitting you up."

Barrett froze. Losing your partner was like losing your wife. Barrett had already lost his wife. He could hear the ocean roar in his ears. Cricket spoke up—

"Captain," Cricket spoke like a diplomat. "I can fully see a suspension from CID. Understandable. But Barrett and I—we're partners."

"Too long." Altmiller handed Cricket a file. "You're going back to Lambeck's office."

"You mean back to Drugs."

"He means back to a desk," Barrett supplied.

"You weren't always a wiseass, Raines. Here." Altmiller practically threw Barrett his change of assignment. "Take it to Records. You can be goddamn sure that'll be a desk."

Altmiller leaned back in his desk. "This is purgatory,

gentlemen. Do your work, with a little luck you can get back. Fuck up one more time, and I mean *anything*, and it'll be your pension."

"Little steep, isn't it, Captain?" Cricket spoke softly, deferentially.

"Call it the straw that broke. *Don't push.*"

"Yes, sir." Cricket fell silent.

"And Raines . . ."

"Sir?" Barrett swayed off guard.

"I'll need your piece."

"Sir?"

"You've skipped a half year of qualifying rounds, Agent."

"I can get current," Barrett protested weakly.

"Your piece."

Barrett fumbled his handgun from its holster. Agents were very possessive of their sidearms. A firearm was a different kind of tool than a saw or hammer or drill; it was the kind of tool whose selection said a great deal about its owner. Barrett's was a 9 mm Smith & Wesson, Model 5946. Semiautomatic. Double-action only. Barrett had chosen it mostly for safety.

Altmiller forced the weapon's surrender with a nod. Barrett placed the butt into his captain's hand. Altmiller popped out the clip, cleared the chamber and then, without a glance, "Next time it'll be your ass."

Moments later Cricket was legging toward the big Ford. Barrett could barely keep pace, "C'mon, Cricket, we've been through worse than this."

"Felt good every time, too, didn't it?"

"We do our job!"

"No, Barrett." Cricket stopped so fast Barrett almost ran into him. "That's where you're wrong—We don't do our job. We used to! We used to do our job and do it right!"

"Nobody can touch us, Cricket. Remember? We're shit on a stick!"

"Ancient history."

"The Dynamic Duo!"

"CUT THE CRAP, BEAR!" And for a second Barrett thought he was going to get slugged. Cricket towered over his partner. "I'm owna tell you something, Raines, I gave you slack for a long time. Man gets problems at home maybe he drinks a little. Maybe he needs to. But this job *means* something to me—You got that?!"

"I hear you."

"Hear me good. You wanta fuck up your own life? Go *ahead*! But if I lose my gig because of something *you* did, 'partner', this Canuk is gonna be in your face!"

"They won't pull your ticket, Cricket. You're too damn good."

"Got news for you, boy . . ."

Barrett had never heard Bonet use that word.

"I don't need you to tell me what's good."

Cricket practically ripped the car door from its hinges, slammed it shut. The cruiser fired to life. Barrett found himself a pedestrian without a partner.

People told Laura Anne that nobody would come to the restaurant once owned by Ramona Walker. First off, nobody'd come without Ramona. Memories of her rape and death were too close, Laura Anne was lectured, and was reminded, too, sometimes not delicately, of her own proximity to the homicide of that fabulously gifted and popular white woman.

Besides, other folks said, lots of Ramona's customers were people she drew from out of town. Tallahassee and Gainesville. Miami. Atlanta, even. Who's gonna come that far to see you, girlfriend?

"They'll come for the food first," Barrett's wife declared. "Then they'll see about me."

Running a restaurant had not been Laura Anne's life ambition. She had been happy teaching music at the local school, giving the occasional piano lesson, encouraging the youngsters' gifts. That's what she had done for ten years at Deacon Beach. That's what Bear told her she'd be doing in Tallahassee, too. The new job wouldn't change anything, he'd told her. Things would be just the same.

It hadn't worked out that way. Laura Anne came to Tallahassee a gifted teacher with good recommendations. Before interviewing for any full-time position, she substituted at a variety of schools, intending with that exposure to find the best place for her own goals and situation.

It wasn't hard to find a job teaching in Tallahassee. But Laura Anne quickly discovered that this was not going to be the experience she had so cherished in Deacon Beach. The levels of bureaucracy here were maddening. School principals ruled capriciously; teachers, on the other hand, had almost no real authority, either within the classroom or with regard to curriculum or evaluation. Those problems, to some extent, Laura Anne expected.

But what she did not expect, what she could not tolerate, was the level of violence and intimidation, student to student, which she routinely observed in schools all over the city. Administrators were in a constant state of triage, putting out one brush fire after the other.

Even that frustration might have been endured, for Barrett's sake. For his career. He had been so excited, so honored, to be moved up to the FDLE! He'd presented her a house twice as large as their home on the beach.

"Built on the old Velda dairy," Barrett beamed as he swung into a private drive off Thomasville Road. "Two storeys. Oak trees. Cul de sac. How do you like it?"

"Can I have a garden?" Laura Anne had asked.

"Sugar." He aped a vaudeville smile. "You can have whatever you likes!"

It was a nice house. Very nice. But it was mostly empty. Barrett was gone from home much more than usual, traveling about the Second District. Even working shifts back home he'd been able to stop in for a breakfast or supper with his wife and boys. And speaking of the boys . . .

They were only nine years old, Ben and Tyndall. Third grade boys. Ripe for new thoughts and new experiences. But still innocent. Without the kind of scar or blemish that turned good boys into mean men. But what Laura Anne saw on her sons' faces that first week of school did not look innocent.

"What's this, Ben?"

"Slip from the teacher."

Laura Anne had seen those slips. Many times. She took it in at a glance.

"Fighting?! You, Ben?"

"Yes, ma'am."

"Why, Ben Raines? You tell me! Why were you fighting?"

He wouldn't say a word. Not a word.

"Tyndall." Laura Anne turned to Ben's twin. "This is not tattling. This is your mother asking. What happened with your brother to fight?"

"He had to."

"Why?"

" 'Cause mama, some white boy called Ben a . . ."

"A what?" Laura Anne had asked even though the pit in her stomach told her she already knew.

"He called me a nigger!" Ben burst into tears.

"Oh, Lord, come here, babies." She had gathered them both into her arms. "That was a bad thing he said, boys. A bad thing! I'll talk to the teacher."

But Laura Anne knew too well how limited the teacher's influence would be in this situation.

"It's the city," she told Barrett that night. "The place. The people. The parents. It's computer games and cable TV. It's everything."

"And it's everywhere," Barrett rejoined too quickly.

"Not in *my* house!" Laura Anne's reply struck Barrett like a whip. "And not at Deacon Beach, either. This *never* happened, not even when it was bad. Not even with Ramona."

"But they knew us, hon. That's why."

"You're right," Laura Anne had nodded quickly. "They know us on the beach. They know who we are . . ."

And before Bear could offer a word she went on—

"That's why we need to go back."

The notion of separate lives didn't occur to Laura Anne soon or easily. She tried to support Barrett in his new career. He'd got off to such a good start! Doing so well! And there were good, well-meaning people to lighten Laura Anne's frustrations. But every time she took her children to school or picked them up from the playground, Barrett's wife saw something gone from her children's eyes.

And the taunts, the terrible, overt, racist slurs, did not stop. Not just from white children. Black children, too. Black children hurling racial epithets as casually as twigs. But the straw that broke was when Laura Anne heard her own boys hurling the insults back.

She snatched up Ben and Tyndall from the school yard, dropped them by a neighbor's home, and went straight to find Barrett at work.

"What you doing here, baby?" He'd been surprised.

"I'm taking the twins, Bear," Laura Anne declared. "I'm taking them home. *Now.* I have to."

Leaving had not been as hard on the boys as she expected. "Daddy's just working here," she had explained. "We'll see him just the same."

"Then we won't see him much," Tyndall declared solemnly.

It took less than an hour to get on the road. An hour later Laura Anne was back at Deacon Beach. The moment she pulled into the driveway of her old seaside home and saw her garden out back with its shrubs and flowers, Laura Anne knew she'd done the right thing. To her neighbors she simply said that she'd moved back home, that Barrett would commute as his schedule allowed. A few locals actually did commute from north of the beach to Tallahassee, so Laura Anne's fiction was allowed if not totally believed.

But Laura Anne wasn't taking any chances on her future with Barrett. She had a family. She needed an income. She tried the community's school, naturally. She had been a music teacher, yes, but she could teach things beside music. Certainly she could. There were no positions to fill, however. And no prospects.

"You can sub, of course," Mrs. Miles offered sweetly. "But that's about all I have. I'm sorry."

It had been distressing news. But driving back from that disappointment, Laura Anne saw Ramona Walker's dormant restaurant.

Ramona had no immediate family. Her cash assets had gone to some nieces and nephews, but the restaurant itself had been left with words of appreciation to Doc Hardesty, a widowed M.D. and Ramona's tireless drinking buddy. Laura Anne used to give Doc's daughter piano lessons. A car wreck had taken that little girl. Some senseless joyride. Laura Anne sang at the funeral. When Laura Anne told Doc what she was about he practically gave her the restaurant.

"You make it go, we'll arrange a lease." Doc wouldn't have it any other way. "If it goes well you'll need an option to buy. Better tie me to it now; you make good I might get greedy!"

It took a lot of work. The kitchen and dining area had to be scrubbed down and restored. The pier was a mess. Plumbing was a nightmare. Laura Anne had to do most of the labor herself; she couldn't afford to hire jobs out. But friends black and white came unasked to help. And Laura Anne made sure the boys worked, too.

"This isn't my place," she told the twins when they balked at their new responsibilities. "This is *our* place which means *you* are taking care of something that's *yours*."

In three short months the Pier's End was on its way to matching a former glory. The last thing to be refurbished was the front door. It had been a door off a Costa Rican cruiser which Ramona, while alive, salvaged from the bottom of the sea. Everyone who knew Ramona knew that door, and the story behind it. Laura Anne was adamant that it be preserved.

"I don't want folks to forget her. *I* don't want to forget her."

The place was an instant success. Laura Anne made everyone feel at home. Didn't matter if you came in cut-offs or an evening gown. And she liked having people experiment a little, try new things. Oh, sure, you could have a T-bone steak if that's what you wanted, but Laura Anne would urge you to "just try a taste" of hush puppies and grouper. Or maybe you'd like to mix some catfish and swamp cabbage. Laura Anne knew most of Ramona's recipes and added more from her own heritage bringing a home-grown feast every night to a growing circle of regulars and tourists. The food and service were excellent and as for the ambiance . . .

A grand piano was not what you'd expect to see in a restaurant on Deacon Beach. Music in this region normally meant Garth Brooks or Willie Nelson, but even rednecks had to admit there was something nice about a baby grand. The boss lady would leave a customer's table or shuck her apron to tickle the ivory; diners would then enjoy their shrimp or steak with a Rachmaninoff aperitif.

People didn't talk about Ramona so much anymore. They talked now about Laura Anne.

She had a visitor this evening. The gentleman reclined across a candlelit table. A long-stemmed rose swayed in a vase set beside a glass of wine. Cook's night off allowed Laura Anne a rare appearance in an evening dress. She had a mane of jet-black hair that fell silk-soft past long muscles which worked firm and knit down her back. Her skin was distinctive, a kind of light chocolate that stops hearts, a golden patina on an African frame.

She rarely used perfume. Her body's natural chemistry was spiced now from the kitchen—cinnamon, red pepper, cayenne. Not much salt. She had long, spectacular legs. A face etched somewhere on a pyramid.

Barrett Raines thought she was the most beautiful woman he had ever seen.

Laura Anne glowed across the table from her husband, inhaled the rose, "Nice of you to remember."

"Nice of you to think it's nice," Barrett smiled though he ached inside like a jilted freshman.

"Where'd you get it?" Laura Anne put the rose into its vase.

"Dropped by the house. Took it off your bush."

"Barrett!"

"Then I got Roy to scrounge up the vase."

"Something like a homemade valentine?" she smiled, still.

"Sort of. Except you own the rose, the vase, and the restaurant."

"If that's a congratulations, I'll take it."

Barrett wanted to congratulate her. He wanted a lot more. But he stalled over an issue more painful to his pride.

"What is it, Barrett?" She sampled her burgundy.

"My, uh—paycheck's hung up. Everybody's is."

"It's okay."

"But I should have it for you. I put the house on the market. . . ."

"Shhhh. Listen, Bear." She leaned forward. "It's no hurry. Things are picking up here, can't you see? Couple of months I won't need another paycheck."

"Well, thank you, ma'am."

"Baby, don't do that! I can make a living off this place. We have friends here. The boys are happy. All we need's you."

"You want me to just chuck what I got? Just throw away my career? My work? Is that what you want?"

"Life isn't always about 'wants', Bear."

"You got that right."

"That your way of saying, 'Happy Birthday, Laura Anne'?"

Barrett scrounged up a Marlboro.

"Thought you were quitting."

"I am. Can't you tell?"

"You're drifting, Barrett. Getting any sleep?"

"Not getting any, period."

"Will you be straight a minute?"

He sighed, "Okay, it's true. I'm not sleeping—with anyone. I'm smoking. I'm eating pickles and eggs for breakfast. Cricket is flying a desk because of me. And I owe Shark forty-eight dollars and fifty cents."

"That would be a nice meal at my place."

"Meal for you. Mortgage for him."

"Let's talk about Cricket," she said and took his cigarette away.

"You're a jewel, you know that?"

"And you're a diamond in the rough. Now what's this about Cricket?"

"I have a fantasy, sometimes."

"You and Cricket?"

"Me and you."

"There's always hope," she observed.

"Dwells eternal," Barrett agreed. "I see you on the beach. The Gulf. It's a blustery day."

"Like Winnie the Pooh?"

"Not exactly." Barrett wet his lips, "You're there on the pier. Legs up to your ass. All that hair loose beneath one of those floppy white hats—"

"Are you trying to seduce me, Barrett Raines?"

"Is the Pope Catholic? I'm just come home from a big case. I'm a hero. We kiss!!!"

"And I loan you forty-eight dollars and fifty cents."

The balloon burst. Barrett sagged wearily. But not Laura Anne.

"Now," she continued, "I want to hear about Cricket."

"He's my conscience," Barrett replied.

"He's your second wife," Laura Anne amended.

"My second divorce, too, if I'm not careful."

"Don't say divorce, Barrett. Don't say it."

"Isn't that where we're headed?"

"Is it?" She looked him straight in the eye. He couldn't hold it.

"Tell me about Cricket." She let him go.

"We're split up. Sacked to a desk. Different desks as it turns out. My fault. Damn near lost our butts over it."

"If it'll wake you up, maybe it's for the best."

"I lost you. That aint waking up anything."

Laura Anne turned then to a waiter. "Roy—can you clear these?"

"C'mon, Laura Anne," Barrett coaxed. "You know it's true. I can trace my slide downhill to one date. One time!"

"Funny how thing's looked up for me," she replied as Roy took their glasses and wine. "Not to mention the boys."

"Well now that's the damn truth." Barrett sat back. "I can't argue that."

Roy came back for the vase and rose. "No, thank you," Laura Anne stopped him. "I'll keep it."

"Second time you've been nice tonight." Barrett thanked her.

"I'm going to leave you with something, too, Barrett," she said.

"You can post-date it."

"You got yourself a lip, now, haven't you?"

"Okay," he surrendered. "Sorry."

"Come here."

She held the rose close, leaned to place her face close to his. "You are the best lover I ever had, Barrett Raines. The best friend I'll ever have. But you've changed, Bear. You're livin' a half life."

"Half life. The hell's that mean?"

She settled back. "Ever since you moved to Tallahassee all you've thought about is being a cop. Not me. Not family. Always good guys and bad guys. Act like you don't need anything else."

"I was wrong."

"Barrett, listen to me. When you're in Tallahassee all you think about is being a cop; when you're on the beach all you think about is being married. Don't you think you can have both?"

He thought about it. "I did once."

She shook her head slowly. And then, "You used to be a good cop. Maybe damn good. Don't throw that away because you found out it's not everything. Awright?"

"All right," he said. Though he did not believe it.

She rose from the table, took her thorny corsage from its vase.

"I always did like things homemade."

That was about it for Spring Break.

3.

Hunting Season

November came to Lafayette County on the toes of wild fires, tornadoes, and torrential rains. A Canadian front and cooperative jet stream combined to plummet temperatures into the forties. But Miles Beynon knew better than to ditch his summer clothes. This break from the heat wouldn't last; it was still too early in the year.

Miles Beynon looked like something that had once been substantial before it was pulled through a sieve. Even in his loose, Gore-Tex parka, Miles presented a tall, guant figure. A scarlet bandanna draped over a neck about the size of a Coke bottle. A beaked nose and jaundiced complexion didn't help his overall appearance. But appearance notwithstanding, Miles Beynon was an experienced woodsman. With the exception of one six-year hiatus, he had hunted and fished the fields and streams of northern Florida all his adult life.

Miles welcomed the rain and the wet chill which huddled him inside his parka. Any woodsman, after all, knew that water in the ground meant more squirrel, more whitetail, more ducks. The problem nowadays, for farmers and hunters, was keeping water *in* the ground.

Beynon could recall when spring and even summer

rains used to fill the flatwoods of northern Florida. The Suwannee River, that last great southern artery of water and wildlife, would regularly swell to its banks. In earlier years a series of ponds and swamps and slews corroborated with the Suwannee to catch that rainfall. Limestone acquifers then received the captured precipitation as it filtered from above through sand and topsoil. A bounty of water would be stored forever. That used to be the case.

But the natural balance of things had changed pretty quickly and you couldn't blame it all on global warming or El Niño. Northern Floridians couldn't palm it off on a swelling population, either. South Florida, where Miles himself resided, was growing beyond the reach of any resource. But there was no population problem between Tallahassee and Gainesville. What northern Florida did have, though, were pulpwood companies and ditches, farmers and irrigation.

The pulpwooders were Miles's favorite target for ire. Flying over the coastlands you could see enormous grids which marked off tens of thousands of acres of land owned by corporations like St. Regis which harvested slash pine trees off sandy loam soil for conversion to paper products. In past years, efficiency alone guided the planting and irrigation of these vast tracts of timber. Pine seedlings were therefore planted in rows as straight as possible. Firebreaks were pushed up every half-mile or so and ditches dug to drain the land so that roads and trucks could easily access the interior for cutting and hauling.

It's not true to say that nobody thought about what would happen to the water table when rain fell on those pine stands, collected in those straight, uniform ditches. The folks at St. Regis Paper Company weren't stupid. They knew what would happen.

What happened of course was that water which normally collected in natural ponds and slews routed instead to the Gulf of Mexico. Fresh water that normally seeped into limestone acquifers now ran to desalinate the marshlands along the coast. Water resources inland depleted and so farmers began to use artificial irrigation, tapping the surviving lakes and slews to sustain their crops. When those sources tapped out they dug wells. And more wells.

Within a decade the state of flowers found herself water poor. Legislators authorized millions for consultants who argued the extent of the damage done. Lobbyists representing paper companies on one side and environmentalists on the other spent fortunes on hydrological essays, consulting fees, and impact surveys which supported their contrary assertions.

Miles snorted derision. He could have told them as much. And saved a ton of money to boot.

A fleeting impression of silhouettes flashed across the gray sky. Miles took aim as he had thousands of times before on a squadron of ducks. The mallards had already circled once, too high to hit. A smart duck would always do that, fly downwind too fast, too high so as to tease a man with a gun below. Miles held his fire where a more inexperienced hunter might have cut loose. The law allowed three shells in an automatic shotgun aimed at these migrators. Miles's twelve-gauge Browning was plugged to conform to the restriction; Beynon took pride in that. He almost always got his limit of fish and game. He never cheated. He was patient.

That patience was rewarded as the mallards circled back, their leader nosing his flock into the stiff, chilly wind. The birds could smell better into the wind, could land more easily and could take off more quickly into the wind. They dropped like a formation of Spitfires from a slate-gray sky. The law required game birds to be taken in the air. Miles could hear it now, that peculiar whistle that only comes from the wings of ducks flying at sixty miles an hour. They crossed at about forty-five degrees overhead. Miles found a bird, swiveled his ventilated barrel to lead. A thousand calculations of wind and bird and shot and angle were accomplished in the smallest part of a second.

The woods shook with the first explosion. Miles felt the satisfying recoil against his shoulder, felt the warmth of the chamber as the shell ejected. When Miles first hunted he used a light load, usually Number 2 chilled, but federal law protecting migratory birds now prohibited lead shot so Miles had switched to a magnum load and Federal BBs. One bird was already going down when the hunter took his second shot. Another shot, another recoil, another bird. And now the virile, acrid smell of powder mingled with moss and water and wind.

Miles liked the purity of it all. Unlike most hunters he did not drink. Did not smoke. Those habits tainted the world of moss and water and shot and blood. Miles set the safety on his Browning. He could see both his mallards, brilliantly marked in about a waist of ice-cold water. The woodsman left the shore and the cover of his small, camouflaged boat to retrieve his twin kills. Two beauties were these. Miles smiled as he placed the birds in his bag; it was only the first day of hunting season and already his skill and judgment had proven true. It had taken many years to gain this skill, this knowledge of the weapon, of the game, and especially of the land. Miles was not a native of the counties between Tallahassee and Gainesville. Like many men who loved rods and guns and game, Miles had sought out the regions west of the Suwannee. There were, in fact, working plantations which catered to men like Miles. Some of these hunting and fishing camps were famous. Ted Turner owned one near the Georgia border. Kenny Rogers was rumored to have himself a place.

Miles was not likely to keep that sort of company. He squatted now at a cypress knee beside a sheet of water that mirrored the gray sky above. The Sand Pond, as it was called, was really a series of spillways which in earlier years received water running off the river and flatwoods. Bone dry for years, it was easy to see how the ponds got their name, blinding white sand set in what looked like gigantic bunkers inside a belt of ancient timber. But November's rain had come in buckets and deep-running creeks forged channels beneath limbs and berries of mayhaw and hickory to fill the Sand Pond with fresh, clear, life-giving water.

Water was precious. But it was the oaks that brought Miles Beynon to this isolated spot, a grove of water oaks, actually, which thrived dead center in the middle of the pond. Miles had poled his small flatboat for two miles seeking that particular configuration of water and tree. In some of the more shallow stretches he'd had to drag the boat behind him, a substantial effort, but worth it, because the oaks would bring ducks.

Mallard migrating this time of year needed a safe place to find shelter, water, and food. And right here before Miles's small boat was the most ideal combination imaginable. First of all the place was, from a duck's point of view, safe. It hadn't been hunted in years. Why would a hunter bother? It had been ten years at least since water had collected beneath these oaks. But this year the water had come and the oaks had dropped their acorns onto its mirror-smooth surface. Ducks found a floating feast. Miles was waiting, the only hunter on the ponds. That was fine. Miles wanted the ducks to himself. He was as irritated, therefore, as he was surprised to find another hunter at his back.

It was a tall man who stood there cradling a shotgun like some kind of Mohican above a bandolier of shells. Dressed too nice for real hunting. Not like a local. A tall man, still rugged in his late forties. A handsome, creased face. If Miles were better traveled he might have speculated that this was a Slavic face, which would have been true. But being untraveled it was the intruder's eyes that got Miles's attention; silvers of agate they might have been. A pale and pitiless blue.

"Christ, you always sneak up on a man?" Miles slipped a pair of shells into his shotgun.

"Always nice to see what the other man has," the newcomer replied.

Miles didn't like the voice. It was foreign. Like the clothes—it did not belong.

"Nice birds." The tall man examined the mallards in Miles's bag. Their dead eyes stared vacant atop long, fluted necks.

"Not bad." Miles didn't look at them.

"But stupid." The stranger went on about the birds. "Like beautiful women. Don't you think?"

"Don't know." Miles spit out some Redman. "Never shot a beautiful woman."

The man threw back his head and let out a roar that echoed through the woods. Miles grimaced. So much for shooting fucking ducks.

"You're a visitor here, aren't you?" It was the foreigner who asked the question.

"What makes you say that?" Miles fingered the safety on his weapon.

"Passed your truck," the tall man shrugged. "Saw the plates."

"Truck's a good two miles from here."

"Good two," the man agreed and then without pausing, "As a matter of fact you're from near Orlando, aren't you? They call the place Ocala. Indian name, isn't it? Seminole."

". . . You want something mister?" Miles was getting pissed with this character.

"Information," the intruder replied. "I'm especially interested in armored cars."

"I don't know what you're talking about." Miles pulled his scarlet bandanna closer around his neck.

"Oh, I think you do, Mr. Beynon."

It bothered Miles that this bastard knew his name.

"It's been nearly seven years, hasn't it?" The pale man went on. "Miles Beynon and another man robbed an armored car. Near Miami. You spent six years in jail. Six years without hunting. Must have been difficult for you."

"Wasn't no fun."

"You spent six years incarcerated," the man repeated. "Your partner, however, a Mr. Brandon Ogilvie—? He simply disappears."

"You a newspaperman?" Miles couldn't believe this character was a cop.

"I'm a curious man." The voice that answered carried no hint of sarcasm or threat.

"Better read yer paper again." Miles wadded some more Redman between his cheek and gum. "Brandon din' disappear. He was kilt."

"Ah, yes. Drug-runners, I believe you said."

"They hired us to hit the car," Miles nodded. "Paid us pretty good, too."

"So you did the job?"

"Sure."

"No problems?"

"Not with the job, no."

"Then why would these people kill your partner?"

"Woulda kilt me, too, if the cops hadn't got me first."

"You haven't answered my question." The fellow's accent had begun to grate on Miles's nerves. "Why did these drug-related persons kill your partner?"

"We got greedy. There was a ton of money in that car. Cash. So we helped ourself to a little extra."

"How much extra?"

"Thirty thousand dollars."

"You're lying." The man said it calmly.

Miles released the safety on his shotgun. "Interview's over, mister."

"Your partner's still very much alive, isn't he?" The bastard didn't seem much concerned about Miles's gun.

"I said yer interview's over," Miles snarled.

But ole' Blue Eyes just kept pushing. "In fact, there never was a drug connection, was there, Miles? Just two hoods working on their own. All you expected was a payroll. Correct? And perhaps some petty cash. But you hit it rich, didn't you, Miles?"

"Go to hell."

"Half a million British pounds," the hunter continued. "Packed neatly in a code-locked aluminum case."

"Who the hell are you?" The faintest tremor, now, in Miles's voice.

"I kill people," the Slav answered shortly and then, noting Miles's response, "You know it's interesting to me. People go to great lengths to contact me. Put themselves at extraordinary risk. Pay me large sums of money to do what I do. But they're always squeamish about that word, 'Kill.'

"Which brings us back to your armored car. I had been engaged, you see. A good client. It was a big job. Political. I received expenses up front but the rest—cash on delivery. Half a million pounds sterling. The money was routed to my account through an American bank. It was robbed."

"The bank?" Miles croaked hopefully.

A smile withered below the stranger's blue, blue eyes.

"No. The money was in transit. It was the armored car that was robbed. The car *you* robbed, Miles. You and your very silent partner."

For a moment there was complete silence on the lake.

The assassin smiled genially.

"You had no idea how much money was in that case,

had you, Miles? Probably had never before seen a pound note. Not once in your short, brutish life."

That's when Beynon jerked up his Browning. The killer slapped the gun aside like a twig. A boot to Miles's collarbone. Miles heard the crack and felt a stab of pain shoot like fire from his neck to his shoulder.

"*Goddammit!*" Beynon cursed as he writhed on the ground.

The tall man emptied Beynon's gun, slipped the chilled shells into his bandolier. "Where is my money, Miles? Where is Brandon?"

"The fuck would I know?!" Miles tried to find his feet.

"Ah, but you do," the stranger assured him. "And sooner or later, so will I. You see, Miles, that was my property in that car. And one way or another I intend to get it back."

Miles tried for his boat. Slipped and fell. The birds were there, both of them, staring up at Miles Beynon from their fluted necks, their long, fluted necks. Miles struggled to his knees. That's when he saw the corkscrew. That's when he saw the knife.

"Where is the money, Miles? Where is Brandon?"

That's when Miles began to scream.

Barney Pearson had been a game warden for thirty-three years. A game warden's salary wouldn't go far, not even in Lafayette County, but Barney loved the work. He'd seen some bad things in his years in the woods, mostly cruelty with regard to animals. A buck might be left to rot, his antlers taken for some city-slicker's trophy. But mostly there was just greed, folks who treated the woods like a footlocker. Some fellah with a car worth more than Barney's house might try to get away with about twice as many quail or bass as the state allowed. Barney was used to that kind of meanness. Beat the hell out of the days when he guarded a chain gang. Pearson still had a momento from that year. His wedding-ring finger wouldn't support a ring; it was shot off below the knuckle. That nub still ached now and then, especially in these first, chilly days of the hunting season.

Barney could feel the nub now as he poled a johnboat through the Sand Pond, but that minor ache couldn't take away the thrill which came with seeing the ponds filled again and running. A tell-tale V overhead told the game warden that ducks would find the place and feast. Barney was so fixed on the game above he almost missed the barrel which peeked over a shallow-draft boat near the shore.

"*H'lo.*" Barney called out his challenge loud and clear. It was easy to go to sleep out here, man stuck in the cold, waiting for game and Barney had no intention of startling a hunter dozing with a twelve-gauge.

"State Warden," Barney called again over to the boat. But he was close enough now to see there was no hunter. Just a Browning automatic propped pretty sloppily along the flatboat's gunwale.

"Not a safe way to secure a weapon," Barney reproached the air.

That's when he saw the bandanna. It floated a scarlet lily pad ten, maybe twelve feet offshore. Barney tested the water's depth with his pole. Knee-deep here. Probably no more than waist-deep or so over the whole pond. Be hard for a man to drown out here but not impossible. Barney'd seen it before.

He waded out, tugged at the scarlet choker with a meaty forearm. It wouldn't come.

"What the hell?" Barney could haul a twelve-point buck over his shoulder with a single hand. An ice cube seemed suddenly to settle in the warden's stomach. He seized the bandanna again with a ham-sized fist, gave a yank—

"God from Zion!"

A corpse bobbed from the pond's sandy bottom. Ago-
nized eyes stared from a skull flayed like an onion. But
even that wasn't what emptied the game warden's guts.
"*Jesus God.*" Barney let the thing go.

The corpse floated full-bodied to reveal a final insult. A
duck stared stupid and sightless from what used to be a
human face. It was a mallard that gagged the victim, even
in death, its long neck rammed like a faucet down Miles
Beynon's throat.

4.

A Fall From Grace

If there was one thing Barrett couldn't stand it was being tied down in front of a computer screen. It wasn't the technology he decried; it was impossible to deny that computers and a host of other technologies had greatly benefited law enforcement. Computers were now essential and became ever more valuable as fewer cops were called on to catch ever-growing numbers of criminals.

In an astonishingly short time Barrett had seen desktops and mainframes mated with other technologies to accomplish tasks that simply could not be handled by humans alone. The AFIS system offered the most familiar example. Called the Automatic Fingerprint Identification System, AFIS could take a single fingerprint from anywhere in the States, match it against every single fingerprint filed with the FBI. A job like this would be impossible to do by hand. There were close to a million prints filed with the FBI. There were tens of thousands of requests for matches made daily by sheriffs and detectives from all over the country.

AFIS combined a computer's processing speed with the same kind of digital imaging used by space-faring satellites. The same technology that displayed a canyon on

Mars, in other words, was used to create a digitized image of a fingerprint. A print taken from a crime scene in New York State or Texas was routinely scanned, digitized, and entered into the AFIS mainframe computer. A list of fifty possible matches would be produced from the prints on file. A fingerprinting expert then compared those fifty possibles to the print in question, determined whether the print from Texas or New York could be matched. A human being always made the final call, but he made that call from a sample of dozens rather than millions.

The old kept meeting the new in law enforcement. DNA analysis, or genetic fingerprinting as it was sometimes called, had not yet replaced ordinary fingerprinting as a conclusive means of identification; juries still didn't completely trust probabilities over fingerprinting's unblemished certainty. But digitized algorithms were already making DNA profiles as accurate as the older technology's.

Even the most ordinary procedures benefited from digital intrusion. Take parking tickets for instance. New York State police nailed the infamous Son of Sam by matching parking tickets issued to the killer with locations proximate to his victims. The problem was it took a legion of cops tens of thousands of man-hours to accomplish the task. Your kid's desktop would do it in minutes. Sam could have been caught months earlier. A dead girl or two or three might still be alive.

Barrett knew that. He knew that anything which could collect and sort information in nanoseconds could save lives and solve crimes, and he knew nothing shit and git faster than these sheet-metaled brains. But Barrett worried that months and months of looking at a computer screen would take away those skills that let him see the crucial detail of a scene or suspect, or that it would diminish whatever Gestalt it was which enabled him to put apparently disparate pieces together into an unexpected whole.

Bear's new supervisor was unsympathetic with the veteran's concern. Bear distrusted zealots of any kind and was goddamn positive that the fresh-faced, eager, young tax-sucker before him now would have leapt to follow Jesus or Hitler or any other prophet. It was just the luck of the draw that computers got the little bastard first.

Barrett had been stuck in Records with this little turd through the hottest summer on record, charged with the amorphous responsibility to, in the jargon, "create a data base of cases" (showing no potential for resolution) which would "interface" with every case recorded by any law enforcement entity in the state to be linked by a "real-time, on-line, fiber-optic network capable of processing at ungodly speeds."

" 'Scuse me," Barrett had raised his hand during that initial briefing.

"Yes?" The youngster regarded Barrett like a truant.

"What is a gigabit?" Barrett asked.

For a long moment the consultant said nothing. Finally, "Tell you what, Agent Raines, why don't we dedicate you to Input?"

November found Barrett still separated from Laura Anne and the boys and stuck with the turd at a keyboard entering license tags and Vehicle Identification Numbers in a collage that eventually assumed the significance of paste on the wall. Barrett met Cricket in the quad one day. The two men shared a Styrofoam of coffee, the only thing they'd shared in months. A stiff wind combining with the precipitous drop in temperature chilled Bear to the bone. Park bench weather, of course, for the Crazy Canuk.

"Know what I miss?" Cricket made the first stab at conversation. "Is the Fall. Autumn. Wisconsin, Minnesota you get a real change of seasons. Weather breaks, leaves change. But *here!* Christ, we get days like this in the forties, next week, hell it can be ninety-five and hurricanes. It's nuts."

Barrett barely noted a sky gray as lead.

"I'm going crazy," he stated flatly, squeezing honey from a plastic pack into his coffee.

Cricket sighed as he shredded the stir for his coffee into toothpicks.

"Not exactly thrills for me either, pard."

"Don't know how it could be any more worthless than what I'm doing."

"I haven't been on the street in a month," Cricket offered.

"I haven't been off my ass in a month," Barrett countered. "I'm sitting there typing in tags and VINs for cases that've been dead since Christ was a corporal."

"Never can tell what'll turn up, Bear."

"I feel like Sisyphus."

"Not familiar."

"He was a god. Greek god. Had it good but then he pissed Zeus off."

"How?"

"Ratted him out. Kidnap case, I think it was. Point is my man Sisyphus gets his ass condemned."

"They killed him?"

"That'd be too easy. No, what they did was they made ole' Sisyphus roll this big-ass boulder up this big-ass hill."

"Doesn't sound too bad."

"He had to do it forever, Cricket. Every time he'd get to the top, every time he'd finally get that fucking boulder to the top of that fucking hill, the gods would kick that rock down again. Sisyphus would have to go all the way back down, down to the very bottom. And start over."

The Bear tossed his remaining coffee into the frost.

"Makes me think Sisyphus had to be a black man."

*   *   *

It was only a couple of weeks later that Barrett got the call. He was staring somnolently at amber characters swimming on his screen when Mary Perkins waddled her state-paid ass over an acre of desktops to deliver a summons. "Altmiller wants you."

"Is that sexually?" Barrett inquired.

"You should be so lucky." Mary popped her gum. "Captain said make it ASAP. Over at TMH."

That got Raines's attention. Tallahassee Memorial was the hospital affiliated with FDLE. Autopsies that used to be done on-site were now farmed out to the Medical Examiner at TMH. That meant they had a body. A dead body, probably, unless Doc Thorpe was expanding his practice.

"Sounds like that boulder's up that hill for the last time." Barrett grinned to an uncomprehending face.

But then the gods intervened.

"You're just pulling a case." Perkins slapped a post-it on his terminal and waddled away.

"What's that mean?" Barrett called after her. "What case?"

"On your screen, stupid."

Barrett scanned the handwritten note pasted on top of his amber characters: Beynon, Miles Richard / Arrest# 112334 / SSN 267-53-6791.

Barrett, Cricket, and Captain Henry Altmiller waited silently beside a doctor, an intern, and a corpse. The autopsy was almost finished. Most people's notion of forensic investigation traces to sparkling white icons grafted onto the subconscious by TV shows like *Quincy* or feature films claiming more realism. Whether television or film, viewers enter a world where the Medical Examiner inevitably wears a shining, white cloak, the corpse lies serenely on what looks like an operating table set beneath what looks like a surgeon's lamp with a welter of hi-tech diagnostic and recording apparatus. You don't see the hose which washes blood by the buckets down industrial-sized drains. You don't see cigarettes curling smoke from plastic ashtrays or coffee pots plugged in next to corpses. You don't see mops carelessly stuffed into pails of disinfectant left alongside a man of thirty, say, or a girl of thirteen. You don't see the scales they use to weigh livers, kidneys, hearts, and, oh yes, the brains of human beings whose lives cut short bring them to this medieval place of inquiry.

You don't smell anything on TV, either, but there are smells here. All these things are here, because this place is real. Body drawers chill corpses in a room that might otherwise be taken for a meat locker. The examining room is right next door. A short gurney down the hall carries the stiff in for dissection, oops pardon, autopsy. There's no lobby for Doc Thorpe's office. Why would there be?

The tile on the floor matched that to be seen in Doc's Mexican kitchen. Doc had a place down there. The Pacific coast. The tile reminded him of tortillas, señoritas, and tequilla. For an aging man those were important memories. The lights in this house of death were ordinary fluorescents that you might see in a drugstore. A surgeon's lamp swiveled about the table for peering into eyeballs, cavities, orifices, and such. A concession to convenience did bring a goose-necked microphone down from the ceiling to the table. The C-clamp which secured the apparatus to the ceiling had given way to the yanks of weary ME's. Thorpe had secured the mike with duct tape and that's the way it was secured now. The Medical Examiner mumbled his findings into an ordinary Sony tape recorder which rested on a scrap of plywood salvaged from Handy Dan's. There were white-starched lab coats here, but Doc preferred the rubber apron which he wore over an ancient madras shirt, seersucker slacks and weejuns.

With these amenities Thorpe had more work than he could possibly do in a state where medical examiners underwent strict examination and review. He was the best forensics man in Florida. There was a time when Barrett would have been eager to see the master at work, a time when he would have looked forward to viewing this body, to pursue the cause, the killer. To enjoy the hunt. And there was certainly a time when Barrett would have been glad to have the chance, even in this place, maybe even especially in this place, to work with Cricket Bonet, but that was not the way Barrett felt now.

He felt old. He felt alone. He felt like Henry Altmiller, neatly pressed behind his Windsor knot, was waving a bone in front of his face and expecting Barrett to beg.

"Died of suffocation," Doc's attention was on the rail-like corpse which stretched on his stainless table. The skull was awful. A pair of eyes still cried out from a cranium stripped to the fat and muscle beneath. Lots of blood. A pair of messy holes punctured a kneecap. Not hard to figure what that was about. Barrett tried not to notice Beynon's genitals. It was hard. Miles's penis was nearly as thick and long as his forearm, the only gifted part, so far as Barrett could tell, of the dead man's anatomy.

"Guy'd make a run at Dillinger's record, wouldn't he?" a young intern piped up.

"You want me talking about you in here?" Doc inquired mildly and ended the chitchat. "I found traces of amphetamines." Doc turned his attention back to the victim. "At least two injections. Victim was revived at least once before death."

"Christ." Cricket had a hard time keeping his eyes on what used to be Miles Beynon. Most folks would.

Doc shoved his eyeglasses aside to massage the bridge of his nose. "Victim was bound, hands pulled behind and back to the ankles. You can see the welts. Nylon, I'd guess. Or something similar. Certainly not cotton or hemp. Multiple injuries to the right patella and into the knee joint. Way in. Left clavicle was broken. And of course the skull."

"He was found by a game warden near Alligator Point." Altmiller supplied the background. "Taylor County Sheriff got out there, had the good sense to realize he needed help. We sent down a mobile."

A "mobile" was a Mobile Crime Unit. Florida's counties were like counties everywhere, rich with crime, short of money. At a sheriff's request the FDLE supplied a van and investigators to completely work a crime scene. Agents from Tallahassee had already photographed this victim and the scene of his murder, had even gridded off a hundred-foot perimeter around the site sifting for every scrap of physical evidence. That sort of investigation was completely beyond the resources, not to mention the expertise, of most county law enforcers.

"We got this." Doc pulled a plastic bag from an ice chest at his feet. A mallard's stupid eyes stared from a head and neck gone stiff.

"Made him choke on it?" Altmiller asked. Doc affirmed with a nod.

"Bastard enjoyed his work, didn't he?" Cricket moved from the flayed skull to the whorled wound on Miles's kneecap. "What did this?"

"Something with a screw on the end."

"Like a power drill?"

"More likely a hand tool. Awl of some kind."

"Which came first, Doc?" Altmiller's turn to look smart. "The skull or the knee?"

"Knee." Barrett couldn't resist.

"I'd guess the knee," Doc winked at Barrett. "If the skull

were flayed first, considering the temperature and wind-chill, the certain loss of blood, the victim would have lost consciousness. If you look at that knee it's obvious the victim was kicking back. Or trying to."

"You're saying whoever did his wanted the guy awake to feel it?" Cricket looked to Doc for confirmation.

"I can't read minds." Thorpe was famous for this remark.

"Then what have we got, a visiting sadist? A crazy med student?" Altmiller was talking to Barrett and Cricket, now, and for a tenth of a second it felt like the old days.

"Drill to the knee used to be a signature for the IRA," Cricket observed. "If the perp is professional maybe there's a connection."

"Okay," Altmiller nodded. "How about motive? Was he tortured for fun, or was there some other reason?"

"Why should we give a shit?" Barrett had the feeling Altmiller was leading him someplace.

"Read the file," the captain replied.

Barrett scanned a computer printout. "Meet Miles Beynon. Outdoorsman it says here. Claimed to have never done drugs. Never drank or smoked. Liked his Redman, though."

"A clean liver," Cricket remarked and Doc Thorpe laughed at the totally unintended pun.

"Lessee," Barrett scanned the file. "Miles spent a hitch with Uncle Sam. Last tour, Saudi Arabia. Worked odd jobs after the army...Lessee. Here we are: Released from Raiford last December. Served six years. Sent up for an armored-car heist. Says here the robbery was drug-related."

"One of our first cases." Altmiller chewed a lip. "Story was Beynon and his partner hit the car for some runners in Miami. Got greedy, apparently. We picked up Miles—"

"—but the dealers got his partner, I remember. So now you figure the druggies came back to finish the job?"

"Miles might've held back. Might have stashed away a little retirement."

"Says here we got the cash. Little over thirty thousand total."

"One item was unaccounted for, though." Altmiller pulled out some Chap Stick. "An aluminum camera case. Locked. Uninsured."

"Could have been cash in the case." Cricket seemed glad to move away from Doc's table. "Or it could have been drugs."

"Hell, it could have been catfish or condoms. It could have been anything!" Barrett went back to the file. "Look—this robbery's nearly seven years old. Statutes ran out three years after the crime. Why not let it die?"

"What about Miles's partner?"

"Who gives a shit? He's dead!"

"You don't sound too enthusiastic about this problem, Raines," Altmiller observed dryly.

"Why is it I get the feeling I'm on a wild goose chase?" Barrett shot back.

"Beats where you are, doesn't it?" Cricket gave Barrett the sign to shut up.

Barrett did. For all he knew this was Cricket's chance to get off a desk. If it was, Barrett wasn't going to screw it up.

"Now," Altmiller went on. "Do we have a name for the victim's partner?"

"Brandon Ogilvie," Barrett answered.

"Anything else?" Cricket took it up.

Barrett went back to the file. "According to this, Ogilvie did the skill work. Lessee. Used to be some kind of commercial diver. Had a thing for redheads and unfiltered Camels—that's according to Miles. But as far as a photo, driver's license, military service, library card—Nothing."

"And no body either," Altmiller chimed in.

"Say again?"

"We know Miles had a partner, a man in a ski mask." Altmiller was licking his lips. "But we never found a body."

"There probably wasn't enough left to find." Barrett remained unimpressed.

Something like disappointment flickered briefly over Altmiller's stern countenance. "A missing body. An uninsured satchel. Aren't you curious?"

"Curiosity killed the cat," Barrett shrugged.

"What about Miles Beynon?"

"Maybe it killed him, too." Barrett suddenly wanted no part of it. Not the body, not the case, not the FDLE. None of it.

A short silence gathered like a storm. Cricket intervened. "Say, Captain, ah—when do we start?"

Altmiller regarded Barrett cooly. "I've got an address near Orlando."

Raines was sure then that he was headed back to Records.

"Waste of time." Barrett handed over the file.

"Probably." Altmiller pocketed his Chap Stick. "That's why I'm sending you."

5.

Disney World

The captain said he was sending them to an address near Orlando. That struck Barrett as a remarkable lack of precision. He and Cricket picked up their car at the Avis counter in the Orlando airport, fought traffic a half hour to clear a town once hailed as lake-filled and traffic-free and were now eight miles southwest of the city on Interstate 4 headed toward Kissimmee and Disney World. Barrett was halfway inclined to suggest they hit Disney World and forget about Miles Beynon but his reunion with Cricket was too recent and too fragile for that kind of risk.

Cricket was in hog heaven. He had a car. He had a gun. He had the full weight of the law, a dead man, and a mystery.

"This is a waste of time," Barrett grated at last.

"Beats where we've been, pard," Cricket chirped merrily.

"There is no Brandon Ogilvie, Cricket." Barrett loosened his tie another notch. "Not alive, anyway. Brandon, if that's even the bastard's name, has been dead damn near seven years. And now the same guys that offed him took care of his partner."

"You don't do something like that to a man after seven

years, Barrett. Not if you're a professional. Not for thirty thousand dollars."

"Oh, I think Miles was lying about the money," Barrett yawned. "Probably had drugs in that uninsured case. Coke or heroin. I can see Miles and Brandon helping themselves to a cache like that. The druggies find out. And make 'em pay for it."

"Seven years is a long time to wait."

"We're talkin' drug dealers. Come on, Cricket, they whack guys from the Ice Age."

"Don't ruin it for me, all right, Bear? I'm enjoying myself."

They took Exit 26 off the Interstate. You could see billboards all the time now advertising Disney World. Barrett couldn't help but reflect that he was seeking a corpse and a killer in the land of Mickey Mouse and Donald Fucking Duck.

This would be the second time Barrett visited Disney World. The first was with Laura Anne. In fact, it had been Laura Anne's idea to visit the amusement park. Barely engaged, Barrett's future wife was already enthusiastic about having children, a prospect Barrett ranked right along with constipation and thumbscrews. He tried to dissuade the idea at first with humor, "Can't stand the little rug-rats. Yard-apes. Hungarian clabber-lappers." Didn't work. Laura Anne had always wanted children, loved children, and assumed that Barrett's derision of little ones was feigned to hide a genuine affection. She was wrong. If Barrett was trying to hide anything it was fear.

A confident man would simply have told Laura Anne of his apprehensions, of his doubts. He would tell her of the times he had been beaten and then locked inside a closet so that his father could turn on Barrett's mother at leisure outside. Barrett could hear her screams inside that closet. He could hear the sound of bone on bone, of a fist across a face. But he could not cry himself, he could not scream in that closet, because he could not breathe.

Barrett had not told Laura Anne these stories. She'd learned them, of course, gradually, incrementally, by default. They'd been married for years before Laura Anne fully understood that her husband, so patient with Ben and Tyndall, so affectionate, was still in some ways afraid of them.

Barrett could remember driving this road for the first time, trying to share Laura Anne's enthusiasm for the coming adventure, her sense of anticipation. They were on the road to recover innocence, after all. To recapture childhood. And so he had laughed beside Laura Anne trying to be a kid. They emerged, Barrett and Laura Anne, from a grove of slash pine in hellish heat to find the theme place. The first thing you saw, after you wended through the trees, was an enormous, asphalt parking lot. Lazy johns rippled from the tarmac as thousands upon thousands of men, women, and, yes, kids fell upon Disney's fabled park. Barrett estimated the line at the gate to be a quarter of a mile long. Forty minutes later Raines entered Disney World fighting heatstroke and reminding himself he was supposed to be in the recovery of childhood when he saw Minnie Mouse. Minnie and Mickey and Donald and Daisy—these were the first things you saw when you went through the gate. They were sculpted in shrubbery.

Barrett's father, pressed by an absolute necessity for alcohol, indentured his youngest son to work at a nursery on the beach. There were no childhood names at this garden, no lilies or daisies or black-eyed Susans. Everything was in Latin, hundreds of genera, thousands of species and subspecies, all strictly enumerated in Caesar's tongue.

Every day after school and every day of the summer, Barrett labored in that thankless place, his three dollars per day confiscated by the father for conversion into whatever gin, beer, or whiskey best suited the day's particular fury. Barrett learned in that place of dead names how easy it was to despise labor whose reward was confiscated or thwarted.

"What's this called?" Laura Anne had asked, fingering Daisy Duck's waxy leaves.

"Ligustrum," Barrett answered automatically, and then told her quietly that they must leave.

Barrett Raines and Cricket Bonet arrived at Miles Beynon's apartment complex in Kissimmee shortly after noon. There had been no break from summer here; Bear stepped from the rental's cool interior into a suffocating blanket of heat. A swimming pool looked inviting.

"Get done maybe I'll take a dip," Cricket grumbled.

The Coral Manor was conspicuously distant from reefs or water of any kind. It was a place of tennis courts and sports cars. And a pool, of course. Barrett wondered how Miles's mud-caked truck would look beside the camel-tan Alfa Romeo which purred to a stop beneath a sheltered slot. A party house set beside a bikini-decked pool and balconies loaded with toys of the twenty-somethings went on to tell Barrett that Miles was a fish out of water here. That impression was confirmed when after producing identification and a warrant Barrett informed the apartment manager that Beynon would no longer be needing his apartment.

"Good." The manager placed a balding head and cut-offs between himself and a blistering sun. A native, here. A real cracker. "When can he move out?"

"He can't move at all." Barrett took an instant dislike to this Bubba. "He's dead."

"Shit, who's gonna pay the rent?!"

"Somebody who's not dead," Cricket said and then

went on to politely inform the cracker that Miles's apartment was being legally searched, and admonished the manager to leave the apartment alone until it was determined whether the place needed to be designated a crime site.

"Are we gonna have all that yellow tape and shit?"

"With any luck." Barrett smiled as he took the keys.

Miles had occupied the Coral Executive Condo which meant he had two storeys of four-ply industrial carpet with a view of tennis courts, foreign cars, and pines. Miles would not win marks for interior decorating. Art Deco, Southern Colonial, and junkyard mixed about equally. The paintings on the wall, all prints, looked like they'd been salvaged from some graduate student's office. But what interested Barrett as he scanned the condo's garish walls were Miles's toys.

There were no mountain bikes, here, no Rollerblades or cross-country skis. Instead, a sea bass shared space with a Ryobi open-face reel. Barrett noticed that the rod was custom-made from a graphite blank and fitted with Fuji guides. And as if that weren't enough an entire set of "S" series Penns were rigged with varying tests of line and lure beneath. A black bear was expensively mounted on a facing wall; a Sako .375 magnum occupied that place of honor. A cabinet beneath secured a king's ransom of firearms. Barrett counted four Brownings, everything from .243 to a .375 magnum, a pair of Remington small calibers, and four Smith & Wesson handguns.

Cricket whistled between his teeth. "Where'd you say our Beynon worked?"

"K-Mart," Barrett replied. "Part time."

"What say we get busy?" Cricket was loosening his tie.

"I got upstairs." Barrett's hand was already on the rail. A half-hour later, he was still sorting out crap in Miles's bedroom. "I can't believe the fucker ever slept here!" Barrett yelled down the stairs. Socks and underwear piled unwashed beside an enormous chest of drawers. Barrett found nothing in a rolltop desk beside the bed but when he yanked on a drawer from the stand-alone a mound of crap spilled to the floor.

A lot of junk in that drawer. Playing cards, matchbooks, girlie mags. Letters and bills and credit card receipts.

"Anything?" Cricket appeared at the door.

"Visa Card." Barrett sifted through it all. "American Express. But somehow I don't get the feeling this guy was into deficit spending."

"I think you're right, partner," Cricket smiled. Barrett froze. It was the first time Cricket had called Barrett "partner". Barrett looked for something to do with his hands. Finally he dropped the receipts back into their drawer, and then, without looking at Cricket, "Let's bag this stuff."

"Roger, that," Cricket nodded. "And then I got something else. Not gonna be easy to bag, though."

"Where?"

"In the kitchen."

The murdered man's kitchen looked out over a waist-high counter to the rest of the Coral Executive Condo. It was a modern kitchen which meant that everything ran on radar and timers. But that wasn't what made the place interesting for Cricket.

"What about this?" Cricket ushered Barrett inside to find something that definitely looked out of place. A freezer squatted on cement blocks inside the kitchen. It was a ton-and-a-half freezer crowded into a very small place. It sat in the cookery like a coffin.

"See for yourself," Cricket looked ill.

"Okay." Barrett opened the freezer's lid. And nearly gagged. "Jesus."

Rows and rows of fish stuffed the icebox. Hundreds of

pounds of some smelly water creature. All identical. They rolled dead, dark eyes toward Barrett and Fish Heaven.

"What the hell are they?" Cricket croaked..

"Mullet." Bear's reply was definite.

"What the hell's a mullet?"

"Fish," Barrett answered.

"Really. You get that from *Field and Stream?*"

"They're a saltwater fish." Barrett let the freezer lid fall. "Bottom feeders. Real common. Closest place to fish 'em from here would be on the Atlantic side. Titusville. Merritt Island. Any number of places, really."

"Never seen an uglier creature." Cricket still looked ill.

Barrett snorted, "People in Japan? Indonesia? They go for the roe *big* time. But there are still lots of Floridians, you show 'em a mullet? They'll *gag.*"

"Miles did gag," Cricket reminded him grimly.

"Maybe we better see the manager."

The manager was irritated to find out that his new vacancy would not be immediately open for rent. "We're just gonna do a sweep," Cricket explained to the man. "There's a regional office in Orlando. We'll have 'em in and out of here by tomorrow afternoon."

"Some shit," the Bubba replied leaving Barrett's opinion of his IQ and attitude intact.

Barrett flew back to Tallahassee with Cricket and a garbage bag of trash. It felt right, somehow, like someplace they'd been before. The two agents didn't talk too much. Cricket was crammed beside a window. Barrett was lucky to get an aisle seat and was actually dozing off when the Canuk's question nudged him awake, "Bear. About those mullet."

"Mmm?"

"Do *you* eat 'em?"

Bear chuckled. "Sure. But then my granddaddy used to say only coloreds and crackers would. I know in Texas they still won't use a mullet for anything except chum."

"You mean bait. To catch other fish?"

"Yeah."

"Well, I won't be eating any, I can guarantee you that. Not after looking into that freezer. And smelling it!"

"Now don't be prejudiced. You need to come out to the restaurant. Let me have Laura Anne fix you some."

"No."

"Gotta broaden yo' horizons, white boy."

"I'm broad enough, thank you."

"Have a steak, then. Laura Anne misses you. 'Fact, you're the only thing in Tallahassee she does miss."

"I doubt that." Cricket winked, turned back to his window and within seconds was asleep.

Barrett glanced through his partner's window to see the sun catching a rib of clouds. He couldn't sleep. Questions which nagged him in Miles's apartment now returned. Why had Miles Beynon placed himself so distantly from the things he apparently enjoyed? What was a fisherman and hunter doing in an apartment complex filled with singles and city dwellers? How'd he pay the rent? There was something that Bear knew he wasn't seeing. Something in that room of rods and guns. Something in that freezer filled with fish. Bear shook his head gruffly. Too much time sitting on his ass. Way too much.

But at least he could look forward to seeing Laura Anne. The weekend visit was already planned. And now Cricket was coming, too.

There was a ritual at Pier's End. Sunset came with a piano concerto. Sometimes Laura Anne would play. But this evening a young waitress surprised customers by trading her apron for the baby grand. A Chopin concerto wafted light and breezy from the Steinway. A salty wind scattered pink-tinged cumulus clouds over the horizon like cotton fugitives. The water was as green as jade.

Laura Anne Raines bared copper shoulders in a light, denim dress. She took her husband's arm as they lounged on the pier.

"I'm glad you came."

"Me, too."

Cricket was still inside eating. He started with a steak and kept on grazing. It was easy for Laura Anne to excuse herself and Bear for a private moment outside.

"Cricket's enjoying himself."

"Yeah. He is."

"I'm glad you brought him."

"Me, too."

"Barrett, you're here in body." Laura Anne had to smile. "But your mind's a million miles away."

" 'Miles'—that's appropriate."

"You've got that look."

"Lessee, that'd be the hungry look? The horny look?" Barrett turned to face her.

"Try the 'I'm on a case' look." Laura Anne smiled wider. "How's it feel?"

"Beats driving stakes in vampires' hearts."

They were both grinning, now.

Barrett took her hand. "You've got something special here, Laura Anne, you really do."

"Thanks."

"Thanks, be damn. You did this all on your own."

"Oh, I had help." She blushed. Nothing sexier than a genuinely beautiful woman who can still blush at a compliment.

"So how'd it go in Disney World?" She squeezed his hand warmly.

"Went fine. Good in fact."

"Catch any bad guys?"

"Nah."

"Maybe you can surprise somebody."

"I'd have to surprise myself, first." Barrett sipped a Samuel Adams. "We've got one dead ex-con, an apartment in Kissimmee, and seven years of loose ends."

"Sounds like a challenge," she smiled.

"Don't start, Laura Anne."

"Why not?" She teased him with a smile. "Why?"

"I guess," he faltered. "I don't want too many expectations."

"Better to reach and fail than never to reach at all," she intoned.

"That sounds like something you'd glue on a poster and stick over the commode."

"What do you want, Bear—?"

The breeze caught her hair as she let his hand go. "—What do you really want?"

"More of this for one thing." Barrett pointed to his beer.

"No, really, what would you like to have most?" she pressed. "Right now?"

"Besides forty-eight dollars and fifty cents?"

"Yes."

"Okay." Barrett searched for her hand. "I want a whole life again. You and me."

"Floppy hats and legs up to my ass—is that it?"

"Sure."

"That's not a whole life, Barrett. Remember? It's just a piece."

"Damn fine piece." He looked her up and down.

But Laura Anne wasn't buying.

"What about your job? What about being a cop?"

"They don't need cops anymore." Barrett went back to

his beer. "They've got their printouts and their labs and their lawyers. Their goddamned computers."

"You're scared," she declared. "Scared of failing. Maybe scared more of succeeding."

"Think so?"

"You haven't broken a case in so long you're afraid to try."

"I'm on a case now, aren't I?"

"Cricket said you did everything you could to lose it."

"When did you talk to Cricket?" He straightened up.

"Never mind."

"What the hell—are you checking on me?"

"Never mind," Laura Anne said sharply.

The wind dropped suddenly.

"Maybe we better get back inside."

They entered the dining room to find Cricket hip deep in culinary slaughter.

"Good food." He squashed a belch.

"Glad you liked it," Laura Anne smiled politely.

"You should go into business," Cricket chirped.

Normally Cricket's small humor broke whatever tensions played between Barrett and his wife. An uncomfortable silence broke with the waiter's arrival.

"Everything all right, Ms. Raines?"

"Of course, Roy," the boss lady smiled winningly.

"Mr. Raines?"

"Good food, Roy."

"Mmmm, say." Cricket polished his plate with a hush puppy. "What was that?"

"Sir?"

"That side dish. There. What was it?"

"Why, Cricket," Barrett had to chuckle. "That was mullet."

"*Mullet?*"

Cricket reached for a napkin. "You fed me a plate full of *bait*?!"

"Oh, Cricket!" Laura Anne was genuinely concerned.

Barrett roared.

"Gotcha, partner. Got your ass!"

"You son of a bitch," Cricket growled good humoredly.

"You two stop it," Laura Anne chided and pressed a glass of water into Cricket's hands. "Now, what's goin' on here?"

"Your husband! Got me eating *chum*, for God's sake!"

"You mean the mullet? But you liked it." Laura Anne tried hard to keep a straight face. "In fact, you wolfed it down!"

Roy offered to refill Cricket's glass.

"No, no, that's all right," Bonet waved him aside. "It's just a new delicacy. For *me*!"

Laura Anne smiled sympathetically. "People 'round here have eaten mullet for years."

"We just found a whole freezer full," Cricket told her. "If I'd known I'd have hauled 'em up for you."

"Oh, I wouldn't take them," Laura Anne smiled.

"Why not?"

"Well, because mullet don't keep very well. They get a taste. You have to catch 'em fresh and cook them the same day if they're to be any good."

"So where do you get yours?"

"Down the coast," she replied, sweeping a copper arm to the south. "Around Steinhatchee? They've got slews of mullet. Blacks, mostly. We get a fresh catch nice and iced every day."

And for the first time in a very long time the tumblers long dormant in Barrett's brain began to fall.

"Barrett? Bear, are you all right?"

* * *

Every building has a dungeon, a place where old desks are stored or files wilt in antedeluvian cabinets. The FDLE was no different, though Altmiller had marked the place for destruction. "Not needed," he said of the ancient desks, lamps, and files which crowded the place. "A waste of space." A gray-templed security guard was astounded for more than one reason, therefore, when late one night he entered the dungeon to find Agent Barrett Raines.

"What're you doing here?" the guard demanded.

"Overtime," Barrett replied and went back to work.

There were no computers down here, no windows, no oak trees, no distractions. A single gooseneck lamp tunneled a corridor of illumination to a Florida road map. Scotch Tape anchored the map onto a bulletin board. Barrett hunched over a GI-issue desk pulled up beneath. Carboned receipts lined up like solitaire cards in three orderly columns on the desk. Barrett fished a receipt from his garbage bag on the floor, checked it, then fingered a location on the map. In goes a pin to mark the locale on the cork board. Down goes the receipt to its appropriate column. So it goes, receipt after receipt, pin after pin to complete a string of scarlet-tipped beacons which stretched from Kissimmee to—

Barrett checked the map once more—

"Hells bells."

6.

Fish or Cut Bait

Barrett's Scotch Taped map spread over Henry Altmiller's desk. Three color-coded lines connected the pin holes dot-to-dot on the map. Red, green, and hot-pink lines stretched from Miles's apartment to the south to a town in northern Florida.

"I got an idea on the Beynon case." Barrett moved aside so Cricket could see the map with Altmiller. "See these? These are three trips Miles made in the year he's been out of prison. Three trips—almost exactly three months apart. February thirteenth, May twelfth, and then again in mid-August. Always to the same spot."

Cricket thumbed a town near the coast. "Right here?"

"That's as far as the receipts go," Barrett nodded. "A Seven-Eleven in Perry, Florida. But that's not where our man stopped."

"How do you know that?" Altmiller interrupted.

" 'Cause of the mullet. Remember the mullet, Cricket?"

"Ah. Sure."

"I naturally figured Miles fished for mullet someplace close to home. Somewhere on the Atlantic side. But then I thought about these receipts, I did a little checking, and, sure enough, there's our man driving to Perry. Way north. An' on the *Gulf* side, now why would he do that?"

"To fish?" Altmiller was singularly unimpressed.

"Why not?" Bear replied. "He came up here to hunt, didn't he? And there's a community fishes mullet south of Perry. But you have to go past the town all the way to the coast and down before you find it."

"You check for Brandon's name while you were at this?" Altmiller still wasn't hooked. "Motels? Car rentals?"

"Not a car," Barrett said emphatically. "A boat. He always rented a boat."

"Why?" Altmiller inquired mildly.

" 'Cause you can't get there by car." Barrett smiled as if this were the most delightful revelation since Copernicus.

"Get where, Raines?" The captain's patience was wearing thin.

"Get to where Miles got his mullet," Barrett answered. "And I'm betting where he got his cash, too."

Bear turned to Cricket. "Look. Why would a man like Miles, a real woodsman, catch so many fish if he didn't intend to eat them?"

"You tell me."

" 'Cause he was never there for mullet," Barrett answered. "He was there to get money. But he'd need a reason to go there, wouldn't he? Something that looked natural."

"That's one hell of a leap," Altmiller grunted sourly.

"We're fishing anyway."

A long moment passed. It looked for a moment as if Altmiller was going to sweep Barrett's map into the trash. But then—

"All right, Agent Raines, let's start with the heist. The armored car. Say Miles did find something he didn't expect. Drugs, cash, whatever. Why stash anything on the coast? Why not just find a local bank and put it in a safety-deposit box?"

"He's right," Cricket frowned. "Why drive a hundred and eighty miles when you can stash your winnings just as safely down the street?"

"I don't think Miles ever had the winnings to stash," Barrett replied. "I think his partner did—Brandon Ogilvie.

"Couple of days ago you said Ogilvie was dead," Altmiller reminded him.

"Couple of days ago I was acting like an asshole," Barrett replied.

Captain Altmiller looked him in the eye.

"I'm listening."

"Say Ogilvie wasn't killed." Barrett laid it out. "He took whatever was in that armored. Maybe it was money. Maybe it was drugs. Or jewels, I don't know. But Miles sure as hell knew. And Miles also knew when he got caught that if he took the fall, served his time . . ."

"He'd collect his share when he got outside," Cricket finished the thought.

"Or maybe more than his share," Barrett amended.

"So you think Miles's own partner killed him?"

"It's a possibility," Bear nodded. "If his partner's still alive."

"Only one way to find out." Altmiller ran his finger down the coastline. "Say you can't get there by road?"

"No." Barrett shook his head. "And there aren't any phones, either. No phones, no faxes, no computers. No outsiders, either."

"I don't see a thing on the map," Cricket declared.

"It's there," Barrett insisted.

"Has it got a name?" his boss inquired.

"Locals have one, yes, sir."

Bear put his finger on the spot.

"They call it Dead Man's Bay."

7.

Sittin' on the Dock of the Bay

There is a Florida that doesn't have anything to do with Disney World, nothing to do with palm trees or Holiday Inns. Tourists are not abundant or even particularly desired in this Florida, and you can go a hundred miles and never see a golden arch.

Barrett could almost feel his chest go tight as he left the rolling hills and arbored streets of Tallahassee for the crowded tangles of palmetto and scrub oak which withered south along US 90. Down here roadside shops sported plywood windows and empty gas pumps. Black people fished ditches with cane poles and corks and earthworms kept moist for survival in coffee cans. Barrett saw frayed patches on filthy overalls and skirts made of flour sacks.

"You remember somebody in Washington talking about trickle-down economics?" Cricket draped one paw casually over the wheel.

"Yeah."

Cricket nodded out the window.

"Here's where it's trickled to."

Barrett lowered his window for a better view. The cold front had pushed through, warmer temps and humidity rolled in from the Gulf with a vengeance. A musty smell of humidity and fetid ditches now flooded the car.

"Do you mind?" Cricket loosened his tie.

Barrett closed the Crown Vic's window. A thin shell of safety glass could not disguise evidence that the prosperity taken for granted elsewhere in the state was conspicuously absent here. Some people blamed the government for this errant state of affairs. Native old-timers claimed that big business was to blame, that in years long past the region had been raped by cynical Yankees who took the region's hardwood, sapped its turpentine, and then left. Both views were partially true. But Barrett knew that individual choices also shaped the destinies of the counties between Tallahassee and Gainesville. And many of those choices had been bad.

One bad choice had to do with tobacco. The cash crop for years, tobacco had been grown to the exclusion of almost everything else. It took hand-labor to seed, transplant, tend, and harvest tobacco. It was hellish work, not only because of the hours, the drudgery, and the heat, but because tobacco poisoned those who worked in it. Farmers knew what it meant to get bear-caught, but they put their children in the fields, anyway, swapped them back and forth with other growers to cut costs and increase profits. When those children got able they bolted from that work. Black labor was then recruited or conscripted to replace white.

It didn't last. African Americans retired from tobacco's hard labor and slave wages for Wal-Mart and welfare; immigrants came to fill the vacuum which their exodous created. Latin American families camped now on fields where Spanish hadn't been spoken since Ponce de León. But at the very moment when government subsidies and cheap labor seemed to have solved the growers' problems, domestic demand for cigarettes began to sag. Then came law suits, foreign growers, foreign markets.

It was just a matter of time before the bottom fell out. A few growers tried to diversify. Dairies. Watermelon. Chicken houses. The newest industry saw Mexicans harvesting straw which cracker middlemen sold to road contractors or nurseries. Some people found prosperity along those lines, but in the main the plight of a woefully uneducated population was to join the ranks of the working poor.

Poverty had by now taken root with the pines in north Florida. Barrett could see the signals everywhere: Roadsigns riddled by shotguns and rifles. Mobile homes propped on cement blocks at erratic intervals on pastureland or beneath the cover of trees. And there were subtler indicators of decay.

The region pierced by the ribbon of road on which Barrett now traveled used to be a place rich in story, culture, and community life. But that heritage had not borne up well against other influences which seeped or hammered in from outside. The Aryan Nation now scrawled its propaganda on the walls of abandoned stores. The Klan, never dead, hid now behind the guise of local militias. And there were other signs, unexpected, which caught Barrett's attention. A billboard badly painted in block letters, for instance, offered something he'd never before seen.

FIRST ABRAHAM THEN JOSEPH, JESUS, AND MUHAMMED
DIAL 1-800-44ISLAM

What version of the Koran, you had to wonder, would callers to *that* number receive? And, of course, there were the already-dated apocrypha which had attended the millenial craze. Y2K-YAHWEH, a roadside church bannered that cryptic message for consideration, mating computer clocks, Barrett supposed, with the Almighty.

But the most pervasive influence on local culture came as everywhere from television. TV brought the worst of the wider world to these farms and hamlets. Even the poorest shelter had a satellite dish anchored outside; Barrett was certain that the same residents who now suckled on that hi-tech tit once ridiculed welfare recipients for the inevitable antenna that rose above their sharecropper shacks.

"What goes around comes around," Barrett murmured.

"Fine." Cricket's gorevan hair seemed afire in the afternoon sun. "So when do we get to Perry?"

It took around an hour and a half to reach what was officially designated the "Perry Metro Area". Wasn't much to it. A pulpwood mill. A string of motels and/or whorehouses. A solitary traffic light marked the intersection of US 90 with Highway 27. Just about every other route followed a trail originally made by a pig, a deer, or a dragline. Barrett was reminded that, among other contributions to civic pride, Perry, Florida, had been called the capital of the state's Ku Klux Klan. He pulled over to a self-serve to ask for the sheriff's office.

"You wanta find it, I reckon you can find it," came the redneck's laconic reply.

Barrett produced his ID.

"Agent Raines. Florida Department of Law Enforcement. Now, sir, would you like to try this again?"

A deputy shuffled Agents Raines and Bonet into the Taylor County Sheriff's office. A largemouth bass mounted over the sheriff's desk along with an eight-point buck. The original boy named Sue examined the agents' credentials from behind the implacable veneer of his Ray-Bans. Barrett would not have been surprised to learn that Sue bought the sunglasses years ago after seeing the boss in *Cool Hand Luke*. Bear wondered briefly if the man might actually be blind.

"Agent, I get that right?" Sheriff Driggers lingered over Bear's identification. "FDLE? Why, you must be one of a kind."

An added window unit pumped Arctic air into an already centrally cooled calaboose. The sheriff passed gas without apology and Barrett felt his normally cheerful smile take on the rictus of a corpse. The county sheriff was still god in the state of Florida. Popularly elected, a sheriff ruled over all law enforcement within his jurisdiction. Technically he or she could tell the FDLE to go to hell. Most of them didn't, of course. Most of the sheriffs were professionals who appreciated the FDLE's support. Some were lazy and loved the FDLE's support. And of course there were always one or two who liked nothing better than to be a burr under your butt. Taylor County's sheriff ranked in this last category.

"I could go out there myself, ask around, save the tax-payers a hell of a lot of money." Sue wormed a toothpick from one side of his mouth to the other.

"Except the murder didn't take place in your county." Cricket offered that incontrovertible fact as pleasantly as possible. "Our investigation relates to a crime committed outside your jurisdiction. That's why we need to follow up on our own."

"If there was a Brandon Oliver . . ."

"Ogilvie, Sheriff."

"Right. Well, if he was here doncha think I'd know it? Doncha think I'd a'heard?"

"We're not sure he goes by that name," Barrett pointed

out. "All we know for sure is that his partner was killed in Lafayette County. We're concerned there may be a connection."

"Cavalry to the rescue, that it?" The sheriff winked to his deputy.

"Just routine." Barrett's smile felt by now as if it were stapled to his face. "A few days, week tops, we'll have collected all our yeses and nos and wrapped this thing up."

"Waste o' time," Driggers bit it off.

"We know," Cricket smiled magnanimously. "That's why they sent us."

Harold's Marina was the last point in what passed for civilization before you skirted along the coast to Dead Man's Bay. On each of his three trips Miles Beynon had rented a boat at Harold's. For more than one reason, therefore, Harold's was the logical place to start. Problem was Barrett didn't exactly know how to get there and he sure as hell wasn't going to ask Sheriff Sue. The map Cricket fished from their cruiser's glove box was about as detailed as a globe. Fortunately a county roadworker knew the way.

"Harold's? Why, sure." The worker leaned over from a Caterpillar to answer Cricket's question. "See this here two-lane you're on?"

"Yeah," Cricket nodded dubiously.

"Just stay on it."

"Just—straight?"

"Straight to the water. Harold's usually there. If he ain't, just honk you horn. Or wait. He'll be back."

"Thank you, sir," Cricket nodded.

"You welcome," the worker smiled through a set of broken teeth, and Barrett was struck that the only polite human being they'd met so far in Perry, Florida, was a black man.

Their road was an unmarked blacktop which ran straight as an asphalt string through the flatwoods to the coast. Within a few miles the regular rows of company-planted pulp gave way to the wild, unregulated contours of native growth, of cypress and yellow pine, of blackberry and deer's tongue and vines thick enough for Tarzan and a gaggle of apes. This was the land with which Barrett had once felt intimately familiar, the land of the rattler, the panther, the black bear, the kingsnake, and alligator. It was on land like this that Seminole Indians outlived the Spanish conquistadors, Andrew Jackson, and measles and refused a white man's treaty until well into the twentieth century. The Bear was born in this region, had been raised in just this kind of flatwood and swamp. Why then did it all seem so unfamiliar?

There was virtually no shoulder on the road which sliced thinly through this sweltering wilderness. The sensation you had hurtling toward its terminus was one of vertigo. There was no horizon. No point of reference. Even the weaving yellow line which pretended to center the road had faded with time so that, after an hour, you had the feeling you had gone nowhere. Were going nowhere. But then finally the asphalt gave way to rock, and the rock gave way to sand, and then you burst out of the flatwoods into a place which could not be called a beach but which did give a view, finally, of the water and the Gulf of Mexico.

The sun was a swollen ball of fire an hour or so past zenith by the time Barrett and Cricket piled out of their Crown Victoria beside Harold's Marina. Not a human in sight. But there were birds. Birds were omnipresent here, ever-vigilant, predatory. There were heron, cormorant, and pelican. A host of others.

Bear spotted a kingfisher propped atop a massive, black cypress. The tree had been hit with lightning. No leaves and not many limbs left on this watchtower. Just a black skeleton with a hunter on top. The fisher-king plunged suddenly thirty feet or more to the water below. A heart-beat later he broke to the surface, a fish struggling in his long beak. A silver belly winked wet and bright as a dime before being swallowed whole. Barrett shivered, suddenly, in spite of the heat.

Cricket honked the car's horn a couple of times to no visible effect.

"Let's just go on over," Barrett suggested finally. And so the two men stretched stiff joints as they walked over to a pier mounted on legs so spindly Barrett was sure the tide would wipe it out.

A tin-roofed shack perched on the pier, it's thin walls perforated with windows. No screens. The shack looked out over maybe a dozen tire-buffered slips. About half that many boats, outboards mostly, tied on to cypress pilings. Barrett could see a single gas pump on the water's side of the shack. A badly painted sign stirred in the breeze alongside; HARBORMASTER, the sunbleached placard declared.

"A little pretentious, don't you think, for a place like this?"

Cricket shrugged.

"People got to have their titles."

Barrett and Cricket walked the pier to the shack, arrived at the door, and found a bib-capped old coot sipping a Coke inside.

"Afternoon." Barrett tried not to get irritated.

" 'Noon," the coot acknowledged.

"We, ah, honked the horn," Cricket pointed out.

"So you did," Harold nodded.

"We're not disturbing you, are we?" Barrett's sarcasm rolled off like water on a duck's back.

"Not yet," Harold replied. "What can I do you for?"

"Boat," Barrett answered. "I need to go to Dead Man's Bay."

Harold looked Barrett over. Then Cricket. Finally, "No boats today."

Barrett displayed his ID. "We're with the Florida Department of Law Enforcement, Harold. We're here on an official investigation. Call Sue if you'd like to check us out."

"No phone." Harold sipped his soda unabashed.

"Isn't that a radio I see over there?" Cricket nodded to an ancient, vacuum-tubed set.

"So it is." Harold looked pained. As if he'd been caught.

"How about a boat?" Barrett suggested.

"Take the green one yonder." Harold jerked his head to a fifteen-foot Boston Whaler. The center-mounted console was familiar and Barrett could see a big Merc mounted on a transom at the stern. Barrett had a young detective in Deacon Beach owned a whaler. Great for fishing. Taylor even used the boat to ski, delighting to leave roostertails of water on the decks of homes reputed to be owned by drug dealers.

"That's a lot of boat," Barrett grinned. "Do I really need it?"

"Take it or leave it."

"We'll take it," Cricket replied. "How do we pay?"

"Cash. I don't take no credit cards."

"Since when?" Barrett challenged sharply.

Harold squirmed. Barrett produced a MasterCard.

"Just get the boat."

Seagulls quarreled over scraps of bacon that Harold tossed from a small, flat-bottomed skiff which the old man now secured by a nylon line to the whaler. Barrett lowered himself into the whaler. Cricket handed Raines an overnight bag. "I don't know about this."

"Cricket, it's routine." Barrett peeled the clip-on tie from his Arrow shirt.

"I should go with you," Cricket maintained.

"Look, all I'm gonna do is ask a few questions. Get some background."

"Still think I oughta be there." Cricket ran a pale paw through his hair.

"We've only got a week." Barrett padded sweat from his face with his tie. "We've got to check the motels Beynon used in town. The gas stations. The restaurants. That's a lot of stuff."

A grin broke over Cricket's face. "You're back in the saddle, aren't you, partner?"

"Hey, just makes sense, right? One guy does the bay. Other guy does the town."

"You smell something, Bear?" Cricket's eyes narrowed.

"Fish," Barrett reassured him. "Anything else comes up I'll have the boat's radio. Provided it works. Does it work, Harold?"

"Last I looked." The harbormaster fired up the whaler's inboard. The Mercury purred smoothly enough, but Barrett had to grab a rope to keep from falling.

"I'll expect a call," Cricket relented. "Soon as you get over. And one other thing," Cricket nodded to the overnight bag. "Check it."

Barrett opened the overnight. There was a handgun inside. It was a familiar shooter, Smith & Wesson, 9 mm, double-action only. Freshly-cleaned and holstered.

Cricket winked at his partner. "Never leave home without it."

Cricket remained on the pier as the harbormaster steered the whaler clear. Barrett waved once to his partner, a little alarmed that something like a sense of loss came so quickly. Was there something archetypal about setting out to sea, even a sea so flat and calm as this? Barrett waved again, broadly, to reassure Cricket, and maybe himself, and then turned away. The whaler's low rumble brought a fresh scent of gasoline to that of breeze and brine; its hull slapped the water. Barrett could feel the pounding and vibration in his feet. Something archetypal, Barrett thought as the breeze almost chilled him. No doubt about it.

The harbormaster checked once to make sure his skiff was secure in the whaler's wake, then turned to port. "You familiar with this rig?" the old coot demanded of Barrett.

"Sure," Barrett lied. "But why don't you jeep me in."

The harbormaster went over the basics. Fuel, starter, throttle. Fire extinguisher and radio. A lift for the outboard. "That's all there is to it." The briefing ended. And Harold slowed the whaler to a wallow. The boat rolled to a halt in the swells.

"Wait a minute, why—why are we stopping?" Barrett tried to keep his feet.

"How the hell am I 'sposed to get to my skiff?" The old-timer looked at Barrett as if he were an idiot.

"But we're going to the bay." Barrett had the sudden feeling he'd missed part of a very important conversation.

"*You're* going to the bay," the coot corrected him. "I'm just gettin' you a boat."

Barrett turned then to find the pier. Even though he had been raised practically on top of the Gulf of Mexico, Barrett had spent very little time on saltwater. That was common for black people in his community. In fact, many black people from his rural, coastal setting could not even swim. After all, there was no beach, only a tangle of pine and saw grass that marched right up to the edge of the water. There were no pools which weren't private and those weren't likely to be owned by black people.

Barrett himself could barely stay afloat, gaining what little skill he had from the ponds and slews and hammocks unwanted by white folks. He had ventured offshore on a boat, occasionally, usually within sight of shore. But this—! This was not something Barrett had expected.

He scanned the pier nervously. Cricket was already gone, or to be more accurate, was going. Barrett could just make out the wink of the sun on the rental car as Cricket drove away.

"Well, what the hell, make up yer mind." The harbormaster spit into the brine.

"I don't exactly see a road map," Barrett grated. "Maybe an exit?"

Harold nodded ahead to a finger of cypress. "Buoy a hundred or so yards starboard of that point, see it?"

At first Barrett couldn't see anything. And then he did see. The harbormaster's buoy was nothing more than a cypress pole stuck straight into the sand.

"That your North Star?" Barrett tried to joke.

Water off a duck's back.

"Stay on the starboard side of that point." Harold's bib-cap bobbed as he spoke. "Follow the coast. You'll run right into her."

Barrett had to remind himself that starboard meant the right-hand side.

"How long," he asked, "till I get there?"

"Half-throttle," the coot shrugged. "You should make her a' hour. Hour-half. The tide depending."

Just like an afternoon off Deacon Beach. Except this place had no houses, no docks, no visible navigation— probably no druglords, either, Barrett ruminated.

"I guess you've done this before," he said to the older man's back.

"Few times," the coot allowed, timing, as he did so, the whaler's roll to step deftly from the larger boat into his waiting skiff.

"Cast off that line, would you?"

Barrett fumbled the nylon line free, tossed it to the old mariner. A single pull brought Harold's outboard to life.

"Anything else?"

It was Barrett's last chance.

"No," Barrett shook his head.

"Be seeing you," the master nodded.

And then he was off. Not even a glance back. Barrett watched his guardian disappear. Nothing now for company but the birds and the sea. A rocking sea, at that. And then it came.

It hadn't come in a while, now. Not in a long while. But there it was, the door, the closet door. A hammer went suddenly crazy in Barrett's chest. He could not breathe. The door was closing!

"Easy, Bear." Raines forced himself to exhale. Forced himself to ignore the door. You couldn't open it once it closed, that wouldn't work. You had to turn inside. It wasn't that bad inside, Barrett told himself. Lots of room in that closet. Plenty. There were thick, cotton bathrobes in there. Flannel shirts and lingerie. Dirty socks. Lots of things to smell. Lots to breathe.

Once Barrett's heart subsided to something less than a gallop he groped for the whaler's chrome-plated wheel. Found it. Now the throttle. The boat's bow rose with a smooth rumble of engine. A fresh breeze swept over Raines with the aroma of gasoline. Barrett resighted the finger of cypress which the old man had mentioned, confirmed which of these tight-knuckled hands was starboard and port. And then—

"Go Seminoles!!"

Barrett Raines launched to sea on a swollen sun and a cypress star.

Two hours later the Bear could find no buoys, no markers and no bay. There was no shore to be seen along this coast, no strand of sand giving way to more discernable features. Pine trees and saw grass marched, it seemed, right to the water's edge. Bear started out distinguishing the myriad patterns of grass and tree and water which slipped by on the portside of his boat, but by now everything looked the same. And there were other concerns. A strong tide kept pushing Barrett toward shallows barricaded by oyster bars that could rip through the whaler's hull like a can opener. Barrett checked his fuel. Was there an hour left? Twenty minutes? Two?! He had no idea. He also had no water, or more accurately, he had water, water everywhere. But not a drop to drink.

The sun had swollen to a red rubber ball which kissed the horizon. A spectacular array of ochres and oranges and purples painted a vast canvas of clouds. In another mood Barrett might have marveled at the sight. But all he wanted to see now was Dead Man's Bay. Soon it would be dark and he'd be stuck offshore.

An hour and a half at half throttle, that had been the harbormaster's instructions. Barrett checked his watch. It had been at least that long. Barrett was sure he'd followed the coast. All he could see now was a creek or slew that cut into the shoreline. Beyond that the coast stretched what seemed forever.

"Halloo! Hallllloooo!" he called to the shore.

No answer. Barrett checked his watch again. Once it got dark he could go by Dead Man's Bay and never know it. Or maybe he'd passed the bay already. Best to hold up, get some help. Barrett didn't want to be out on the water after dark, best to find a safe place to beach, then use the radio. The Coast Guard was used to picking up amateurs. So, probably was the harbormaster. Barrett could just imagine what a kick Cricket was going to get out of this: Agent Raines rescued from the sea by a tobacco-chewing curmudgeon with a bib cap.

That's when Barrett picked out one of the oddest things he'd ever seen. It was off the water a little bit, at the mouth of some kind of creek, or maybe it was a slew. At first Barrett thought it was a wrecked boat that had drifted into that eddy. But a homemade crucifix had been freshly painted on the bow of this boat. And Raines would be damned if it didn't look like a crude set of doors had been punched into the hull. Something like a shelter or shack leaned on behind.

"*Halloo ashore!*" Barrett cupped his hands into a megaphone. "*Anybody home?*"

No answer. But at least he had a place to beach. Barrett lined up his bow on the homemade crucifix, idled back his engine, and headed for shore engaging as he did so the powertrim mounted on the whaler's throttle. The powertrim used a hydraulic lift to raise the boat's outboard. No sense in losing a prop on a rock or some other shallow-water obstacle. Raines also didn't want to chance slicing his boat open on an oyster bar so, as soon as the water's depth allowed, he gathered the anchor's line, hopped over the side, and towed the whaler up a salty inlet toward the ragtag shack.

Barrett expected to find rocks or oyster bars or sand on his way up the inlet. Within just a couple of steps he found something else. Within a couple more Barrett knew he was in trouble. The bottom along this stagnant eddy was muck, organic material deposited for eons and accumulated layer upon layer into accretions of something like living mud. With each step the muck collapsed around Barrett's shoe and knee to suck him under. When Barrett lost a shoe he realized with alarm that he was mired in quicksand!

He tried to pull out. Another shoe came free with the struggle. Luckily, there was the rope. Barrett grabbed hold of the nylon tether, allowed the boat's momentum to extract him from the mire. Once free of that hazard, Barrett sidestroked for a shore that by now couldn't be much more than fifteen or twenty yards away. The Marlboros didn't help. Barrett's lungs were on fire. His heart hit a target range appropriate for a marathoner, and his legs were turning rapidly to Jell-O. Fortunately the tide had not yet begun to the Gulf. Barrett was carried to shore as much by a gentle swell of saltwater as by his own efforts. He heaved onto a tangle of palmetto and saw grass right at the lip of freshwater. And then he vomited. A day's worth of nicotine, coffee, and fast food retched onto the damp shore.

"Cricket you . . . Oughta . . . Be here!" Barrett sank gratefully to his knees.

That's when a cottonmouth big as a man's leg unwrapped from a yellowheart pine, and raised his flat, ugly eyes to face a weakened target. The snake hissed angrily.

"Oh, God," Barrett backed away. The moccasin pursued.

The hair rose even from Barrett's well-soaked neck. There must be some congenital fear of snakes that runs especially deep for anyone raised in rural regions where vipers can pose a mortal danger. It sure as hell ran deep in Barrett Raines. This was not only a snake. It was a poisonous, venomous snake. It was the biggest damn snake Barrett had ever seen and it was a cottonmouth.

Most people raised on Westerns think the rattler's the meanest critter around. Forget that. A rattler, given his druthers, will avoid people. A rattler unless suprised is not an aggresive reptile. Not so with cottonmouths. A cottonmouth moccasin is born with a permanent and irritating itch which, combined with hunger, seasonal change, and shedding skin makes him a much more dangerous encounter.

The moccasin hissed again. Barrett couldn't believe it.

He'd burst bicycle tires that didn't sound that loud. The moccassin snaked into the water. Folks would tell you these creatures didn't strike under water. Those folks didn't know a hell of lot about moccasins.

Barrett tried to scramble up the bank. His bared feet could not find purchase; Barrett went slipping back down to the water's edge and into the opened fangs of the snake.

The moccasin plunged straight for his crotch.

Bear's scream rang out terrified with the sharp, flat report of a rifle.

"*Jesus!*"

The viper writhed without a head in Barrett's horrified lap.

"*Jesus fucking Christ!!*" Barrett scrambled to shore and almost bowled over his savior.

A mid-aged, stubble-faced white man regarded the new and Nubian arrival with the dispassionate interest of a botanist.

"Ought not take the Lord's name in vain, young fellah," he said, cradling as he did so a bottle of bourbon with an ancient, hexagonally barreled 30.30 carbine.

Barrett thought at first that the man who'd saved him was Ernest Hemingway. This man had the same large, round skull as Hemingway, the same features. He was well weathered, this man, lean with labor and had a salt and pepper stubble that grizzled his face and jaw. Barrett could easily see this guy picking fights at a bar in Key West. Older now, of course. The old man now settled by the sea. Except for the snake and the fact that Hemingway was dead, it all fit.

"Sorry about the language." Barrett felt a new surge of bile.

"S'awright." The older man's absolution was instant. "Better secure that boat. Anything inside?"

"Just an overnight," Barrett replied automatically.

"Get it." Hemingway's clone reached past Barrett to sweep up the moccasin and throw it into a burlap sack.

"The Lord provides a ram." The old man grinned and when he turned for the crucifixed shack Barrett knew that he was being invited to supper.

After securing the whaler, Barrett fumbled a tattered pair of running shoes from his overnight. He then followed Massah Ernest to the shack.

The first thing Barrett noticed on entering a jerry-rigged door was a frayed Bible propped on a cedar chest. Great, he thought, I'm saved from a snake, then fed to a snakeater.

That idea, at first ludicrous, began to assume the awful dimension of possiblity. This was after all a pretty crazy place. Things were definitely out of joint. The grizzled old-timer tossed his burlap beside the Bible.

"Nice place you got here," Barrett said uneasily.

"Not my place." The other man produced a long, well-honed knife.

Can I run? Barrett asked himself. Out of the question. Can I get his rifle? Doubtful. Is there a weapon I can use? Of course! My gun! But the gun was holstered in the bottom of Barrett's overnight.

"It's a gift to God." The other man opened the burlap.

"Looks like a boat." Barrett was ready to make a break.

"It's a church," the older man corrected his guest.

Holy shit, Barrett fought panic.

"You, ah—have a phone?"

"Telephone?" the grizzled man laughed.

"You, ah—an evangelist or something?"

"Don't much like evangelists."

Well, at least he has that in his favor, Barrett was thinking when he noticed that Ernest Hemingway was skinning the moccasin.

" 'Spect you could use a drink."

Barrett found himself suddenly presented with a bottle of Jack Daniels. He reached for the bottle on instinct, then hesitated.

"I'm not crazy," the man reassured him patiently. "And I won't harm a hair on your head."

"I hope you understand my concern," Barrett hesitated still over the bottle. "It's been a long day. I'm a little disoriented."

"*Little?*" the older man laughed again. "Son, you look like a dying calf in a hailstorm. Go on. Take a drink."

Barrett took a long pull. It felt good all the way down.

"Preacher O'Steen."

The way Barrett's benefactor introduced himself it wasn't obvious whether he expected a name in return.

"Barrett Raines." He gave him one anyway.

"What brings you here?" The preacher had already gutted the snake, tossed the entrails casually out a shuttered window.

"Work." Barrett felt another turn in his stomach. Fought it. "I'm a detective."

"Sure as hell aren't a seaman."

" 'Parently not. Thanks for your help. Especially with the moccasin, we don't get many moccasins in Tallahassee."

"Well," O'Steen rubbed his salt and pepper jaw, "We don't get many detectives."

"Have yourself much of a flock, Preacher?"

"Service every Sunday. People come when they like. You're welcome."

"Thank you. But I need to find Dead Man's Bay."

"Mean to say you're lost?"

" 'Fraid so. Can you show me the way?"

"The way, the truth, and the life." The preacher pocketed his knife and bagged his snake without ceremony. "Come on."

Barrett grabbed his bag and followed O'Steen out of the shipwrecked sanctuary. It was dusk. Shadows fell in a nearly impenetrable grove of cypress and palm trees and pine. Barrett got a glimpse of his boat over his shoulder.

"Well, come on," the preacher beckoned not a dozen steps away atop a ridge of sand.

Barrett clambered up.

And found at last Dead Man's Bay.

The sun was just closing ochre lids on a distant and grass-shrouded crescent of water. A pair of pelicans scooped low, then disappeared into the marsh. A channel zigzagged in from the bay, ruby red in the sunset, to reach a row of pilings propped below the solitary pier.

An aging, tin-roofed structure was propped on stilted legs beside the pier to overlook an odd assortment of watercraft. Low-hulled runabouts and bassboats berthed against the rising tide with more unfamiliar hulls. There were also airboats; Barrett was surprised to see a pair of those prop-driven craft. Only one shrimper, pulling in now to the pier, her nets hung like widows' scarves from her rigging.

"This it?" Barrett asked though he knew it was.

The preacher nodded. And then, "Best if I show you in. No one likes surprises."

Coleman lanterns hissed over a plywood bar and ship-to-shore radio. An ice chest of the sort usually seen in high school gymnasiums commanded customers to DRINK COCA-COLA, but there was nothing but beer inside. A well-weathered matriarch dispensed the beer and everything else within reason. Esther Buchanan packed a hundred and fifty Irish pounds into a five-foot frame. Esther was Catholic, originally and still, was originally and still from northern Ireland, from Ulster. She'd left the Emerald Isle after her father was killed in the ongoing slaughter which passed for political dialogue in that region. Esther knew then that she could not live among these men, was not certain in fact that she could live among men at all, but here she was, thirty years later, still auburn haired at fifty, passing out Budweiser and obiter dicta to the roughest kind of men like some kind of Gaelic Solomon. And it would take a Solomon tonight to sort out the tangle which Esther now faced in her makeshift bar.

A clan of fishermen convened around Esther's ice chest. Red Walker, Jawbone Greer, and Splinter Townsend lounged like a trio of trees on one side. Rough-looking men in soiled T-shirts and torn jeans. Mac MacGregor looked out of place alongside, might pass for a silver-haired physicist but for the rope-burns and sunburn which marked his trade. And then there was Jeremy. It was he who concerned Esther most, Jeremy at twenty with a wife eight months down the river and starting a trade with no more sense than God gave a goose.

The only steady heads in the lot were older than hers; Ben and Sarah Folsom had been husband and wife for forty-three years. They still held hands. Sarah Lynn was almost completely blind, now. Would need an operation. Something else to think about.

And then there was Talmadge. Talmadge Lawson made a point of standing apart, had always stood apart. A gaunt figure, tight as banjo string, he ruined a toothpick near the bar's only door.

Well, Esther said to herself, nothing beats a try but a failure. She placed her own shot of whiskey on the bar. And then—

"Jawbone says the mullet's good once ye get past Whipping Post. Anybody vouch for that?"

"Belongs to Talmadge." Red Walker hung a thumb inside his waders. "Oughta ask him first."

Esther knew it was Talmadge's water, of course. She'd

just made Red put the question everyone else was trying to avoid.

Talmadge spit his toothpick to the floor.

"Talmadge?" Esther let the toothpick go. There were more important things just now. "What about it, man? Are there any fish to catch over by the Post?"

"Depends." Talmadge was curt.

"Not much of an answer." Esther wasn't having it.

"The catch is reasonable good," Talmadge allowed when he saw Esther wasn't about to let him off the hook. "Good for one boat, that is."

"Maybe two," Esther amended.

"Doubt it." That was as close to dispute as Talmadge was willing to risk.

Esther sampled her whiskey before she changed course. "Who's the greatest need here? Who needs the water most?"

Ben Folsom pulled himself erect beside Sarah Lynn's rocker.

"Young Jeremy's got a wife expectin'. An' a boat in dry dock."

"That right Jeremy?" Esther knew that was right.

"Yes, ma'am." The boy's affirmation made it public. A community matter. "But I reckon Talmadge has got troubles, too," the boy went on to say.

"So does Ben have," Esther pointed out. "So's Sarah Lynn. So have we all."

"I wouldn't want to sponge, Miss Esther." But even as he said so you could see Jeremy's swollen wife seeking his hand.

"Nobody's the sponge, boy." Esther put an end to that. "We share and take our licks together. Isn't that the right of it, Talmadge Lawson?"

"Licks is right." Talmadge prided himself on the entendre.

"You don't sound convinced." Esther decided this was the time to take him on.

"I'm convinced enough," Talmadge growled out.

"You had a breakdown last fall, as I remember," Esther was reminding everyone including Talmadge. "An engine blew up on you as I recall. And no way to fish."

"I didn't figure you'd forget," Talmadge spit.

"Why should she?" Jawbone spoke up at last. "Why should any of us? Who tended your water? Who made the catch? Who paid for yer boat?"

"I remember." Talmadge found another toothpick.

"Good," Esther nodded. "So now young Jeremy's following his father to the sea. He needs a place to try his luck."

Mac MacGregor brushed aside a shock of silver hair. "I can share my grounds," Mac said. "I'm not half a fisherman anymore."

"A goddamned lie, MacGregor," Esther smiled. "You're twice the hand of any man here. But well said. And you, Talmadge—What do you say?"

There was a long pause. For a moment Esther wasn't sure how it would go. And then—

Talmadge dropped his second toothpick to the floor, "I'll share the south end, below the double buoy."

"Grand." Esther kept her smile. "So there you have it, Jeremy. Odd days you'll split with Mr. Lawson. And evens with MacGregor."

"I thank ya'll," Jeremy nodded to no one in particular. "Much obliged."

"No obligation," Esther corrected him. "You'll work for it."

"By the looks of his missus he's been hard at work already!"

That from Splinter Townsend. Laughter broke out quickly, like a thunderstorm, to clear the air. But just as quickly fell again with the stranger at the door.

"You need something, mister?" Esther was first to speak up.

The Colemans cast Barrett Raines in gargoyles of light and shadow. The only black figure among these Gaelic and white. Preacher O'Steen crowded past the detective to approach Esther Buchanan.

"I brought him, Esther." O'Steen might have been addressing a judge. "He come all the way from Tallahassee."

"I understand a man can get a beer here," Barrett opted for humor.

"For two dollars you can have one." Esther's reply was dead serious.

"Two—?" Barrett looked at the ice chest.

"Or you can take your drinking somewhere else," Esther nodded.

"Two's fine," Barrett replied.

"Beers or dollars?" Esther hadn't moved an inch.

"One beer will do."

Barrett pulled two soggy bills from his wallet. Esther took the cash, nodded to the ice chest. "Help yourself."

Barrett had to crowd between Jawbone and Splinter to retrieve a Bud.

"You're not a fisherman," Esther observed.

"I'm a criminal investigator." Barrett popped a top. "FDLE."

"A fisher of men." The Preacher spoke solemnly and garnered a few nervous chuckles.

These people did not like strangers, Barrett could see that and could not possibly miss the fact that there were no people of color here. No blacks, no Latinos, no Asians. Even Deacon Beach, isolated as it was, nurtured some range of humanity. Not here.

Was that why the faces about him looked so hostile? Was it just local xenophobia? Or was there something else?

Barrett glanced to the bar. The redhead was dead on him. Eye to eye. Now there was an interesting woman. What was that accent—British? Australian? Barrett's speculation cut short with a new arrival. He strolled through the door, hair perfectly trimmed, khakis pressed fresh to mock the fishermen's tattered attire. But the locals allowed the newcomer through without a ripple of protest. Barrett watched the man help himself to a beer from the ice chest. Definitely not a fisherman, Barrett decided and wondered how the hell this guy made his living when Esther intruded with a question.

"What brings you to the bay, Mr. Raines?"

"I need to ask a few questions." Barrett left the guy in khakis for a moment. "Follow a few leads."

"And how long will that take?" she pressed.

"Depends how many rocks I have to turn over," he replied.

"I doubt you'll find many rocks, here," Esther told him. "Mostly sand."

"I'll need a place to stay." Barrett met her eye.

"This isn't a motel."

"Just a few days," Barrett said as low-key as possible.

Esther scanned the bar. No suggestions. No takers. She turned to Preacher O'Steen. "Might he bunk with you, Preacher?"

"If he'll bunk on the porch."

"Up to you," she shrugged.

"Then he's welcome." O'Steen turned to Barrett. "Third shanty down. Right over the water. You can see it from here."

"Thanks." Barrett offered a smile.

"Take the sea-side," Esther chortled. "Maybe that way you won't hear 'im snore!"

Laughter broke again like thunder in the bar except this time it was at the preacher's expense.

Barrett finished his beer. "Hope I didn't disturb anything."

"Not at all," Esther denied it firmly.

"Good." Barrett left his can on the bar. "I'll see you in the morning."

"God willing," she answered but Barrett had the feeling God had nothing to do with it.

By the time Barrett trudged home with Preacher O'Steen the moon had risen half-full above the pines. Barrett tried to check the time but his waterproof watch was digitless. He threw it away. There were no streetlights, here, nor any glow from competing urban enviroments. There were also no clouds. Barrett realized that it had been over a year since he had seen stars like these, bright as diamonds and hanging in the sky.

"Pretty, ain't it?" Preacher smiled.

"Yes, it is," Barrett had to admit and then they went inside.

Preacher's home was really a cedar-planked dog run. The front door opened onto a single room whose back wall was opened to the sea and sky through a pair of enormous unscreened windows. You actually had to step through a window to get to the porch out back, an error in original architecture which Barrett found charming. The porch itself was quite large, was mounted as was the rest of the place on cypress pilings which elevated the whole structure only a foot or two above high tide. Indeed the slap of water onto the pilings or even the porch itself was constant. There was a faucet and sink on one end of the porch, a cutting board, and what Barrett guessed to be a kerosene stove.

"You look tired," O'Steen told his guest.

"Haven't slept much lately," Barrett admitted. "Don't have a smoke, do you? Mine got soaked coming ashore."

"Could probably rustle up something." The preacher ran a hand through his hair.

"I'm supposed to be quitting," Barrett confessed.

"Then I won't tempt you." The preacher turned to leave. "You won't need nicotine. Porch'll be good. High tide, right now. You can hear the water on the wood. Hear it?"

Barrett could indeed. *Slap-slap, Slap-slap.*

"Nicest sound in the world," the preacher grinned. "Pretty soon you won't give a shit if syrup goes to a dollar a sop."

That euphemism, at least, was familiar.

"It'll take more than water to get me sleep," Barrett declared tiredly.

Preacher nodded to a cot which straddled the porch's widely spaced planks. "Yours," he said. And then, as if in benediction, "God bless us all."

Barrett took off his shirt, stepped out of his shoes, stripped his trousers and let them fall. Underwear? Why not. Nobody here to give a damn. Then Barrett fell onto the cot. No springs. Just some kind of foam laid over plywood. There was a cotton blanket underneath the cot and even a pillow. That was nice. Barrett propped his head on the pillow and saw a star. It was low and large and bright. Close to the horizon. Looked like an earring for the moon. But Barrett could not remember its name. Drew a complete blank, in fact. That was irritating. Barrett was supposed to know those things. What the hell was a liberal arts education for if you couldn't remember things like these? He thought of Laura Anne, briefly. She'd like this place. Except for the snakes. A sudden breeze brought up the blanket. Barrett could hear the water hit the pilings below, *slap-slap, slap-slap*. He sank into the pillow. *Slap-slap, slap-slap.*

8.

A Fisher of Men

lap-slap, slap-slap . . . The next thing Barrett knew it was morning and he was watching water splash below his cot. Raines rose like Lazarus to a sparkling sky, a crescent of water, and the unfamiliar smell of kerosene. Preacher O'Steen slapped mullet into a pan of hot grease.

" 'Bout some breakfast?"

A cat pawed at the laces on the preacher's brograns. O'Steen dug into his pocket and produced, of all things, a condom.

"What the hell?" Barrett scrounged a pair of swim trunks from his bag.

"Watch this," the preacher winked, reaching as he did so for a shaker of salt.

The cat quit pawing O'Steen's bootlaces, now. She crouched, expectantly; the tip of her tail twitched back and forth.

"Damn kitty." The preacher slid the condom over a scarred finger and then, to Barrett's amazement, sprinkled the prophylactic with salt. "She'd rather have the salt this way than the fish. All right, kitty—"

The cat leapt a good four feet vertically to reach the cutting board. There were two fresh fish on that board. The cat ignored them, walked straight past them in fact to tongue the salt off the preacher's Trojan sock.

"That's pretty unusual," Barrett smiled, but he was already thinking about work. "What time is it?"

"Breakfast." O'Steen teased the cat with the Trojan.

"Gotta get a move on." Barrett banged sand out of his Nikes.

"Won't be ready to eat for a lick or two. Why don't you freshen up?"

"You've got a shower?!" Barrett was on his feet.

The preacher winked.

"I got the Gulf of Mexico."

Seconds later Barrett launched as flatly as he could into Dead Man's Bay and still damn near drug up the bottom. The water was barely waist deep. He surfaced to see the pier and Esther's bar seventy, maybe eighty yards dead ahead.

Fuck it, I'll swim it, Barrett thought to himself. How tough can it be?

Well, the truth is seventy yards in open water of any kind when you haven't done anything more strenuous than lift a pitcher at Bullwinkle's is a hell of a lot of work. College days were long gone. Marlboros didn't help. And Barrett was not a swimmer; he floundered from a dog paddle to a kind of breaststroke, tried his side, his back, and wound up quite literally staggering in waist-deep water to reach the pier.

There was only one boat still moored. The shrimper. Paint peeled from the hull. The nets seemed stiff as wire. Barrett wondered how often she was used. He noted a conveyor belt leading from the pier to what Raines recognized as an icehouse. The icehouse was tacked onto the back end of Esther's bar. Weighing scales and dollies were arranged outside. Barrett started to swim for shore when Esther stepped out of the cooler tossing an apron of fish heads practically in the detective's face.

"Hey!" Barrett hauled himself upright and waist-deep below the Irish-headed matriarch.

"I meant to feed the crabs. Not you." She dusted her apron of guts.

"Preacher's taking care of breakfast, thank you," Barrett replied. "You run the icehouse?"

"That I do," Esther nodded.

"And the bar?"

"That, too." Esther shook out her apron. "Is this the way you usually go about your work?"

"Just happened to be in the neighborhood," Barrett grinned and then— "Ouch . . . Ouch!!"

Barrett danced in the water.

"Ouch!!!"

Esther smiled serenely.

"Crabs," she said. "Guess they thought I threw them something extra."

Barrett took the shore back to find a feast. O'Steen had to chuckle as his guest gorged on plates of grits and hush puppies and mullet.

"Here." The older man reached for a firkin of coffee. "Wash her down good."

"I gotta tell you, Preacher . . ." Barrett mumbled through a mouthful of fish.

"Yes, sir."

"I don't feel like a police officer this morning." Barrett accepted the coffee.

"No? What do you feel like?"

" 'Bout fifteen," Barrett replied and got a hoot from his host.

"More coffee?" O'Steen offered.

"Hell, yes."

"Never did say exactly what you wanted," O'Steen observed as he poured the thick, rich brew into Barrett's chipped mug.

"Not sure I know," Barrett sighed. "But I do know why I came. Man died a couple of weeks ago. Actually he was murdered."

"There is a difference," O'Steen observed dryly.

"You're telling me." Barrett mopped his plate with a hush puppy.

"How was the man murdered, then?" O'Steen inquired.

"He was tortured," Barrett answered. "Tortured and then filleted like a fish."

"My God."

"Name was Beynon," Barrett went on. "Miles Beynon. Ever had a visitor around here by that name?"

"No." O'Steen shook his head. "But then a man can use all kinds of names."

"You're right. Just a second." Barrett wiped his hands on his shorts, went for his overnight bag. He fished around in the bag, pulled out a pair of photos.

"Here." Barrett gave the preacher a photograph. Miles Beynon posed for a police camera.

"He spent some time in jail," Barrett explained.

The preacher grunted acknowledgement and turned for the second photo. This one had been taken from Miles's apartment. The long, thin hunter grinned beside a four-point buck.

"Hunted regular?" Preacher inquired.

"Yes." Barrett took the photos. "But I'm pretty sure he was fishing here. Fishing mullet."

"He looks old," O'Steen said.

"He wasn't," Barrett replied. "You seen him?"

"Sorry." The preacher shook his head sadly.

"One other name, then." Barrett took the photograph. "We're trying to locate a man name of Brandon Ogilvie."

"Got a picture?"

"Just a name," Barrett apologized.

"Doesn't ring a bell," O'Steen frowned. "But anybody comes here had to've come by boat."

"Right," Barrett agreed.

"So you need to check with the fishermen. If they'll open up to you."

"I'll do that," Barrett nodded.

"Check the harbormaster at Harold's, too."

"I've got a man on that right now." Barrett nodded again.

"And Esther, too," O'Steen finished.

"Esther?" Barrett sipped his coffee.

"That woman," O'Steen shook his head. "She knows everything about everything."

Barrett Raines was strolling down the pier in nylon trunks and a knit shirt drinking iced-tea from a mason jar and wondering if he looked quite professional enough to conduct an "interview." He'd come looking for Esther but a deerskin rocker now claimed his attention. The rocker and its occupant creaked away on the pier alongside the village's single shrimp boat. Sarah Folsom's silver hair caught the breeze beneath a wide-brimmed straw hat. Barrett thought she was knitting but when he approached he saw yards and yards of net spread around the older woman's rocking chair. How many yards? Barrett could not pretend to make an intelligent estimate. He knew in general terms that Florida law banned commercial netting along coastal estuaries, in part by imposing tight limits on the size of fishnets and their application. But as to the size of the nets being knitted before him, or their purpose—Bear decided to leave those mysteries alone.

He had, after all, other fish to fry.

Sarah ignored Barrett's approach, her fingers subtle as a witch's to find a tear, here, a knot gone loose there. Raines did not want to intrude, thought perhaps he should wait to have his presence acknowledged.

She seemed in no hurry to acknowledge him. Just sat there, fingers flying over the nets, ensconced in her deer-skin rocker. Barrett found himself wondering briefly how many white-tails had lost their lives giving this woman a place to sit. Oh, well. He could take the initiative. Break the ice.

Barrett cleared his throat. "Looks like they've got you busy."

"Oh," she smiled, and Barrett could now see a life's worth of wrinkles below a pair of cheap, plastic-rimmed shades. "You must be Agent Raines."

"That's right," Barrett affirmed. "Got the feeling for a minute there you didn't want to see me."

"I can't see you, Mr. Raines," she smiled sweetly. "I'm blind."

"Excuse me for being a jackass," he said.

But Sarah only laughed. Light, silver laughter. It filled you up on the inside, that laughter. It made you smile.

Barrett imagined the woman before him now to be one of those rare aunts or grandmothers who, never demanding affection, always receive it, the kind of woman who always keeps cookies in easy-to-find jars and was sensitive enough, come time for supper, to have you properly diverted while she wrung the chicken's neck. Barrett never had an aunt like this, nor a grandmother, but if he had, Raines was sure she would laugh like silver-haired Sarah.

"I'm not a bear with the brightest brain," he apologized again.

"It's all right." She waved it off. "There's always hope."

Which reminded Barrett of Laura Anne.

"Anyway." Sarah was back to her nets. "Esther's going to take care of it."

"My brain?" Barrett wasn't sure he was tracking here.

"My eyes," Sarah smiled. "Or are you blind, too?"

"Right now I feel like a blind hog rooting for an acorn." Barrett's confession was frank and vivid enough to elicit another peal of laughter.

"Why don't you . . . sit and visit?" Sarah managed to invite him between chuckles. "Have some tea, there should be a glass there somewhere."

"You're sure?" Barrett was already filling a mason jar from a plastic pitcher.

"Oh, you won't be able to shut me up once I get started. I'm Sarah Lynn Folsom."

"Barrett Raines." He gathered up a handful of the net. "For shrimp?"

"Mullet," Sarah corrected him. "These are gill nets."

"I see." Barrett watched those nimble fingers. "How's Esther going to be able to help you, Sarah? I mean, with your eyes?"

"They're going to give me an operation," she said proudly. "Dr. Markellos in Pensacola. He used to operate on jet pilots, you know."

"I'm sure he's a fine doctor."

"The very best." It was the second time Sarah had corrected him. "He uses lasers instead of knives—can you imagine that? He'll take out my cataracts and then do something to my retinas, some kind of technical thing, I don't know. But I do know when he gets finished I'll be able to see."

"Must be one hell of an operation," Barrett said.

"I understand it is."

"Expensive, too." Barrett led her on.

"Oh, yes. But Ben—that's my husband. Ben says we've got insurance."

"Well, Sarah Lynn, if you have insurance, why do you need Esther?"

"Same as most of us."

Barrett turned around to find the new voice and almost dropped his jaw. A pair of long, toned legs ran rock-hard and tan to an ass framed in faded cutoffs. A tank top trapped full breasts over a firm belly with a navel as deep as the Grand Canyon.

She was mulatto. Barrett recognized the play of white and black genes which so often turned out beautiful children. And this child had grown to be a stunner.

Where had she come from?! She had a white woman's hair, cut in layers, brown and loose and short like a boy's. She had broad shoulders and a smooth, dark, bare back. Eyes like amber. And wide-set as a deer's.

She couldn't have been much over twenty, walking, fairly deliberately, for Barrett's inspection to give Sarah Lynn a pert kiss on the cheek.

"Morning, Megan." The older woman sought the younger's hand.

"Mornin', Sarah." The younger woman gave her hand gently.

"Don't believe we've met." Barrett was about to stand.

"You're the police officer." She cut him short. "I'm Megan. Looks like you've met Aunt Sarah."

"We were talking about her operation."

"Blue Cross and Blue Shield," Megan said curtly.

"Beg your pardon?"

"You wanted to know how Sarah's paying for her surgery. We all pretty much use the same thing."

"Blue Cross won't cover everything." Barrett wondered how she kept so fit.

"We all pitch in," she said.

Barrett scanned the single pier and scattered shacks which ringed the bay.

"Doesn't look like there's a lot to pitch."

"Just a redneck little fishing village, is that it?" She faced him squarely.

"That's not what I said," Barrett backtracked.

"You didn't have to say," she retorted.

"Megan! That's no way to be!" Sarah Lynn's fingers stopped their quick flight.

"I'm sure I don't have a hell of a lot more in my wallet than you do." Barrett offered the confession as a truce.

"Doubt you have nearly as much," Megan refused it.

"I see." Barrett sipped his tea. This wasn't going to be easy.

"I 'spose you work here?"

"Me and Mama both," she affirmed brusquely. "We go for snapper and grouper in deep water. Mullet in the shallows. Whatever. That's on top of the icehouse and the bar and everything else."

"Sounds like a pair of hard-working women."

"Spend a day with us. Judge for yourself." It was Esther Buchanan who made that suggestion over Barrett's shoulder.

Raines did the proverbial double take, and turned back to Megan. "Is this—?"

"Her mother. Yes, it is," the gorevan-haired mother answered for her daughter. "You know, Mr. Raines, for a detective you seem a slow man. We ready to go, Megan?"

"Need another hundred of ice," the daughter replied.

Esther turned to Barrett with a smile.

"Well, now, Mr. Raines. Would you like to make yourself useful?"

*   *   *

Barrett Raines labored under a hundred pounds of ice and a hundred unasked questions as he trailed behind Esther Buchanan and her half-black daughter on their rough-hewn pier. Esther was even more interesting, it seemed, than first appearances suggested. Barrett wondered if there was a diplomatic way he could inquire about her husband? Or Megan's father? Probably not. It was a mark of the woman's hold on this place that her daughter was accepted by its people. As an equal, he wondered?

That speculation got cut short as Esther stopped short before a fisherman's throwback.

"Welcome aboard."

It was what old-timers called a birddog. An old-fashioned mullet boat. Her name was painted sternward, bold and black—*The Debra Kaye*. Barrett was reminded that the last craft of this kind he could remember seeing was propped up as a planter outside a bait shop. Birddogs had virtually disappeared, at least along this stretch of coastline, the State of Florida making its restrictions on mullet fishermen more palatable by buying their boats as well as their nets. And yet here was a well-preserved vessel carrying in her stern what seemed to be endless yards of netting.

Esther and Megan leaped lightly into their atavistic craft. Barrett, timing a gentle swell to follow, barely avoided a hernia.

"Wasn't much more than a hull when I bought her." Esther wrapped a rough hand around a long tiller with no apparent concern for the detective's inspection. "Restored her meself."

It was an unusual construction. A very wide stern kept the nets beneath a pair of railroad ties. There was a water well built more toward the bow than Raines first imagined, but the well wasn't for fish or bait. It was for an outboard motor. A hundred-horse Evinrude mounted on a transom inside the well to drive a prop situated forward of amidship.

"Give me six inches of water I can make forty miles an hour," Esther claimed loudly. "I can skip easy as you please where any other boat'd have her hull ripped to shreds on the mounds."

The oyster mounds, she meant, of course, those centuries upon centuries of accumulated shell and mineral with edges sharp as knives.

Esther's ice had Barrett's shoulder aching to the bone. Between the nets at stern and the engine boward Bear could see a fish box, a big one, five or so feet long, three feet deep and as wide, partially filled with a slush of ice and saltwater.

"There?" he grunted.

"Don't drop it," Esther nodded.

Barrett eased the ice as well as he could into the fish box.

"Don't see many birddogs anymore." Barrett glanced to gauge the remark's effect on Esther.

"And are ye now a game warden, Agent Raines?" She seemed amused.

"No, ma'am," Barrett shook his head.

"Good."

The Evinrude sputtered to life.

"Yer nets ready, Megan?"

"Yes, ma'am."

"Come along then, Mr. Detective."

"On the water?" Barrett demurred.

"Well, where else? Look around you, man. Everyone but the lame and the blind are at sea. And if you plan to interrogate me—" She eased the throttle forward. "It won't be where it's dry."

They followed a channel which ran for miles, it seemed, in a sea of grass. Esther goosed the Evinrude; the bow rose slightly, seeming to pull the boat's white hull over a gash of dark water. Barrett felt the spray of brine in his face. A good feeling. Bear glanced astern to Megan. She was standing to meet the rush of briny air, the wind filling her top along with those other fine attributes. That washboard belly. Barrett returned his attention to Megan's mother.

"Had no idea you were married, Ms. Buchanan." He leaned in close to make sure he was heard.

"Was married," she told him. "And call me Esther."

"Call me Barrett," he rejoined. "I'm married, too. Don't know for how long."

Esther didn't seem interested.

"Why so much ice?" He tried a different track.

"Mullet have a higher fat content than most fish," Esther replied. "If you don't chill a mullet out of the net and keep him chilled he'll rot."

"I see." Barrett knew now why mullets were best served fresh. "And where are we going to find the suckers this morning?"

"Hold yer britches." Esther reached for the throttle. "And you'll see."

The channel wound in a maze which had to be negotiated before reaching Dead Man's Bay. Esther opened up her outboard, running her 'dog along a featureless ribbon of water with nothing to guide her but a series of cypress poles stuck at low tide into the sand.

There were no proper buoys, here. No formal aids to navigation. Everything from oyster mounds to sandbars to wrecked hulls conspired to snag a fisherman's boat. Esther weaved past those obstacles on her pole-marked course like a skier on a downhill slalom. And just when the waterway seemed interminable, the channel widened out, abruptly, to give a full view of the bay.

Barrett saw a boat far off to starboard. One indistinct boat. Nothing else. Esther turned hard south.

"We've got a low tide running," she explained. "That's good. Most generally we'll net in six to eighteen inches of water."

"Inches?" Barrett exclaimed.

Esther nodded. "You go to bird-dog mullet, you better be ready to work shallow."

" 'Bird-dog'?" Barrett had not heard the term used as a verb.

Esther apparently didn't feel the need to clarify.

"Here. Take a hat." She pulled a sweat-stained and filthy thing from a map box.

Barrett hesitated.

"Put it on," she ordered. "I don't want you sunstruck. Then help Megan with the nets."

"Nets?"

"Just see Megan." Esther swerved for the shoreline. "She'll show you what to do."

Barrett staggered back to find Megan securing buoys and weights to the nets. The buoys, it turned out, were nothing more than a pair of plastic milk jugs jerry-rigged to support either end of the net.

"How much net you got here?" Barrett eyed the coils warily.

"Hundred and fifty," Megan smiled wickedly. "That's yards. Not feet."

The bottomside of the net was anchored with everything from discarded flatirons to window sashes. This is the South, for sure, Barrett said to himself as Megan showed him the right way to feed the net. In the Northeast or out West somebody would manufacture a buoy for these nets. Somebody else would make weights to anchor them. And somebody else would put them together. Everything would come neatly packaged and above all, orderly. Clean. Standardized.

Not here. Everything from the boat to the nets

reflected a culture of make-do, of broicilage. Nothing served its original purpose, it seemed, which meant that everything had a cosmos of possibilities.

Barrett tried not to look at Megan while he worked. He wasn't much help, rigging these nets. He sure as hell wouldn't be much help when it came to the netting. Watching Megan's quick, sure labor, the boy from Deacon Beach began to feel like a milk bucket under a bull.

Esther kept her boat close to the shoreline. A bewildering variety of wildlife burst before the boat's patient stalk. The pelicans and heron and gulls were familiar. But other things Barrett had not seen in years. A short, distinctive "pop" brought his attention to a pod of small crustaceans that, breaking to the surface at regular intervals, immediately descended like miniature submariners, leaving a tiny train of bubbles behind.

"Scallops?"

"Aye," Esther confirmed. "You don't often see 'em this late in the season."

There were other things to fascinate a man not often on the water. Turtlegrass. Flying fish. And on the land, too, *rara avises* which Barrett would not have seen at all without Esther to guide him.

"Lynx." She pointed to shore.

A clutch of trees signified some freshwater outflow; the lynx lounged in the arm of a magnificent cypress, twitching his bobbed tail like Preacher's cat. And then Barrett turned to see a dorsal fin slicing across the bow—

"Shark!" He sounded the alarm.

"Cobia." Esther shook her head.

"Really?" Barrett watched the dark shape knife away.

"Never seen one?" Megan regarded him scornfully.

"Not on the water."

"Hell of a game fish." She returned to her nets. "We catch 'em for fun."

*   *   *

Esther turned her boat smoothly to port to intercept some unmarked coordinate leading to a channel that cut through a barrier of rocks and oyster bars that opened out onto a wide plateau of perfectly smooth water.

"My grounds." She offered the explanation shortly pointing ahead to a buoy striped blue and white. Within moments *The Debra Kaye* coasted above sandy bottomed shallows stretching still and calm beneath water clear as crystal. The shallow water ran shoreward against a boundary of saw grass and marsh while extending as far as Barrett could see into the bay.

"Now we look for sign." Esther trolled her craft so slowly it barely left a wake. It was about an hour later and barely in slight of shore that the older woman dropped her bird-dog to an idle.

"In there." Esther nosed her craft into the mild breeze which prevailed. "We've got ourselves a school. Get ready, Megan."

"I don't see anything." Barrett craned over the bow.

"Yes, you do," Esther told him. "You just don't know what it is that you see."

They fished in water that Barrett couldn't believe was much more than ankle deep. He could see shadows from cumulus clouds overhead cast on the shallow bottom. And then he realized there were no clouds. There were no shadows. What Barrett was seeing, shifting on the bottom like phantasmagorias, were mullet.

"Feeding on algae." Esther anticipated the question. And then, "Let's get to work."

Barrett soon discovered that bird-dogging mullet was a lot like beating for tigers. You wanted the fish to panic. You wanted them to panic and run and then charge head-first into into your waiting trap.

"Make sure you don't tangle the net." Esther circled the

school as Barrett scrambled with Megan to spill the gill net off the side. "And make sure it's smooth all along the bottom, I won't stand for losing fish!"

Barrett barely had time to register that command before the boat jerked from under his feet. Esther ran her birddog balls-to-the-wall over the water, around and around in ever-dwindling circumferences. She whooped like a cowboy—

"*Cam on you little bastards!*"

She screamed, she cursed, she cajoled the fish at the top of her lungs. So did Megan. Not Barrett. He hadn't the wind to spare. His heart hammered for the second time that day as Raines struggled with Esther's daughter to draw the net tighter and tighter around their shifting school of fish.

"*They're runnin', Mama!*" Megan looked like a jockey on a winning horse.

Barrett could see them, now, could see the bullet-headed fish panic and run and dart for open water. The first shadows fired like cartridges into the gill net.

"Why don't they just back out?" Barrett asked Megan.

"Can't," she shouted. "Their gills're like barbs. Once the head goes through—they're stuck."

"So that's why we call this a gill net," Barrett regarded the hemp in his hands.

Esther just shook her head.

"And the man calls himself a detective."

Tighter and tighter the circle became, until finally an entire school of fish thrashed helplessly in Sarah Lynn's finely wrought web.

"Haul 'em in," Megan's mother called out finally. And Barrett found himself with Esther's daughter hauling in hundreds of pounds of thrashing, silver-bellied mullet.

Mullet and everything else. Barrett was amazed to see everything from stingrays to pinfish tangled in Esther's net. There were also flashlight batteries and soft drink cans, the droppings from passing boats and ships.

"We got to cull 'em out," Megan said impatiently. "Separate the mullet from the rest."

There was only one way to do that. Barrett reached in gingerly to extract a crab.

"Be all day at that rate." Esther offered the critique dispassionately.

So it went. All morning long they hunted the shallows. The sun rose unmercifully as net after net went into the water, cast after cast. Barrett pulled fish till he thought his back would break. Megan paced herself alongside in the brutal heat, pausing only to gulp water from an ice cooler.

The sun by now burned low in the sky. Esther's fish box was filled with mullet. Esther inspected the day's winnings briefly.

"Good enough," she said at last and Barrett collapsed like a slaughterhouse cow to the deck. Not so with Megan.

"Swim, Mama?"

"Make it quick."

Megan dove tank top and all like a dolphin into the water.

Barrett watched her, amazed. A day's labor that would kill most men and here was this girl swimming to sea for recreation. The water pulled back Megan's hair. She rolled onto her back. Saltwater coursed into the bowl of her belly, between her breasts. It pulled at her top.

Esther dropped a beer onto Barrett's swelling crotch.

"She's too young for you."

"She must be twenty or so," Barrett protested.

"Twenty-three." Esther popped a top of her own.

"No offense, but—Why hasn't she gotten out of here?"

"She had a fellow 'till this spring."

"What happened?" Barrett pulled the beer can across his brow.

"He ran off with some whore from Perry." Esther spit out the words with venom.

"Sorry," was all Barrett could think of to say.

"I'm not." Esther turned to him. "You think I'd want a man like that for my daughter?"

"I meant it's too bad there wasn't better," Barrett replied.

"Ah. Aye," she said and swallowed her beer.

"I've got some questions for you, Esther." Barrett found himself seeking permission for something that, as a law enforcement officer, he ought to be able to demand. Why was that? What had happened in the twenty-four short hours he'd been in this place?

Once again Esther was ahead of him. "I never met a man called himself Miles Beynon. No, sir. Nor a Brandon Ogilvie."

"How in the hell—?!"

"While you were jawing with Sarah Lynn I spoke with the preacher," Esther shrugged.

"I'm beginning to feel out of my league." Barrett cooled somewhat with the simplicity of her explanation.

Esther nodded. "First smart thing you've said since you got here."

"Can't let it drop, though." Barrett faced her squarely. "I know Miles got as far as Perry. The harbormaster identified him. Said the man was headed here."

"That's all you've got?" Esther was looking at her daughter.

"Got some dates from the rental." Barrett risked a look himself. "Miles came up here from Kissimmee on February thirteenth, May twelfth, and August thirteenth."

"Pretty damn regular," Esther observed.

"He'd keep a boat four or five days, usually. Never more than a week."

"That's something at least." Esther bobbed her head. "When the men come drinking I'll ask around."

Barrett paused over his beer. "I am surprised. Thank you."

"Don't thank me." Esther crushed her can with her fist. "I figure the quicker you get what you want, the quicker you'll be out of here." She glanced again to Megan. "That'll suit me just fine."

"One other thing since I'm batting so well."

"Go on."

"Last night. Man came into your place after me, well-kept in khakis. Looks like he keeps his hair cut in town someplace and he sure as hell doesn't earn his living the same way the rest of you do."

"Ray," Esther nodded shortly. "Ray Boatwright."

"Know anything about him?"

"Came in here about a year ago, maybe a little more," Esther paused. "I could tell he wasn't a fisherman."

"Have any idea what he does?"

"None," Esther shook her head. "Why? Is it important?"

I've been behind a desk too long, Barrett berated himself silently.

Bear knew how important it was, especially in the early stages of an investigation, to keep potential witnesses honest. "Just keep in mind," he used to coach rookie interrogators, "that when you're a detective and you're asking somebody a question one of two things are most likely gonna happen: One—they're going to try to please you. Or, two—they're gonna lie to you.

"If a person wanting to please gets the idea that a certain piece of information they've provided is significant they're likely to embellish, or exaggerate the truth. On the other hand if a liar thinks a line of questioning is significant they'll shut down or misdirect."

It was easy to teach, hard to do and Raines knew he hadn't done it in a long time.

"Everything's a help." Barrett glossed over his mistake. "Everything."

"Good." Esther swigged her beer. "Consider it a day's wages."

"What?"

"A day's work for an interview, I'd say that's fair. Megan—" Esther chuckled wickedly.

"Yes, ma'am?"

"Getting late. Best we go in."

It was slower going back on a birddog filled with fish in a rising tide. Esther left the shore for deeper water, took a line across the bay.

Megan stretched on the deck in shorts and a top soaked by saltwater. Barrett struggled to keep his attention on her mother at the well. Esther took them past an island not far offshore. Barrett could see the remains of a dock teetering in the sunset, and then—

Barrett leaned forward suddenly. Was that a crucifix? It certainly looked like the skeleton for one. A solitary post, obviously man-made, was planted ten or twelve feet high. A crosspiece was secured about halfway up.

"Place have a name?" Barrett asked Esther.

"They call it the Whipping Post," Esther replied.

"Whoa." Barrett took another look. "Got a history?"

"Years ago a man found his wife cheating. Story goes he planted that post, tied her on. Then he beat her with palmettoes. Some said till her ribs showed."

"Hard man," Barrett winced.

"No," Esther disagreed. "An ordinary man. And then he left her for the tide."

"The tide?"

"Covers the dock," Ether said. "Covers the island, too, if the moon's right. That's what he wanted, of course. A good moon for her to hang, to bleed, and beg. And then to drown."

Barrett whistled. "Some story."

"Is it?" A hard edge crept into Esther's voice.

"C'mon, you don't believe that kind of stuff. Look—" Barrett waved a hand to the island. "That's just a place where they dried nets or something. Nothing else happened. It couldn't!"

Esther shrugged. "You tell us about a man skinned alive. Could that happen?"

"Whoever did Miles was a professional," Barrett pointed out. "Hard to imagine a regular guy doing something that elaborate to his wife."

"It is hard," Esther agreed.

"What kind of man would go to that kind of trouble?" Barrett tossed it off as ridiculous.

"A hard man," Esther told him. "An ordinary man."

"Anybody remember who he was?" Barrett sipped his beer.

"I do." And for the first time Esther looked with Barrett to the Whipping Post. "He was a black man, in more than one sense. And he was my husband."

Barrett steadied himself on the gunwale of *The Debra Kaye*. He wanted to hear a lot more about the Whipping Post. He wanted to hear a lot more about Esther and her one-time husband. But the pier was already in sight and the day's work, as Barrett was to see, was nowhere near ended.

Once they reached the pier the day's catch had to be weighed and stored in the icehouse. Barrett was shoveling mullet into a wheelbarrow when he noticed a condom stuck in Esther's net; he was reminded of Preacher's cat.

"The hell are you laughing at?" Megan demanded.

"Never mind." Barrett went back to work.

An ice-grinder wailed like a banshee to crush hundred-pound blocks of ice. Jawbone and Splinter tossed the blocks like beanbags onto the coveyor which fed the grinder. A row of boats joined Esther's to offload their day's catch into her cooler. Esther logged the total weight and price per pound for each man's catch. Barrett must have shoveled fish from a dozen boats. Every patch of skin except for what was shaded beneath Esther's loaned hat was burned. (Funny how white folks assumed black people couldn't sunburn.) And his hands! Barrett's hands were in blisters. His arms were on fire. His back hurt more to stand than to bend. Still more fish to shovel.

Megan kept pace easily alongside. Barrett knew, now, how she came to have that back, those legs, that belly. Splinter Townsend grinned to the detective from Tallahassee. "Looks like somebody got a day's work out of you."

"They will if they're not careful," Barrett admitted weakly and even Esther smiled with the laughter which floated from the pier.

Almost done, now, only a couple of boats left when Mac MacGregor came puttering up in a birddog almost a clone to Esther's.

"It's not Lent yet, MacGregor," Esther called from the pier. "Why so gloomy?"

"It's an odd day, isn't it? Wednesday's are odd."

"All day," Esther nodded.

"Young Jeremy must have got confused." Mac was shaking his head as he eased his craft into the pier.

"How's that?" Esther took his line.

"I went to fish my grounds." Mac flung aside his nets. "Nothing there. Not a nibble. I went from buoy to buoy. Saw not mullet one."

"Jeremy!" Esther stood to bellow across the din. "Jeremy Bantham!"

"Yes, ma'am." He came bounding from the icehouse.

"Did you fish Mac's grounds today?" Esther asked the boy when he got close enough.

"No, ma'am." Jeremy stumbled to a halt. "I fished Mr. Lawson's grounds today. I fish Mr. Mac's t'morrow."

"Good lad." Esther placed a beefy hand on the young man's shoulder.

"Maybe I caught the tide's wrong," MacGregor suggested.

"Maybe," Esther mulled, but when she hanged her clipboard on a rusty nail a dead silence fell over the pier. Barrett watched as one by one the thick-armed hunters of the sea dropped their ice and their fish and their nets. Esther looked them all up and down—then strode down the pier toward Talmadge Lawson.

Talmadge's boat wallowed with mullet. Esther watched as Talmadge culled his catch. One by one the other fishermen—Splinter, Red, Jawbone, Mac, and Jeremy—came to stand at Esther's side. Lawson rose from his work to find the whole community standing a silent choir above.

"A good day, Mr. Lawson?" Esther peered into his boat and johnny.

"Good enough." Talmadge ruined a toothpick in his mouth.

Esther didn't ask permission as she dropped into his boat. Talmadge locked his jaws as the woman fished through his nets.

"Something I can do you for?" Talmadge bit it off.

Esther ran work-hardened hands over his nets. "Nearly dry. I'd say you had an early start."

"Gets the worm," Talmadge replied shortly.

"Ah ha." Esther continued her inspection.

Talmadge finally exploded. "You might own the icebox,

woman! You might own the bar and everyone in it! You might think you own the goddamn Gulf, but you don't own my boat!"

"We own a piece of it—in case you've forgotten."

With that Esther plunged her fist into the teeming fish. What she pulled out from under the mullet was a buoy. Red on green, the milk jug had been crudely marked with duct tape. Red on green with a white divider. Esther displayed the jug to her gathered fishermen.

"You all know MacGregor's marks."

"Doesn't mean anything," Talmadge snarled.

"Probably came off Mac's net, sometime earlier," Esther remarked casually. "But you got it today, didn't you, Talmadge? At first tide. You scooped it up when you poached Mac's fish."

"Damn thing could've come off months ago!" Lawson protested. "Could easy have drifted to my grounds."

"God could have put feet on flounder," Esther said coldly. "But He didn't."

"Those are my fish." Talmadge stabbed a toothpick at the mullet.

"Are they?"

"You can't prove they aren't!" Talmadge jeered. He had her now. Bitch couldn't prove a thing.

"No, I can't." The admission came frankly, without a pause. "I cae'na prove these aren't your fish."

Talmadge was about to smile when Esther continued—

"But then again I don't have to buy them, either."

"I'll sell them myself," Talmadge retorted.

"I've got a radio," Esther informed him. "And I know every buyer on the coast."

"Just get me the ice." Talmadge hardened.

"I'm fresh out," she returned.

"The hell you are!"

"Fresh out." She took Splinter's hand to leave Talmadge's boat. "And you'd better hurry, Mr. Lawson," she nodded to his labor. "Your fish are half ripe already."

"You fucking whore."

Barrett didn't like what he saw, then. A whole community of fishermen stepped past Esther toward Talmadge's boat. Jesus Christ, Barrett thought. They're going to lynch him!

But Esther stilled them all with a single, raised hand. The men stopped in their tracks. Esther turned back tiredly to face Talmadge Lawson.

"Whore is it?"

"You heard me!"

"Then hear this, Mr. Lawson: The last man called me whore lugged his guts to the sink."

That was it. Esther turned her back on Talmadge Lawson.

She passed through the bay's gathered men.

Barrett Raines found himself moving aside with the rest.

9.

Blood and Water

Thelma Johnson had just dropped off her dry clean-
ing at The Royal Touch and returned home to fish
whatever it was that was rattling around in the garbage dis-
posal when she heard a rap at the aluminum-framed
screen door that kept mosquitoes and salesmen out of her
trailer home. The double wide had been top of the line
when it was made in the mid-eighties. By now it was an
artifact raised on railroad ties along with nearly a hundred
other mortgage-dodgers who collected with the snowbirds
around Fort Walton Beach.

Thelma was a veteran tenant at the Seaside Courts. She
lost almost everything during her tenure among the
mobile homes—her husband, her youth. Thelma Lou still
retained a residue of strength, though, left over from
active days on the basketball court, softball diamond.
There were pictures and trophies of those early triumphs
all over her cheaply-paneled walls. Those early trophies
had been largely replaced in later years by a ceramic vase
filled with matchbooks. Glossy-covered cardboard adver-
tised places like the Ocean Lounge & Grille, Holiday Inn,
or Sandy's. Thelma collected them after her many futile
evenings beside a bourbon and the sea.

Not that she couldn't still command a good look. Thelma had a wealth of hair that one could have imagined once was strawberry blonde. She retained much of the figure that made locals recall high school shenanigans in a variety of backseats. Labor and loneliness had taken their toll, however, so that by now Thelma thought of herself pretty much as just another artifact propped along with the rest.

A rap at the door drew her attention, if not her interest. Neighbors didn't knock, nor boyfriends. Only salesmen knocked, polite like that, or the occasional Mormon. Then came a second summons. The flimsy screen door shook this time.

"Whatever you're sellin', I'm not buyin'," Thelma yelled as she dropped another matchbook into her vase. There was not a third knock and for an instant she thought she was safe. She did not know that the tall stranger who waited beside her oleander and boxwood was not interested in sales.

He cleared his throat. "Mrs. Johnson? Thelma Johnson?"

Looks like she'd have to come to the door. So she did and for a minute Thelma thought she'd won the Publisher's Clearing House Sweepstakes. This guy was a looker.

"Mrs. Johnson?" he asked.

"Who's asking?" She wasn't going to be easy just because she was desperate.

"A friend of Miles's."

Pale blue eyes never wavered above the assassin's warm, genial smile. He displayed a photograph for her inspection.

The photo was well-worn and wrinkled. A trained eye could see that it was also soaked with water. But all Thelma could see was a snapshot of a shapely woman seven years younger and a skinny, toothy companion poised over her shoulder. A man's hand had scrawled over the back, "Thelma, 305-913-4435."

"My old phone number." She offered the completely unnecessary explanation.

"Miles told me if I was in Fort Walton I should give you this." He let her have the snapshot. "He said it would remind you of some good times."

"Oh, is that what he said?" She laughed as she ran a hand through her hair. "Well, where is Miles, that rascal?"

"Thinking of you, I imagine," the killer teased.

All he had to do now was give her a name. Any name would do.

"Frederick Haus." The handsome man extended his hand. "I knew Miles when he was stationed in the Mideast."

"Well, Fred why don't you come in? Tell me what those good old times were all about!"

He did come in, careful to let the cheaply framed door close behind him. He could see her dry-cleaned clothes hanging still in their cellophane wrapper. He noted the scarlet cords which tied her cheap drapes aside from the trailer's jaliced windows. An extension cord fed a toaster, a waffle iron, and an ancient coffee pot which percolated in a kitchen that looked over a waist-high counter. He closed a second, interior door while she fussed with an air-conditioner. Minutes later he was comfortably seated beside a panel of mildewed relics and a vase filled with matches, smiling patiently to histories which did not interest him, and nursing a cup of coffee which he did not want.

She spooned heaping teaspoonfuls of sugar into the killer's coffee, happy that she'd just manicured and painted her nails. Very pretty nails. Not too long. The polish was labeled "Salmon."

The foreigner watched her hands, her fingers particularly, as he endured the woman's chatter of anecdote and exaggeration. She had met Miles in Miami a couple of months after Beynon was discharged from the army. Miles was stocking vending machines for Coca-Cola. She kept the books for an offshore salvaging operation; she'd see Beynon when he'd stock their machine.

"Those little bottles, you know?" Her chatter was filled with asides. "Like you can't get anymore."

He smiled, understanding with perfect conviction.

"Anyway," she searched for the thread just now abandoned. "Oh, yes. In Miami. Well, Miles would come in there once a week. Regular as church. Everybody else in that place kept hitting up on me," Thelma confided to the stranger. "Especially the divers. Not a diver born doesn't think he's God's gift to women. Miles was the only one nice. Didn't drink, much. Didn't smoke, neither. It's nice to kiss a man now and then, believe me, without beer or nicotine on his breath."

"I take it, then, that you were fond of Miles? Perhaps—knew him well?"

"Oh, we had ourselves a time or two." She smoothed her skirt. "Not sayin' he was a Robert Redford, you understand."

"No," Blue Eyes agreed.

"He was one long drink of water, though," she recalled, stirring her coffee continuously, needlessly, and then, teasing. "Long in other ways, too. Talk about divin' deep!"

She giggled but then added quickly, "He was the only one of them boys showed me any respect whatsoever."

"You stayed in touch while he was in prison?"

"Oh, yes, I'd call once, maybe twice a week. Always from a pay phone. Miles didn't want the police to know anything about us. He said it was our secret."

"You keep secrets very well?"

"Wild horses," she giggled and crossed her heart.

"I suppose prison must have been rough for Miles."

"No. Except for the niggers and queers," she said reflectively, "things never seemed to get him down. He'd just tell me to wait. Said he had a pot of gold at the end of the rainbow!"

She laughed. "I guess they all say things like that."

"I suppose," her guest shrugged. And then, "Miles told me to look up a man, I believe his name was—Ogilvie. Brandon Ogilvie."

She stopped stirring her coffee.

"I don't know anything about an Ogilvie," she said.

"You're quite sure?" He was still smiling.

"You know I'd love to talk more but—Look at the time! I've got chores waiting," she said sweetly, but rose from the table to make clear she was inviting him to leave.

"Have I said something impolite?" Her visitor feigned surprise.

"Look, Fred, I just don't think I should be talking to you about Miles's business."

"Ah. Then Miles did speak with you about Mr. Ogilvie. Can you tell me where he is? Where I might find him? Or do you have a photo? That would be a great help."

"I don't know anybody named Ogilvie." She was pale now. "I don't even know where Miles is now he's out of prison—Say, are you the police?"

"Absolutely not." This time his smile was genuine.

"Then what's all this about Miles? Where is he? How is he?"

"He's dead," the killer said.

"Oh, God. How?"

"I killed him," he shrugged.

She backed away. He rose from the table to block her way to the door.

"Miles did have a pot of gold, you see." The assassin never quit smiling as he stripped a scarlet cord from a drape. "But it was not his pot to keep; it was mine. Five hundred thousand British pounds. Royal currency, you agree? And hard-earned, too, I can tell you. But Miles stole my earnings—with Mr. Ogilvie's assistance—and so whatever luxury your friends have enjoyed, Miss Thelma, has been at my expense.

"I just want my money. I thought Miles would be able to help me more, you see. I thought he'd know the details. I asked him very carefully, 'Does Brandon live in the area? How does he control the money?' And especially—'How do you change the pound notes to American dollars?' I asked Miles over and over to explain everything.

"He didn't. But he did tell me where he went to collect his cut of the deal. He told me who gave him his small portion of the pot. But that's not the end of the rainbow—is it, Thelma?"

"I don't know what you're talking about!" She croaked it out.

"It's very simple, really," he replied helpfully. "I know where the pot of gold is. I know who tends the pot. But I don't know precisely what's in the pot nor how to get it out. I'm sure Brandon Ogilvie could tell me these things, just as Miles told me about you, Thelma, but I cannot locate Brandon. I don't even know what the man looks like. Now, the truth is, I could probably manage on my own, may be forced in fact to manage on my own. But it would be so much easier if I could only speak with Mr. Ogilvie. If you could only help me, here. A phone number. A picture, perhaps."

"I don't know Brandon Ogilvie," her voice quavered. "I don't know anybody."

"According to Miles that simply isn't true." He offered the contradiction politely. "You see, before we were finished Miles said your name to me many times. Again and again. And he said quite clearly that it was you who introduced him to Brandon Ogilvie."

"Doesn't mean I know where he is now!" she protested.

"Doesn't it?"

"That was eight years ago! Jesus Christ, Brandon was working salvage. I knew him from work. That's all!"

"So you don't have an address? A phone or location?"

"No, now get out of here! Please!"

"And you don't know anything about the money?" He saw a radio. Good. That would help.

"What money?" She was looking for an escape, now. Or a weapon.

He unplugged the extension cord from the coffee pot.

"What are you doing?" she demanded.

"You don't have a heart condition, do you?" he asked as if confirming another, useful, detail.

"Leave me alone, please. PLEASE!" She was begging, now. Crying.

"I cannot," he apologized. "I need some information."

"*I don't know anything!*"

"Perhaps not." He pulled out a knife, began peeling insulation from the cord. "But I have to be sure."

10.

Mrs. Brown, You've Got a Lovely Daughter

Esther's iron discipline of Talmadge Lawson was followed by a long, communal celebration at her bar. The restraint which Barrett had previously observed in this fishing community vanished. Splinter was showing his apendectomy scar to some floozy on Jawbone's shoulder. Red Walker was playing some Appalachian ditty on a fiddle that could not possibly be in tune. Ben and Sarah cornered happily with Jeremy and his pregnant, young wife. Preacher even allowed himself a libation by the Coke cooler. Esther teased and cajoled and courted the rough-housed bunch as if she hadn't a care in the world.

Barrett borrowed Esther's radio to leave a message for Cricket Bonet. He wasn't getting through. An antedeluvian TV competed for attention. Black and white and snow came from a Pensacola station. So this was life before cable, Barrett thought as he once again triggered Esther's ship-to-shore. Barrett's contact with Cricket led unfortunately through Sheriff Sue Driggers at the Taylor County Shrine for Reluctant Law Enforcement. Barrett had just about decided to give up on the radio when Sheriff Driggers's drawl broke the ether.

Ten minutes later Barrett was still talking and getting nowhere.

". . . Look, Sheriff, can you just tell my partner I called in? Tell him everything's ten-four, over."

"Tell him yourself, he'll be here in the morning, over."

Barrett jabbed his mike—

"Sheriff, let's cut the Boy Scout, shit, shall we? I have *tried* to catch Cricket at your office. He obviously is *working*. We have only this *radio* to communicate. *Can you just tell him I'm okay? Over.*"

More static. Barrett was sure he heard the sheriff laughing over the wireless. Finally—

"So you want your partner to know you can't get holt of him but not to worry everything's awright. Is that about it? Come back."

"Just about," Barrett said tightly. "And can you give him Esther's call sign here? Over."

"I guess I can do just about anything I want," came Drigger's reply. "Sheriff's office over and out."

"Thank you very fucking much."

Barrett signed off. A local crime report faded in and out over Esther's TV. Some woman found near Fort Walton Beach. Tortured, a local cop was saying as he held up the electric cord that had been applied to the woman now dead. Suffocated at the end, the reporter went on to say and described how a neighbor had found the woman in her kitchen with a launderer's cellophane bag twisted tightly over her head. The Royal Touch.

Barrett shook his head as he left the tube. Must be the season.

A meteorologist's enthusiastic description of a storm out of season went unheeded. Barrett collected a foldout chair, and swung over to an unscreened window to try to enjoy what was left of the day. A spectacular flamingo fire burned where the sky met the water. Barrett kicked back with a Bud and would have watched that sunset forever except that duty kept intruding. Barrett wondered what he would have done, earlier in the day, if Esther's fishermen had assaulted Talmadge Lawson. He knew what he should do, of course. Any law officer would know that. But there seemed to be a big difference in this place between what should happen and what *did*.

Respect for the law involved some degree of separation between those who enforce and those who obey. Cops, particularly street cops, revel in that separation. The uniform, the badge, the gun—all say to civilians that this man or woman is different. Detectives prided themselves on a more subtle distinction, but the fact that there *was* a distinction was never in question. To be accessible was one thing. To be familiar was to breed contempt.

But it was too late now for Barrett to segregate himself from these people, too late to find that Arrow tie and plastic card that set him apart. Barrett had come here essentially a lost man. He had accepted food and lodging. He had worked with these people, blistered his hands on their nets, and discovered what everyone else already knew—That Esther was the real law in Dead Man's Bay.

Barrett sipped his beer. What the hell, he propped up his feet on a neighboring chair. He wasn't doing much more than a missing-person gig, here, anyway—"Where in the World is Brandon Ogilvie?" And it was pretty obvious it wasn't going anywhere. Couple of more days to check out Ray Boatwright, maybe follow up on the Folsoms, and he'd be out of here.

Barrett had just determined to take that course of action and was just reflecting that he had not enjoyed a cigarette in hours when a pair of rock-hard legs took a seat beside him.

"Sit?" Megan asked.

"Please do." Barrett took his feet off a chair. She took it, pulled over to Barrett's side. Now, there was a surprise.

"Seen Talmadge?" Barrett inquired.

"He went north." She pointed up the coast. "Trying to get iced before his fish go bad."

"He won't make it."

"Nope," she was smiling. "He won't."

"Your mom wouldn't make a bad detective," Barrett said.

"Better than you." The edge came back to Megan's voice.

"Look." Barrett planted his beer on the windowsill. "We first met, I came across like a snob. I didn't mean to. Now—can we start over?"

"Where do you want to start?" She'd donned a T-shirt instead of a tank top and it did nothing to make her less appealing.

"I need some background." Barrett tried to keep the bubble in the middle. "Take your mom, fr'instance."

"Everyone depends on her," Megan said. "She came with her papa when she was little. We're Irish, you know."

"You're half-Irish," Barrett replied carefully. "You're also half-black. You know your dad very well?"

"No. He left when I was little."

"Good thing, what I gather."

"You think it's odd, don't you? Me being here with Mama?"

"No, I don't." Barrett shook his head. "It's just been a long time since I've been in a population this—homogeneous, that's all. And you kind of stand out."

"Because I'm mixed."

"Because you're mixed and drop-dead gorgeous," he replied.

She seemed pleased to hear that.

"What about Mac?" Barrett moved to safer ground. "And Ben and Sarah? What's their story?"

"They've been here forever."

"Talmadge hasn't been here forever," Barrett pointed out. "Somehow I don't think Red Walker has either. Or Jawbone. Or Splinter. Any idea where they came from?"

"Who knows?" Megan's shoulders rippled when she shrugged. "Maybe someplace they'd rather forget."

"You going to stay here?" Barrett sampled his beer. "You bust your butt on that water, day in and out. Summer and winter. You gotta know there's an easier life, Megan. Don't you want to leave? Just get the hell out?"

She smiled as she stretched her long legs.

"I almost took a man from Perry. That was a mistake."

"Believe me there are other places than Perry," Barrett said. "What about New York? Boston? Paris, for Christ's sake?"

"That where you live?" She was looking at him, now. Eye to eye.

"Well, no."

"You see," she smiled. "You're telling me to do something you're not even doing yourself."

Barrett surrendered to that argument silently. The sun lost its last smoulder below the horizon. Megan turned her attention outside.

"Evening star," she said.

"What—?" Barrett followed her gaze.

"Over there" she said, and Barrett saw the star he'd seen his first night on the bay. It was there again, that big, silver earring hanging low beneath a half-lemon of moon.

"It's not really a star, you know."

"I didn't, no," he replied.

She reached over to steal his beer.

"It's a planet. Venus."

That's it! Barrett nodded. He'd known that once. Somewhere long ago. Far away.

"Venus." He said the word as if for the first time.

"Venus," she affirmed. "For love."

T-shirt and cutoffs. Long, tawny legs. And there was no doubt now that Megan was allowing him to look. Wanted him to look.

Esther's daughter rose like a dancer.

"You gotta be careful fishing," she told him.

"And why is that?" he asked.

"Because . . ." She gave him back his beer. "You might catch something."

Slap-slap, slap-slap. There was no insomnia here. The tide slapped the floorboards on the preacher's porch. O'Steen snored to high heaven inside. Barrett slumbered oblivious on the porch beneath the stars. The evening star had long retired to be replaced with winter constellations. Orion wheeled by, his feet planted brightly in the heavens, his sword a faint trio of distant suns strung from a well-lit, hydrogen-fueled belt.

Barrett was dreaming. It was a blustery day. He'd just made The Big Case. Henry Altmiller was offering him a cigar when a low-slung convertible drove up. Laura Anne got out. The breeze whipped up a gossamer-thin skirt beneath a wide, floppy hat. She was smiling. She was radiant.

"Wake up—*wake up!*" she said.

But she was not Laura Anne. Barrett drifted up from his dreams to find Megan pounding on his cot.

"*Wake the hell up!!!*"

Apples would fall from a tree so shaken. Barrett barely rolled over.

"*Oh, God!*"

She was crying. That's what brought him from the depths.

"What—? What is it?"

"Oh, thank God. *We need your help!*"

"I want to sleep," he groaned.

"*No!!*" She tossed him his shoes while he fumbled for shorts.

"What the hell is it?" Barrett grabbed a shirt.

"Baby-time!" Megan said.

"Shouldn't we kiss first?"

Moments later Barrett found himself racing on an airboat beneath ten thousand stars on what would otherwise be a deliriously exciting first date. Megan cut through the bay's cedar-staked beacons like a slalom skier. Barrett took a death grip on his webbed seat belt.

"It's Louise!" Megan yelled to Barrett when conversation was still possible. "Jeremy's wife—It's her baby!"

That was all she got out before an engine rescued from some drunk's wrecked Corvette screamed like a banshee, a MacCauley fixed-pitch propeller kicked in and Barrett found himself launched over a saltwater buckboard at a speed he conservatively estimated to be one thousand miles an hour.

"Try not to kill us, all right?"

The wind caught his words and flung them into the howling prop out back. Megan kicked the rudder, the airboat slammed into a long, skidding turn. The sea pounded the shallow hull, hammering Megan and Barrett like a mallet. Barrett was seriously concerned he'd fracture his back. He could feel his eyes bulging in their sockets.

"Megan!"

Barrett screamed to his pilot for restraint. It was no use. She couldn't hear him and even if she could she would not slow, would not spare herself or him or anyone else. She was going to Louise, going to a woman in childbirth, in pain, and in danger. That's all Megan knew. And all she needed to know.

Barrett's head snapped as the airboat hit a swell at sixty miles an hour. They sailed a hundred, hundred and fifty feet through the air before they landed another bone-cruncher into the water. Strap in, son of a bitch, Barrett told himself. She's got bigger balls than you.

Twenty harrowing minutes and a lifetime later, Barrett arrived at a prefab house raised on telephone poles off the Gulf. Barrett pounded after Megan up the stairs. Louise Bantam barely noted their arrival. She labored pale as death on a four-poster which looked inordinately ornate in this primitive place. Esther was propping Louise up on pillows soaked with blood. Blood trickled, now, from Louise's birth canal. Jeremy rushed a pail of steaming water to the bed. Esther spoke over her shoulder to Barrett.

"I radioed for a doctor. Two hours at least. She can't wait."

"Wait for what?" Barrett asked stupidly.

"The child has to come out," Esther said angrily.

"I'm no doctor." Barrett suddenly realized what was expected of him.

"I thought they gave you people training." Esther dipped a towel into the water.

Sure they did, Barrett thought. They gave me sixteen hours of training nearly a decade ago confident that I'd have a radio, access to paramedics, and obstetricians nearby. I could probably even manage a delivery in a taxi provided the woman did all the work.

But that wasn't what this was. This was life or death. This was where the rubber met the road and Barrett Raines suddenly felt more inadequate than he'd ever felt in his life.

"I told her you'd know what to do." Esther drilled him coldly.

"I thought you knew everything," Barrett cracked back.

Esther flushed suddenly scarlet and Barrett thought for a moment that if Louise had not previously claimed

Esther's attention the older woman would have gotten a knife and killed him.

"Good God, man!" she finally managed to hiss. "Is everything for you a damned joke?"

Louise screamed, then. It took Barrett off guard. He had heard that scream before. It was his mother scream- ing. His father was beating her. Barrett was locked in the closet. If Barrett opened that door, if he so much as cracked that prefab, Handy Dan portal, his father would slug him with a fist hardened on grown-up jaws and women. But to stay, oh! There was never enough air to breathe. Always too many of those flannel shirts, a suffoca- tion of cotton, and sweat-drenched socks.

Barrett heard another scream. He saw his mother. She was on the floor, he could see through that crack, that tiny crack between the door and the carpet. She bled on the floor. Bled from the mouth. From the ears. His father cursed above her and then Barrett could see himself pick- ing up the baseball bat that propped beneath his mother's lingerie. He could remember bursting, screaming from that closet. His father grinned drunk as a sot to meet that bat. Had watched it all the way in. You had to do that when you played ball. Watch it all the way in. Barrett's father went down.

"*Jesus Christ, do something!*" It was Esther, now, who screamed.

The closet door stayed open.

"Okay," Barrett hauled a barrel of air into his lungs. "Okay, first thing first—Jeremy, you need to wait outside."

"No."

"It's all right, lad." Esther's voice was not so steady.

"No!"

"Come on, Jeremy." It was Megan who coaxed him, "We can do more for her out here."

Megan steered him out of the room, telling him they'd

need to be outside, to look for the doctor, that they'd need more water, and that, yes, she'd be all right, all right, all right.

Barrett felt a pang in his chest watching Megan shepherd Jeremy out the door. Bear knew what it meant to wait outside. He had waited for the twins, not allowed to be by Laura Anne's side, not allowed to see his boys enter the world.

"Louise, I'm just gonna check you out." Barrett heard himself speaking to Jeremy's wife.

First the pelvis.

"Looks wide open to me," he remarked.

"Her water broke at noon," Esther said tightly and then cooed things to Louise in her Irish brogue, that she was not to worry, never to worry, dear, that, yes, we'll bring your wee-one, bring him whole.

"Louise," Barrett interrupted firmly and clear. "I'm going to help you out."

He eased his fingers into a womb where there was not room. A moan broke in reply.

He had to go further. She screamed. But he was in, now. And what Barrett could feel, lodged there in the mother's vagina, was a foot.

"Easy, girl," Esther told her and then to Barrett— "What's to do?"

"Looks like a breach," Barrett replied grimly. "I'm gonna stick my hand up there—Where's that water? Soap? Good. I'm going up your canal, Louise, and turn your little one around."

"You ever done this before?" Esther whispered once they were down under.

"Not unless you count a calf or two," Barrett admitted.

"I'll count them." Esther held Louise with beefy arms. "Then let's get started."

*   *   *

Talmadge Lawson was unaware of Louise's ordeal and even if he had known couldn't have cared less. Lawson had returned to his houseboat, anchored not a half-mile from Esther's pier, filled with an impotent fury. The public humiliation hurt him more than the day's loss. The fish had gone bad, of course. The whole day's catch. Talmadge dumped them rotting into the Gulf.

Maybe it'll poison your goddamn grounds, he cursed Esther silently. Maybe they'll rot and drift into your fucking bay. Maybe a shark will find you and them and take you both.

Frustrated fantasies for revenge chased with whiskey do not make for a good night's sleep. Talmadge tossed in his rolling home until well past two. He did not notice the rowboat which glided silently up to his houseboat, did not hear the screwdriver which jammed into the lock at his door. The door burst open and brought Talmadge erect in his bed—

By then it was too late.

"Who's there?" Talmadge fumbled for his flashlight.

No answer.

"Who's *there?*"

The flashlight switched on to trigger a weaving circle of light.

Red Walker, Splinter Townsend, and Jawbone surrounded Lawson's bed like a circle of trees.

"You bastards!"

Talmadge lunged for a window. No use. Three brawny pairs of arms pinned their prey as surely as a net.

It was almost a half hour before Barrett Raines got Louise's little one turned around. He could feel a head that was too large breached in its perilous canal. Barrett wedged his fingers like forceps around that pliable skull.

"*Now,*" he commanded.

"Push, Louise," Esther urged her. *"Push like hell."*

"It's coming," Barrett watched in amazement as the woman's pelvis surged open. Her crotch ripped like a sack.

Louise screamed. A misshapen head burst through. You could see the eyes, still closed, the ears. And the blood.

"Rest a minute." Barrett cradled the baby's head. Was it even alive? "Rest . . . Rest . . . Okay, big breath."

"Heave it in, Girl!"

"Now," Barrett demanded. "Now!"

A huge push—The small crown dropped out to drag behind a tiny, battered shoulder.

"Keep coming," Barrett commanded as he rotated the shoulder. *"One more push, Louise!"*

She did. Louise Bantham pushed through her agony one final time. Her baby slid like a seal into Barrett's bloody hands. The baby was out. But blue-cold. And not a sound.

"Breathe, baby!" Megan had returned to the room and Barrett hadn't even noticed.

Barrett rolled the baby over, smacked her smartly between the shoulder blades. Mucus spit out. But still not a breath.

"Breathe!" Esther bellowed like Moses to the sea.

"Take it easy," Barrett said sternly. "Okay, here we go."

Barrett rolled the child face-up, pulled that tiny, tiny mouth into his own. He pinched the nostrils shut, puffed in a measured breath like a diminutive bellows into infant lungs.

The baby's chest heaved in reply!

"Mary and Joseph." Esther crossed herself.

A pause. Barrett ventilated the child again. And again. The chest heaved once, twice! And finally a cry broke warm and welcome.

"Baby?" Louise asked the question near shock.

"Gonna be fine." Barrett leaned close to her face.

He had not experienced such peace in a long, long time. It was more than joy, more than satisfaction. It was beyond wonder and weariness.

"What have we got, anyway?" Esther asked the question.

"Looks like a fisherwoman to me." Barrett smiled so wide it hurt. Megan squealed delight. She rushed over, kissed Barrett full on the mouth. Esther allowed a smile, extended her hard hand.

"You did good."

Megan gave him a ride back to the preacher's shanty. Slower, this time. She barely said a word, but when Bear stepped from the airboat, she touched his hand briefly.

"Thank you."

Then she was off. The moon poured like molten lead down the wake left by her noisy craft. Barrett was certain the airboat would wake Preacher O'Steen but the older man never broke a snore. Bear edged past the preacher's bed to collapse on the back porch. He didn't rouse till late the next day. Barrett had barely shaved and had his morning swim when Preacher O'Steen came up grinning—

"Get yourself over to Esther's."

"Why?"

"They got a feast is why. Esther's treat."

O'Steen headed back for the bar without further explanation. Barrett followed a few minutes later and was astounded to find that the entire community knew about Louise and the baby; everyone was saying that it was the detective from Tallahassee who had saved their lives. Barrett enjoyed fish and hush puppies and swamp cabbage while enduring exaggerations of his efforts with perfect aplomb.

"We couldn't find a scissors to cut the cord," Esther

laughed. "So our Mr. Raines takes himself a top off a beer can, saws her through as pretty as you please!"

Esther went on in graphic detail to describe how Louise had expelled the placenta and was finally, finally! able to hold her baby. The doctor had arrived minutes later with a paramedic. She'd need blood, they had said, but Jeremy's wife would live to raise her lovely daughter.

Jeremy was home with his new family, Esther concluded, and returned to her old, terse self arranging neighbors to help Louise until things settled down.

Barrett hoped to see Megan this morning, the taste of her lips still lingering on his. Megan, of course, had returned to Louise and the baby. She was needed there, wanted to be there with the new mother and child and Barrett found himself yearning for that familiar obligation.

Barrett turned his attention outside. There was a peculiar heaviness in the air this morning. A kind of gray haze gauzed the sky. Barrett had about decided to take a stroll on the pier when something on the water drew his attention.

A sleek, new jet boat bubbled up to Esther's bar. A safari-clad skipper berthed a Glastron skillfully into a tire-bumpered slip. Ray Boatwright killed his Burkly pump, climbed from his propless boat, and headed straight for Esther's bar.

MacGregor spelled Esther at the ice chest. Ray relaxed on a bar stool in his desert-tan khakis, fresh-pressed as ever over a beer. Barrett noticed again how well his hair was cut and noticed, for the first time, a tattoo on the man's forearm. It was an anchor and chain.

"I'll have one of those." Barrett pointed Mac to a Bud Lite.

"Did you hear this man got Jeremy's missus past a hard spot?" Mac beamed to Ray.

"She did all the work." Barrett saved Boatwright a reply. Mac handed Barrett his beer. "No charge."

"Why thank you." Barrett displayed his ID to Ray. "I'm Barrett Raines, Florida Department of Law Enforcement. Don't believe you and I have met."

"That mean this is official?" Ray's rejoinder couldn't exactly be called civil.

"Yes, it does." Barrett returned the plastic to his pocket. Ray took a swig of beer. "What do you want?"

"Some answers. 'Course to do that I have to ask some questions. You have a problem with that?"

"Yes," Ray replied shortly. "But I don't suppose that matters."

"I'll try to keep it painless." Barrett beamed goodwill. "Might start with your name."

"Ray Boatwright."

"I know some Boatwrights. Up toward Deacon Beach. You any kin?"

"Not to anybody local."

"Awright. I understand you've been on the bay a while."

"Not so long."

"Well, for a year at least, right? Maybe a year and a half?"

"Might be just about that."

"I can't help but wonder." Barrett settled back. "Everyone here makes a living off either fish or fishermen. How about you?"

"I'm not a fisherman, if that's what you mean."

"What are you, then?"

"Retired."

Was that a bead of sweat on Ray's forehead?

"Retired from what?" Barrett stepped up the pace.

". . . Work." Ray slowed it down.

"Mr. Boatwright, if you want I can take us both someplace where we can actually have a conversation."

Ray tipped his beer.

"I worked offshore," he said finally. "Oil rigs, mostly."

"Company?"

"Marine Drilling. They work out of Corpus Christi."

Barrett made a mental note to have Cricket check that one out.

"You a roughneck? Or you work on the rig itself?"

"On the rigs."

"Which means you repair them?" Barrett prodded.

"I fix 'em," Ray nodded.

"You're a diver, aren't you?" Barrett summed it up. "Started in the navy, probably. That's where you got that tattoo. Then salvage. I'd guess you're a hardhat."

"Was," Ray amended. "Was a hardhat."

"Ever around Miami?"

"No," Ray said shortly.

Barrett could see the sweat clearly, now. Yep. Good old fashioned perspiration was taking the crease out of Boatwright's Eddie Bauer outfit.

"Nice boat you've got." Barrett nodded to the rocket at the pier. "Must've cost a pretty penny."

"It was repossessed."

"Still—can you retire on that kind of money diving?"

"If you're good you can."

Ray dropped a pair of bills on Esther's plywood counter. "Thanks, Mac." And then to Barrett, "Are we finished?"

"I need an address," Barrett told him.

"I've got a trailer." Ray slapped a fat wallet in his safari jacket. "Flag of Dixie raised out front. It's south on the bay. Anyone can show you."

Ray Boatwright slid off his bar stool.

Barrett stopped him, almost casually, with—

"Somebody killed Miles Beynon. Took their time, too."

Ray flinched as if bit.

That put a hitch in your get-along, didn't it? Barrett smiled to himself. You bigoted son of a bitch.

"You've got me confused with somebody gives a shit," Ray spat out.

"Never heard of Miles Beynon, I 'spose." Barrett played him along. "Never heard the name?"

"Forgot it already."

Barrett would bet his balls this character knew Miles Beynon, but that wasn't the main thing triggering the adrenaline which now hammered his heart.

This man was a diver. Dimes'd get you doughnuts he *had* worked in Miami. And then there was money; Raines glanced again at the jet boat that gleamed beside Esther's pier. A very nice retirement.

"One more question . . ."

Barrett leaned close to the man beside him.

"Brandon Ogilvie. That have a ring to it, 'Ray'? Brandon O-Gill-V?"

"Sorry. Can't help you."

Bear saw that the ex-diver would not meet his eye. Barrett let him stew a moment. Finally—

"You need to stay close for a couple of days, Mr. Boatwright." Barrett emphasized the name. Gave him something to sweat.

"That official?" The question came with a bravado Barrett suspected was not genuine.

"Yes, it is." Barrett was not smiling.

Ray Boatwright, or whatever his name was, turned without another word and left the bar.

Barrett Raines departed Esther's Shrine for Recovering Workaholics some good time later. He was barely past the icehouse when a hand snaked out to clamp down on his shoulder. Barrett wheeled on reflex, locked the offending hand and thumb, and took its owner to the mat. A lance of agony rippled across an already shattered face; Talmadge Lawson stifled a groan from the pier.

"Goddammit!"

"What the hell?" Barrett released his takedown.

Talmadge's mouth badly missed a couple of teeth. A laceration over his brow ran nearly to the bone. Barrett helped Lawson to his feet.

"Who did this to you, Talmadge?"

"Who you think?"

"You should file charges."

"I've got something better than charges."

"Better?"

"For you," Talmadge nodded. "But it'll cost."

"I'm the law, Talmadge. Be damn careful what you propose to an officer of the law."

"Fine," Talmadge wheezed. "Take me in—You'll get nothin'."

Lawson coughed up blood. Barrett steadied him, glanced up and down the pier.

"How do I know you've got anything worth paying for?"

"Can't tell you here," Talmadge shook his head. "You got a boat?"

"I do."

"Get out to Whipping Post Island. Early. B'fore seven."

"Then what?" Barrett could feel hair crawling up the back of his neck. Was he being set up? "What then, Talmadge?"

"Never you mind." The broken man grinned through ruined teeth. "Just be there."

11.

The Outsider

The sun was buried under a bank of clouds when Barrett pulled out of Dead Man's Bay in his Boston Whaler. Within a minute or two Barrett could make out Whipping Post Island. He set the whaler's bow onto what was left of the dock. The island's solitary pillar rose like an obelisk to finger a rising sun. Barrett tried to imagine Esther hanging on that rough-hewn post. He tried to imagine a husband, any husband, cruel enough to subject a wife to that ordeal. He tried to imagine a community indolent or indifferent or sadistic enough to consent. He wondered how differently locals might have behaved if Esther had married white, instead of black.

The whaler rose and fell hard on choppy water. There was a change in the sky this morning. The air was noticeably heavier and the sky was red.

Red sky at morning sailor take warning, Barrett reminded himself.

He approached on the lee side of Whipping Post's rotting pier. Nothing to see at first except those cypress pilings. But then Barrett saw something else, something bobbing in the swells generated by his whaler. They were bleach bottles, a dozen or more, riding the swells in a weaving row which stretched out from the dock.

"Never seen one?" It was Talmadge who asked the question and Barrett who jumped out of his skin.

Barrett recovered to see Talmadge's grinning face pop up from the other side of the dock. Talmadge was standing in a small boat tied onto the wind side of the dock and Barrett could see, now, that Lawson was tying a final bottle onto the row which bobbed like ducks on the water.

"Called a trotline," Talmadge supplied as Barrett left his boat for the dock. "Lazy man's fishing pole. Bottles're buoys. Line underneath's got bait an' sinkers. And hooks, o'course."

"I've laid my share of trotlines," Barrett informed the man curtly. "What do you expect to catch out here?"

"I don't expect to catch nothin'," Talmadge grinned. "It's not for me. It's for you."

"I don't need it," Barrett said.

"You need a reason to come out here," Talmadge said, and handed Barrett an open-faced reel.

Be damned, Barrett saw that the rod was rigged and baited, this guy is giving me an alibi! Barrett was almost amused. Almost.

"You can come out like you're checking the trotline," Talmadge explained. "The rod 'n' reel just gives you a reason to stay. Anybody between us and the bay will see you fishing."

"You think this is necessary?" Barrett asked.

"It's not just for you," Talmadge assured him. "If Esther finds out we're talkin' I'll lose a hell of a lot more than a day's work and some teeth."

"Okay." Barrett made a cast past the trotline and sat down. "I'll fish. You talk."

"I don't have to." Talmadge was suddenly obdurate. "I don't have to do shit."

"I've got a badge, Talmadge. I can haul your ass in anytime."

"You can talk to yourself, too."

" 'Long as we understand each other. Now—You ever see this man?"

Barrett pulled Miles Beynon's photo from a pocket.

"Miles Beynon." Talmadge made the ID instantly and Barrett was stunned.

"Seen him recently?" Barrett was reminding himself to stay calm. Don't let him know it's important, Barrett recited the mantra to himself. Keep the target moving.

"Sure." Talmadge was handing the photo back. "He's been here three, maybe four times."

Barrett nodded as if that were the most ordinary thing in the world.

"When?" he asked casually.

"Spaced regular," Talmadge replied. "February, May, and then again in August."

A strike! But Barrett was not on a desk anymore; he didn't betray a thing.

"Any idea what Miles was doing out here?" Barrett reeled his line in.

"Claimed he was a fisherman," Talmadge said. "He'd get himself a birddog and a net. Run mullet all by hisself."

"Was he any good?" Barrett let out some line.

"Never left without himself a locker-full."

"February, May, August. Pretty specific dates." Barrett pulled the line back in. "How come you remember?"

" 'Cause of Ray Boatwright."

"What's Miles got to do with Ray Boatwright?" Barrett kept the question as flat as he could.

But something there pushed Lawson's button.

"First off, I don't owe Ray or anyone else a goddamn thing!!"

"You don't have to convince me," Barrett reassured him.

Talmadge glanced back toward the bay before he continued. Searched the coast, the horizon! Finally—

"I came here four years ago. Didn't nobody offer to help me. Piss-ant place! If you didn't kiss Esther's ass you got nuthin'!"

"What's this got to do with Ray Boatwright?" Barrett prodded gently.

"Well, he's kinda out of place, ain't he?" Talmadge looked for confirmation which Barrett would not supply. Not yet.

"I mean—I'm a fisherman," Talmadge went on. "Been fishing all my life. These damn people wouldn't give me the time of day. But here's this fuckin' Boat-Right with store-bought clothes and a powerboat, why, they take him in like blood-kin."

"Why should I care?" Barrett hardened. "Boatwright is an outsider. So what? They suck up to him. So what? What's it got to do with Beynon?"

"Let's see some cash," Talmadge retrenched.

Barrett peeled out a twenty. Talmadge remained silent. Barrett peeled out another twenty.

"I didn't come prepared for a sting, Talmadge."

Talmadge took his forty pieces of silver.

"One day, it was the middle of February, cold as lock-jawed mullet. I was out checkin' for some new grounds. It was real late."

"And dark, I imagine?" Barrett inquired.

"Yeah," Talmadge nodded. "But I saw his boat."

"Ray's boat?"

"That's right," Talmadge nodded. "He was goin' slow. Had his runnin' lights on."

"How about your lights?" Barrett was trying to remember Talmadge's boat.

"I kilt 'em."

"Why?"

"I tole you!" Talmadge was suddenly defensive. "I was looking for some new grounds!"

Which meant he was poaching on somebody else's.

"I follow you," was all Barrett said aloud. "Go ahead. You saw Ray's boat—"

"Figured I'd see what he was up to," Talmadge relaxed. "Didn't have to follow him, though. Ray killed his engines a couple of hundred yards off port, but not his lights. I watched him drift there like a damn Christmas tree for maybe half an hour. And then another boat comes up."

"From the Gulf?"

Talmadge nodded to affirm, "A big one. Cruiser. I'd say forty footer at least. They put a spot on Ray, pulled alongside. I think he got on board, but I'm not too sure. I didn't want to spook them. Or get my ass shot."

"Sensible," Barrett agreed. Drugs and guns were frequently exchanged for cash at sea. Was that Ray Boatwright's retirement?

"What then?" Barrett made another cast off the dock.

"That was it," Talmadge shrugged. "Fifteen, maybe twenty minutes later, Ray hauls ass back toward Esther's."

"This was in February?" Barrett rolled on smoothly.

"And every February since I been here," Talmadge affirmed eagerly.

"Wait a minute," Barrett slowed him down. "You mean these meetings at sea, with this cruiser, have been going on even *before* you saw Miles Beynon? Before Miles ever came to the bay?"

"That's right," Talmadge bobbed his head up and down. "Ev'ry February since I've been here. Ev'ry May, too. Ev'ry August and November. But this last year some-thin' funny happened."

"Something irregular?" Barrett encouraged.

"More like additional," Talmadge said. "It started in February. That feller there in the picture—"

"Miles Beynon," Barrett supplied.

"Him, yeah. He shows up. Then two, three days later, Ray goes to meet that cruiser. Next day Miles is gone."

"Gone the next day?"

"Yep," Talmadge nodded. "And guess what? Come May same thing happened. And in August, same thing. Miles shows up, then Ray. Ray goes out to meet the cruiser. Next day Miles has iced his mullet and gone."

"I see," Barrett nodded. "And where did Miles stay? Where'd he hide?"

"Didn't hide anyplace," Talmadge replied. "He stayed at Esther's."

Barrett's heart stopped. At Esther's? Miles Beynon?!

"You're sure about that?" Barrett said as casually as he could.

"Miles always went to Esther's," Talmadge insisted. "Right there at the bar."

"Just help me here, Talmadge. Make sure I get this right. You actually *saw* Miles Beynon *at* Esther's?"

"Me and everybody else," Talmadge replied.

And everybody else?!

Barrett closed the drag on his reel.

"Esther told me she never saw Miles Beynon. She said she never saw anyone like the man in this photo."

"Bitch has seen him good!" Talmadge cursed through splintered teeth. "They all have!"

Sooner or later a detective has to decide whom to believe. Talmadge was the most unlikely witness Barrett had met in a long time. But Barrett was convinced he was telling the truth. Which meant that Esther and virtually everyone else in Dead Man's Bay was a liar.

Miles Beynon had been here; Esther and everyone, *everyone* in her little kingdom knew it. They knew. They lied. Why? What could motivate an entire community to collude in such a mass deception? There was one more question Barrett had to ask—

"Talmadge," Barrett looked the fisherman in the eye.

"Yeah? What?"

"Do you know or have you ever heard of a man here at the bay named Brandon Ogilvie?"

"Nope," the answer came without hesitation.

"You're sure, now. You're positive?"

" 'Course I'm sure." Talmadge fingered his twenties like they weren't enough.

"Awright. Okay." Barrett took a deep breath. "I need to know when Ray's going out. Exactly when."

"You mean to meet that cruiser?" Talmadge asked.

"That's what I mean," Barrett affirmed. "I need to know exactly when and exactly where. Time and location."

"I tell you we'll both know." Talmadge was bargaining again.

"I'll pay," Barrett said, knowing he didn't have much choice.

"I take your money now, you'll be able to follow him for yourself," Talmadge said. "Where's that leave me? Hah? On the outside. As usual."

Barrett paused. Don't blow it, he thought to himself. Don't scare this guy off.

"All right, look," Barrett placed his rod and reel on the dock. "For right now I don't give a damn what tips you off. Today's what—? November sixteenth. Cruiser's due any day. Am I right?"

"Should be," Talmadge confirmed.

"Just tell me when the time comes." Barrett pulled out another twenty dollars. "When and where."

"I'll do 'er, but you'd best watch yer back," the fisherman advised as he took another twenty. "They don't call it Dead Man's Bay for nuthin'."

Cricket Bonet was not a happy man. In three days he'd spoken to his partner once and now this honkie sheriff with the shades lets Cricket know that this wasn't the first time Barrett had called in asking to contact his partner.

"You weren't here them other times." Sue slurped a Coke behind his Ray-Bans.

"You could have left a note," Cricket glowered. "Matter of fact, Sheriff, you could have called me in."

"Said he didn't have anything to tell you," the sheriff shrugged. "Didn't seem all that important."

Cricket decided it was best not to murder Taylor County's lawman. At least not in these public circumstances. So instead he said, "Did Agent Raines call in today?"

"This morning, early."

"Why don't I just call him back?" Cricket pointed to the radio mounted beside the sheriff's desk.

"He said don't." The sheriff stifled a yawn. "Said he'd call again at six; it's there in the log."

"I'll just wait, then."

"Suit yerself." The sheriff stretched. "We're goin' for some supper."

"I'll wait here," Cricket repeated and pulled a chair practically out from under an amused deputy to plant himself beside the radio on Sheriff Sue's desk.

The sun lacked maybe a finger from being on the horizon when Barrett finally raised Cricket Bonet on the whaler's radio. Barrett kept Talmadge's rod and reel. He needed a reason, now more than ever, to be alone on the water.

Whipping Post Island receded with the drift of current to a mote on the horizon. Barrett glanced at the setting sun. There were no flamingoes in the clouds this evening. Raines triggered the switch on his push-to-talk, "Pinnochio to Jiminy Cricket. Over."

Cricket started awake with the static that broke Barrett's voice over Sheriff Driggers's radio.

"Pinocchio to Jiminy Cricket, come in, Cricket."

Cricket grabbed the mike. "Very goddamn funny, Bear. What the hell are you doing? Over."

"Just fishing, Cricket. Ever seen a trotline? Over."

"Don't you have a watch?" Cricket asked.

"Matter of fact I don't, Cricket. Sorry. But I do have a line on Miles Beynon. Over."

"I'm copying." Cricket was all business.

"He was definitely here. And something odd's going on, Cricket. Hold on—"

Barrett cradled the radio's mike as an airboat roostertailed off his port. It was Splinter Townsend's boat. What was Splinter doing out here? Barrett dropped the radio's mike below his fishing reel, returned Splinter's lazy wave.

"Barrett, what is going on? Over!"

Barrett picked up his radio.

"The locals here at the bay will not, repeat will *not,* admit to seeing Miles. But I know they *have* seen him. Over."

"It's a small place, Barrett," Cricket came back. "Hear no evil. See no evil."

"Maybe," Barrett had to admit Cricket could be right. It could be no more than that. "Still, I've got something I need you to check. Over."

"Come ahead."

"Esther Buchanan. She buys the fish here. Check her financials: credit, bank, IRS—"

"I got it."

"Okay. And same thing for a white male, Ray Boat-wright. That's 'Ray Boatwright'. Guy claims he's retired. As a diver, Cricket. Marine Drilling in Corpus Christi, Texas. Looks to me like he's got more money than he ought to and when I asked him if he'd ever worked in Miami he damn near jumped out of his skin. You copy?"

"I do. Sounds like things are gettin' warm out there, pard."

"I won't dance without you," Barrett reassured Bonet. "I do have one other thing."

"Got my pencil," Cricket came back.

"I've got a local here." Barrett spoke slowly. "Sarah Lynn Folsom. Caucasian. Mid-sixties. Husband is Benjamin F. Check their insurance, would you? Should be Blue Cross. I'm curious about the coverage."

"That be it? Over."

"That's it. Captain Midnight. Over and out."

Barrett's communication evaporated from the sheriff's radio with a burst of static. Cricket cradled the mike, but he did not leave the office immediately. He waited instead for Sheriff Driggers and his deputy to return from their evening meal.

"I got in touch with my partner," Cricket informed the lawmen stiffly and proceeded to concoct a sanitized briefing of the Bear's activities.

"Sounds like he's all right," Driggers smirked. "Prob'ly catch himself more with a cane pole and a can of worms."

The deputy guffawed along with his boss.

Cricket didn't smile.

"I'm making a copy of your logs for the last couple of days, Sheriff."

"Say what?"

"Your radio log." Cricket put himself squarely in Driggers's face, a head taller and half an axe wider. "The gov-

ernor appreciates all the assistance you give us, Sheriff.
Next time you need help I wanta be able to show 'em how
much you deserve it."

"I don't need your fuckin' help," Sue boiled.

"Put that in writing and I'll pass it along," Cricket told
him. "But if I ever, *ever* get a call from my partner again
and am not notified promptly I'm gonna be all over your
ass like stink on shit. Is that clear, Sheriff?!"

Cricket bounced the door off its hinges on his way out.

He was hard on doors.

12.

Hero's Welcome

A fresh celebration replaced the sun's setting on the bay. Fireworks burst like new stars against a clouded, indigo sky. Colored lanterns swung in a fitful breeze from the bar and icehouse. A community of fishermen, husbands and wives, sisters and brothers, crowded the pier. Barrett eased his whaler between a pair of outboards wondering what the hell was going on when Megan spotted him from above.

She had traded tank tops and T-shirts for a simple cotton dress that clung to a figure silhouetted in bursts of amber and blue and green. Her hair caught the new breeze to dance over bared shoulders.

" 'She doth teach the torches to burn bright,' " Barrett quoted as a Roman candle hooted balls of fire into the air.

"Hey!" Megan waved eagerly and Barrett bumped his whaler into the pier like a landlubber.

"Where you been?!" Megan took the line which he tossed from the whaler.

"Fishing," Barrett replied. "God do you look nice."

"Why, thank you."

Was she blushing? Was she part of the lies the others

had told? She must have known Miles Beynon. Must have seen him often. And then Barrett could not remember whether he had asked Megan about Miles Beynon or not. Did she know about Ray? About the meetings at sea? Barrett found himself hoping that she did not. He wanted desperately to believe she never lied to him. Or if she did lie, God let her have a good reason.

"What's going on?" Barrett asked as enthusiastically as he could manage.

"A christening," Megan squealed with delight.

"A baby?" Barrett asked.

"God, you're slow—No! A boat!"

Megan hauled Barrett onto the pier, threaded him through the celebrating families.

"He's here!" she called out suddenly.

"Good," Esther came striding up and suddenly Barrett found two strong arms locking his elbows.

"You've kept us waiting, Mr. Raines." Esther breathed whiskey into Barrett's face and then Barrett found himself in the middle of a maelstrom of fishermen.

They were all there, all the hunters of the sea, Mac and Ben and Sarah, Splinter and Jawbone and Red. All the men who had beaten Talmadge Lawson to a pulp were there and now Barrett was at their mercy. Barrett had his Smith & Wesson holstered in the small of his back. But Esther had an elbow on one side. Megan on the other.

They closed in. Too close, now, too close! The fishermen swirled around him. Around and around. Megan was there with the rest. She was laughing at him and Barrett knew what he needed now: anger, fury! But the closet door was closing and this time there was no way to open it. Barrett was tossed like a woodchip into a whirlpool. The crowd roared as he bounced from one brawny arm to another. Around and around. The full panic of claustrophobia had not quite hit when a shove from behind threw the detective out of the crowd of fishermen and into the arms of—

Jeremy Bantham. Barrett heaved air into his lungs. What did they want?! What would they do?! Barrett was reaching for his handgun when he saw the baby girl he'd saved from certain death.

She was there, swaddled with a tiny pink blanket inside a wooden crib. Jeremy and Louise beamed alongside their new baby daughter. An aluminum tub at their feet overflowed with gifts of all sorts. Dollar bills. Dresses. Diapers.

There was more. Behind the child and parents, a newly refurbished boat rocked beside the pier. Fresh-hemped nets coiled neatly on the Bantham's birddog. A fiberglassed hull was spotless and white against the water. A starched sheet stretched over the bow was covered with garlands of flowers. And there was Preacher O'Steen beaming with a bottle of spirits and eager to perform the duty his station required.

Esther came to Barrett's side and a hush fell suddenly over the pier. All you could hear was the chatter of children, the wind, the lap of water on cypress posts.

"Go on," Esther said. "We're waiting for you."

"Me?" Barrett looked around. "What for?"

More laughter broke from the fishermen. Barrett appealed to the preacher.

"You mind filling me in?"

"You are here, Mr. Raines," the preacher intoned formally, "to receive a great honor."

Jeremy left his wife and child to stand with Esther at Barrett's side.

Barrett stiffened.

"Easy, man," Esther poked him in the ribs. "All they want to do is thank ye."

"For my wife." Jeremy said the words for the gathered families as well as for Barrett. "For our little girl."

"Then all this—" Barrett saw for the first time the children, the fireworks, the lanterns. "—This is all for me?"

The pier rocked with raucous laughter. Barrett expelled his lungs like a spent balloon.

"Jeremy's just got his boat out of dry dock," Esther's eyes were whiskey-bright. "She's fit as a fiddle. Stem to stern. And he's a baby girl, too. Which leaves us with a serious problem, Mr. Raines."

"A wife, a boat, and a baby—I'd say that's a couple of problems," Barrett joked weakly and the pier rocked with more laughter.

"We got to have a name," Jeremy explained when things settled down.

"Beg your pardon?"

Esther stepped in, "Custom has it you give your boat your daughter's name she'll stand by you forever."

"Why not a son?" Barrett was kidding but the preacher took it seriously.

"A son's a son till he finds him a wife, but a daughter's your daughter the rest of your life."

The crowd murmured approval.

"I see," Barrett accepted the homily. "But I'm—Well, I'm damn sure no good at giving names."

A chuckle rippled all around.

"You don't have to give a name, Barrett." Megan's smile sent a lance to his heart.

Bear turned to Jeremy. "Why don't I?"

"Because we took yours."

"What?!"

Jeremy stood aside. Preacher O'Steen whipped the sheet which covered the birddog's bow and Barrett could see with all the rest the freshly painted name which marched in bold, black letters across the Bantham's new boat.

She was named, *The Grin & Barrett.*

Applause broke with laughter all around the pier, and Bear thought to himself for the hundredth time he would never understand these people. He turned to Megan.

"I thought it had to be their baby's name."

"It does," Megan agreed brightly and winked at Louise.

Jeremy's wife turned then to scoop her newborn from the crib. She cradled the babe gently in the crook of her arm, then walked with great dignity to present her child to Agent Raines.

"I'm real happy to have you meet our daughter, sir. . . . Barrette Marie Bantham."

The roar that rose then would have done credit to a Seminole football game. Men and women rushed to congratulate Barrett, to thank him, to wish him well. Preacher O'Steen shoved his bottle into Barrett's hands. Raines fumbled to twist off the top—

"Oh, no!" The preacher prevented a faux pas. "It's for the boat, son—A christening!"

One goof after the other and the gathered families loved it. Barrett could see Esther smiling broadly. And Megan. A war of conflicting emotions raged through him, now. *Are these the same people who have lied to me?* Barrett's hands were numb on the bottle. And then the thought occurred—*Or* have *they lied to me?! Has Talmadge Lawson played me for a fool?!*

No time to solve that, now. For the second time Barrett found himself carried on a wave of arms.

They propelled him to the edge of the pier. He poised over the Bantham's boat, hesitated, and turned to the new father.

"You do it, Jeremy. It's your boat. Your baby."

"I give you the honor." Jeremy didn't seem such a bumpkin anymore.

"You've given me plenty," Barrett handed him the bottle. "Go ahead. Bust hell out of it."

"Let's see the arm, Jeremy!" Splinter started a call echoed by the rest.

"One! Two! *Three!!*"

Jeremy swung like Hank Aaron. The bottle shattered over the bow. No champagne, here. The Barrett lady soaked in bourbon. A badly-tuned fiddle cut loose. Preacher O'Steen offered Esther his arm.

"No!" she blushed.

"Do you good," the preacher sparkled like a boy.

"I will not," Esther protested.

But O'Steen had the crowd behind him. Someone's fiddle struck up an Irish jig and within seconds Esther showed the men her leg. A shout rose then as other unschooled couples joined in. A bottle rocket burst overhead. Sparks drifted like stars from the heavens.

"Let's go," Megan offered Barrett her arm.

"No, really, I can't!"

"Sure you can."

And the moment she touched him he knew he could. It was a time for fireworks. A time for laughter. A time, maybe, to forget.

Barrett consented to the maelstrom this time. A whirlpool of music and dance and rockets caught him up and rushed him 'round. But this time Megan was there to lead him on strong, supple legs. A fresh breeze off the bay caught her hair like a sail. And Barrett committed himself to a willing surrender.

They danced together, Barrett and Megan, until the wee hours. Esther turned the bar over to the preacher who supervised, asleep beside his bottle. The families and friends and children had long gone. Megan and Barrett found privacy and a table. She ignored a beer which sweated on the windowsill. Barrett fidgeted an ashtray like a rosary.

"Wish I had something to smoke."

"I've got cigarettes. If that's the problem."

"Why wouldn't it be?" Barrett allowed himself to look at what he was only minutes ago holding. A sheen of perspiration made her dress cling to her breasts and back.

"Something's on your mind, Barrett," she teased.

"Doesn't involve you," Raines shook his head. "At least—I hope to hell it doesn't."

"Can't know till you ask me now can you?"

"One thing about being a cop," Barrett avoided her challenge. "You can't get close to people."

"You mean you can't trust them." Megan put it in black and white.

"You lose your edge," Barrett said flatly. "You can't be objective."

"Are you talking about yourself, Agent Raines?" She seemed amused.

"You miss things," he said.

"You sure do," she agreed and leaned across the table. "Maybe I can help."

"No." He was too definite.

"I might see things you'd miss," she pressed.

"I doubt it."

"Maybe see things that—things that people want you to miss?"

That was a jolt. That wasn't what he expected. Barrett put his ashtray aside. Megan wiped the sweat from her brow, from her beer. Both the detective and Esther's daughter missed the new arrival which nudged up from the bay. It was a very expensive boat, by local standards. This particular Bayliner ran thirty-four feet in length, was rigged with navs and radios and radar for deep water. A pair of U.S. Marine diesels powered the cruiser. Her running lights glowed like a small city as an unseen skipper slipped up to Esther's pier beneath a starless sky.

Barrett's attention remained with Megan. She knew

something. Was she willing to tell it? He borrowed a sip from her beer.

"What is it people don't want me to know, Megan?"

"They don't want you to know about that man," she said simply. "That fellah comes out here."

"You mean Miles Beynon." Barrett had to be sure. "The guy in the picture."

"That's him," Megan nodded.

"Why don't they want me to know about Miles?"

"Mama told me not to talk about him. That's all she ever told me. But I can listen."

"That might put you in a bad spot, Megan."

He had to warn her. He had at least to do that.

"You think Mama's done somethin', don't you?!"

"Keep it down." Barrett glanced at the preacher.

"Well, she hasn't!"

Her breasts swelled beneath that cotton dress.

"It's my job to find out the truth, Megan." Barrett was reminding himself as much as he was her.

She pulled back. "I can show you a place."

"What place?"

"A place he stayed. That man. When he was here."

"I thought he stayed with Esther. Here at the bar."

"He came here," she agreed. "An' he always stayed late. But he didn't sleep here. You oughta know better than that!"

Yes, I should've, Barrett agreed silently.

"So where did he stay—Show me."

"Not now," she demurred.

"When? This could be important, Megan. It might help me a lot."

She thought it over a moment.

"T'morrah," she said finally. "After work. You be at Preacher's. I'll come by in the airboat. Anybody asks you just say I'm givin' you a ride."

"Tomorrow, then," Barrett nodded assent and rose with Megan from the table.

But something pulled Bear up short.

A new arrival filled Esther's door frame. A tall man, taller even than Splinter or Jawbone. Late forties or so. A lined and handsome face set off with the palest, bluest eyes Barrett had ever seen.

"I tied onto your pier," the assassin announced politely. "I hope it is no inconvenience."

The diction and grammar were flawless. It was a sophisticated voice. Cultured. Barrett could not place the accent, but hell, he hadn't been able to place Cricket's, either.

"As a matter of bloody fact it's damned inconvenient." A mist of cool air followed Megan's mother as she stumbled bleary-eyed from the icehouse into her bar.

"What the hell?" Barrett grinned. "Little late to be icing fish, isn't it, Esther?"

"What time is it, anyway?" she growled.

"After two. Why don't you let me put up, Mama?" Megan asked.

"I need some ice, please." The man strolled inside just as if Esther had never entered the bar. "A hundred pounds or so."

"We're closed." Esther wasn't too drunk to get riled.

The killer unfolded his wallet.

"A hundred pounds," he repeated. "And someone to fetch it."

"We're still closed," Esther snapped.

"I can grab it for him, Esther," Barrett volunteered.

"He can wait." Esther's objection lacked conviction.

"It's no trouble." Barrett took a moment to meet Megan's eyes.

She nodded. Tomorrow.

Barrett turned to the tall man at the door. Bastard

thinks he can buy anything, Raines thought to himself. And here I am proving he's right.

"Hundred pounds of ice?" he nodded to the newcomer. "Coming up."

13.

Pleasantries

There was a storm brewing somewhere, Barrett noticed when he got outside. Heat lightning flickered over the horizon like artillery. The moon shone fitfully through clouds scuttling across an indigo sky. Barrett didn't get to eye the heavens for long, though. After leading the new arrival to Esther's locker, Raines found himself stooped under a hundred pounds of crushed ice and laboring to keep pace with the tall man who strolled on ahead.

Bear could see the boat, now. It was impossible to miss. The new arrival waited for Barrett at a catwalk which rose from Esther's pier to the Bayliner's deck.

"This yours?" Barrett edged onto the catwalk.

"Just renting. Watch your step." The man fell in behind Raines.

Barrett noted the registration for the boat, Okaloosa County, and the name—*Easy Money*.

Talk about rubbing it in your face.

Barrett tried to balance himself and the ice on a catwalk which rose and rolled with swells whipped up by the wind. But it had been a long day. He'd been drinking most of it. Barrett stumbled. A hundred pounds of ice plunged toward the water. But a strong arm spoke on instinct—the tall man fielded the hundred-pound burden like a beanbag.

"Jesus!" Barrett recovered his balance.

"I can manage from here," the newcomer said shortly.

"Looks to me like you could manage all along," Barrett replied.

"Excuse my sloth." He returned and moved to pass Barrett on the catwalk.

"I didn't catch your name." Barrett planted himself casually.

He had so many names, so many identities.

"Von Stryker," came the cultured voice. "Dietrich Von Stryker."

"What brings you to the bay, Mr. Stryker?" Barrett deliberately truncated the surname.

"Are Americans always so forward?" Von Stryker seemed amused.

"Police sometimes are. Agent Raines. Florida Department of Law Enforcement."

"Ah. A detective. What brings you here?"

"The way it works, sir, I ask the questions. You answer."

"I see. Well, then, perhaps you'd better follow me on board."

Barrett had never been inside a boat like this; the *Easy Money* ran thirty-four feet of wood and luxury. He followed the man who called himself Von Stryker through an expensively appointed cabin, past a console of ship-to-shore and nav gear, to a galley large enough for a condominium.

"Excuse me." Blue Eyes slipped a cassette into a portable Sony player.

A strong, controlled voice rose with a full orchestra through a digitized sound system. *Madame Butterfly* floated once again aboard ship.

"You like opera?" the foreigner inquired mildly as he stowed the ice.

"Not one of my strong points."

"She's American." The man nodded to the cassette as if the diva were inside. "Mirella Freni."

Her voice soared with pain and grief and betrayal. Very powerful. Very precise.

"I've heard of Freni," Barrett volunteered, not wanting to be regarded a total idiot.

"Good!" the killer said and then, smiling, "Not her latest recording, but superb. I happened on it quite by accident. In Bonn. A lady client. Drink?"

"No, thanks."

"Cigarette?"

"Thanks again. I'm trying to quit," Barrett declined.

"Admirable." His host smiled genially. "You mind if I?"

"Feel free."

Barrett scanned the interior. Pretty much what you'd expect. Except that ceramic vase over there didn't look quite right. Not the kind of thing you'd expect in a rental.

Von Stryker pulled a book of matches from the vase. Holiday Inn, Barrett noticed the matchbook's glossy cover. Fort Walton Beach. That was in Okaloosa County.

Ten'll get you twenty I know where he got the boat, Barrett wagered silently.

The killer produced a cigarette, struck a match.

"I notice you haven't answered my question." Barrett timed his reminder as inconveniently as he could.

"Have I not?" Von Stryker lit up, apparently unperturbed. "Sorry. My work, wasn't it? Yes. Well, I suppose you could say I'm a hunter."

"Hunter?"

"A geologist," the tall man smiled. "I hunt for petroleum. Oil. Natural gas."

"There's plenty up toward Louisiana," Barrett said. "Don't know about around here."

"No one knows." Von Stryker exhaled luxuriously. "Producers have speculated for years that there might be some formations along these low shores. I thought I'd see for myself."

"There must be a survey of some kind."

The assassin's hand shot out like a snake. Barrett flinched—

"Sorry."

Von Stryker silenced the cassette. *Madame Butterfly* and Mirella Freni cut short. The killer then reached overhead to open a bin which Barrett could see was crammed full with charts and maps.

"Let's see," Von Stryker mused. "Ah. Here."

He pulled a rolled-up chart from its tube, snapped it open. A choir of contoured lines and topographical data unfolded cryptically over a representation of the north Florida coast. The killer smoothed the chart over the galley's hardwood counter.

"Odd thing about these," Von Stryker mused. "No one who reads them sees precisely the same thing."

"I guess not." Barrett wasn't looking at the chart.

"That's the thing when you hunt." The killer knew Barrett wasn't looking at the chart. "It's always a gamble."

He tapped the map with a long, aristocratic finger.

"A lovely name, 'Dead Man's Bay.' Don't you think?"

"Lovely doesn't come to mind," Barrett said dryly.

Von Stryker plopped a passport on top of the chart.

"Saves us both time," he remarked pleasantly.

Barrett scanned the passport.

"Von Stryker. Dietrich Von Stryker?"

"Yes."

"From Serbia?" Barrett frowned. "Where do we get Serbia from 'Von Stryker'?"

"My father was from East Germany."

That was true enough.

"He settled in what was then Yugoslavia after the war, married my mother."

That was partially true.

"She was Slav through and through."

He declared that truth as if it were the only fact that mattered.

"I've never met a Serb," Barrett said.

"I've never met a—what should I call you? A Negro? African American?"

"Agent Raines will do," Barrett replied tersely, the passport still in hand.

"No offense intended." The assassin never stopped smiling.

"None taken."

"My apologies, nevertheless. One has to be inordinately careful. There is so much to offend in your country; it's impossible to stay abreast. My passport, please?"

Barrett slapped the forgery into his opened palm.

"How long will your survey take?"

"Hard to say." The assassin inhaled his cigarette. "With a little luck a couple of weeks. Perhaps much sooner."

"Well," Barrett faced him squarely. "Happy hunting."

"Happy hunting, yes." Smoke curled from the Serb's nostrils like a dragon. "Same to you."

14.

Rendezvous

A string of bleach bottles bobbed with an ochre sunrise on Whipping Post Island. A half-dozen fish thrashed in Barrett's perforated bucket. There were a couple of snapper which Barrett could identify. One permit put up a hell of a fight before Barrett lost him. And there were one or two other things with fins and gills that Raines could not identify. He didn't care. He wasn't really there to fish. Talmadge Lawson inspected the trotline critically.

"Better run out some more line."

"Looks fine to me," Barrett replied.

"Tide comes up you'll drag those bottles right under." Talmadge gnawed on a fresh toothpick.

Barrett played out twenty or so additional feet of line. The bay's clear blue sky had been replaced with a kind of cotton haze this morning. It was hot and humid. Barrett's eyes stung with perspiration; he was wiping his forehead with Preacher's cap when a pair of diesel engines drew his attention. Dietrich Von Stryker regarded Barrett and Talmadge through binoculars from the bridge of his Bayliner. A wake rocked the dock as the newcomer cruised by.

"Who the hell is that?" Talmadge asked too loudly.

"Geologist."

Barrett still couldn't decide how to read the Serb. Bear didn't want his own prejudice to color that reading; associating Von Stryker with ethnic cleansing was unfounded and unfair. It was possible, after all, that the geologist's reference to Barrett's race was no more than indelicate, a gaffe, in which case his apology had to be read as sincere.

Why, then, did the Bear feel as though he'd been baited?

Hard to sort that out. And there were other things claiming Barrett's attention. This evening Megan was taking him to Miles Beynon's hideaway. Finally, perhaps, he'd learn something that would explain the falsehood which seemed to pervade this community. Perhaps he'd learn more about Esther's dealings with the slain felon. Innocent, according to her daughter. Barrett hoped that was true. He hoped he wasn't making a mistake accepting Megan's help. Those things alone were enough to claim his attention. And then there was Talmadge.

"I might have somethin' more if *you* got somethin' more," Lawson whined as the Bayliner's wake cast swells onto the Whipping Post.

"Time to quit playing games, Talmadge." Barrett tied off his trotline. "You've been feeding me this story about Boatwright meeting some cruiser at sea. I've waited. I've been patient. I've paid! Now it's time you told me what tips you off."

"We been through all that." Talmadge wormed the toothpick side to side.

Barrett pulled the last two bills from his wallet.

"They gave me a week down here," he told Talmadge. "I'm past that already. And I'm broke."

He nodded to the cash.

"Take it or leave it."

Talmadge eyed the twin twenties a moment.

"All right. The first time was when she gave him the box."

"She? Box?"

"The box she keeps in the icehouse."

"You mean Esther?"

"That's right." Talmadge reached for the money.

"Not yet." Barrett pulled it back. "What's in the box?"

"Don't know," Talmadge shrugged. "I'm an outsider, too, remember? But it's always the same. Ammo box, like army surplus. And Ray always puts it inside one of those Igloo ice chests. You know, like the road gangs use?"

"I know the type," Barrett nodded and remembered the first polite man he'd met in Taylor County. "So she gives the box to Boatwright? How do you know that?"

"The first time after I saw Ray meet the big boat, I started kinda followin' his habits. One night, it was close to the middle of the month, Esther ups and closes the bar. Runs ever'body out. Ever'body except Ray."

"How about you?" Barrett wondered for the fiftieth time who was the fisherman, here, and who was the fish.

"Oh, I was run out with the rest," Talmadge replied. "I played drunk, but then once I got outside I climbed up on the icehouse."

"On the roof?"

"There's an eave right there, where the icehouse hitches onto the bar. You can see inside." Talmadge gave the information smugly. "I got up there. I thought to myself, Ole Ray's gonna get him some jelly roll. But then Esther, she brings out the box."

"The ammo box."

"That's right," Talmadge confirmed. "Had a big padlock on it. Banged like a damn cowbell."

"What'd Boatwright do?"

"Put it in an Igloo, I tole you."

"I meant after that," Barrett said patiently. "After Esther gave him the box, after Ray stowed it in the Igloo—What then?"

"Nuthin' at first." Talmadge lowered his voice. "Esther and Ray, they just sat there drinkin'. I got off the icehouse. Ben Folsom's boat was tied about two down from Ray's so I figured I'd just wait in there, wait for Ray to come out."

Talmadge paused. "Fact is, I went to sleep. Watn't for the fact Ray's boat is so loud I don't think I'd o'woke up."

"Ray had the box?"

"Had it loaded on his boat, had his lights off—which I thought was peculiar—and was headed out of the bay."

"So how'd you follow him?" Barrett asked warily.

"I borried Ben's boat," Talmadge answered. "Hell, it was about two in the morning. I knew Ben wouldn't need it."

"So you followed Ray out to the Gulf."

"That's right," Talmadge nodded. "That's when he met the big boat. Turned his lights on then, for certain. Like some damn Christmas tree.

"That was in May," Talmadge concluded. "That's when I knew for sure."

"How many times have you followed Ray out there?"

"Prolly half a dozen." Talmadge nudged the trotline.

"But you never saw what was inside the box?"

"Never did." Talmadge spit his toothpick into the sea. "Tell me something, you plannin' on followin' Ray? You plannin' on going on the Gulf yourself?"

"Any reason I shouldn't?"

"Nuthin' but common sense, I guess," Talmadge replied. "You know the buoys? You know the waters? The currents?"

"It's just past here, isn't that what you told me? Past the Whipping Post a half-mile or so. I can do that."

"I wouldn't let Ray get too far ahead," Talmadge advised. " 'Fact if I was you I wouldn't let him out of my sight."

"If he spots me he won't make the rendezvous," Barrett said.

"Keep him in sight." Talmadge shook his head. "And keep a compass, too."

"I can always see land," Barrett insisted.

"Not at night," Talmadge grinned. "You lose Boatwright at night on the Gulf, you might not never get back."

Barrett wondered if Talmadge's concern was genuine. Or was there some other reason the poacher didn't want Barrett on the water?

"How do you know the exact night, Talmadge?" Barrett fingered the two bills in his hand. "You saw the first exchange. You lucked into it. But after that how'd you know when to follow Ray? How do you know the night he's going to do it?"

"Third Friday," Talmadge replied. "Third Friday every third month."

For a moment Barrett was furious. The third Friday! That was easy! That was simple! Barrett was about to strangle Talmadge for the fun of it, when another thought jogged his mind. "Christ on a raft!"

Barrett reached for the watch that always used to be on his wrist.

"Wait a minute isn't—?"

Talmadge grinned through shattered teeth. "Yep. Tomorrah night."

Talmadge reached over, then, to collect his remaining bills.

"Pleasure doing business with you, Agent Raines."

"Keep it to yourself," Barrett warned him. "For both our sakes."

"You afraid of competition?" Talmadge winked.

"Why? Should I be?" Barrett heard a warning bell.

But Talmadge had his lucre.

"I tell you, we'll both know."

*   *   *

Barrett loaded his reels and fish and left Talmadge Lawson on the windward side of Whipping Post's solitary pole. Talmadge waited a few minutes before leaving, just to make sure nobody was watching who shouldn't be. Satisfied, finally, Lawson pulled his birddog out from under the dock. Ten minutes later he was home to a houseboat anchored almost within sight of Esther's bar. A pair of tires kept the birddog off an enormous set of pontoons. Talmadge hoarded his wealth inside.

A screen door banged open and shut in a fitful breeze. Barrett's informer had not yet fixed the lock where Splinter and the rest had screwdrivered it open. The rest of the houseboat wasn't in much better shape. Talmadge didn't give a shit. He opened his wallet. Barrett's twenties were there to complete the hundred paid by the detective to his informer. A hundred dollars Barrett had paid. Talmadge spit a toothpick onto the floor. A hundred bucks! Not kitty litter next to the thousand which had only recently come. Talmadge smiled. Talk about playing both ends against the middle! Talmadge stuffed the cash beneath his mattress, stripped off to shower.

He took a long shower. Shampooed hair slick with sweat and grease and dandruff. Miss November was carefully scissored from the most recent *Playboy* and taped on the bathroom wall. The shower's steam and the bay's humidity had already taken their toll. Skin that was airbrushed smooth as silk now wrinkled at the edges. She wouldn't last much longer than the month. But she still looked good and served admirably for Talmadge's purposes. He masturbated perfunctorily, got out of the shower, and emerged from the john to find the assassin waiting on his bed.

"I warned you," the blond man chided gently. "When I pay money for information it belongs to me."

"I didn't tell him anything," Talmadge lied. "We were just fishing, that's all. Swear to God!"

The assassin extended his hand. "I take my property very seriously."

"You cain't take it back!" Talmadge wailed. "Goddammit, I earned that money! It's mine!"

The assassin never even looked at his target. The throwing knife came like a bolt from a crossbow. The snitch clawed desperately at the steel blade in his throat. The blade jerked free in his hands. Blood sprayed from his windpipe and carotid artery like a fountain. It bubbled, too, over lips begging windless for another chance, another chance. Another chance.

Talmadge Lawson collapsed at the foot of his filthy bed.

The Serb did not want to call attention to himself. That was why he paid Talmadge for information that could have been gained by other means. And since Talmadge had provided all the information the killer required, he was obliged to kill the fisherman quickly, as painlessly as possible. That was one of his rules.

The killer used a towel to clean his knife. He then rolled back the dead man's mattress and took the thousand dollars he had paid his informant. The tall man also took the hundred Talmadge had conned from Agent Raines. A hundred dollars was not important but the ritual was. He always took something. A final look about. The place was a sty. He'd have to do something about that. Talmadge's killer kicked some sheets into a pile, pulled a lighter from his pocket. Struck the flint.

The nigger knows too much, he mused as he gathered the things he'd need. I may have to do something about that.

But not yet. Not just yet.

*   *   *

A high tide brought the fishermen back to Esther's a little earlier than usual. No one missed Talmadge at the end of the workday; Lawson often did not return to his water-borne roost at the day's end. The other fisherman culled and weighed and iced their catch. Splinter was designated, this time, to take the entire catch up-coast for sale to Esther's buyers. Barrett wondered briefly if some of the mullet in Laura Anne's restaurant came from these nets. He straightened painfully from Ben Folsom's nets to find Megan waiting. Her breasts swelled to break a cotton halter. Her belly and legs rippled beneath.

"You ready?"

"Depends what you have in mind." Barrett sucked some ice.

She leaned forward quickly, slid her tongue into his mouth.

Barrett got rid of the ice.

"Let's go."

The sun was just getting low, the pelicans and gulls and spoonbills just seeking their roosts as Barrett and Megan nudged out of the bay. Beynon's place was off the coast, she explained to Barrett.

"This place have a name?"

"Sure," she nodded. "Convict Springs."

Convict Springs. Barrett was reminded that a fair portion of this entire region's white population was descended from convicts, a family tree of fugitives who escaped the penal colonies of Georgia to follow the Suwannee River south. Why south? To avoid capture, of course. But a convict's flight to Florida in those years also meant facing the moccasin, the mosquito, the Seminole, and malaria. It must have seemed to many of those early felons that they had traded the frying pan for the fire. Only the fittest among them survived.

Barrett looked at Megan again. Her own history was most likely quite distinct from that of her mostly white community. Her mother had come from a ton of troubles overseas. Her father was almost certainly descended from slaves. What brought that man to this region, Barrett wondered? Was he fleeing some Georgia persecution? Or was he also a man in trouble with the law? Either way, Megan's was a troubled heritage. Was there a triple-helixed predisposition for treachery bred into those lovely, well-honed bones? Or murder?

Megan took the birddog for their expedition. They'd be in some grass, she informed Barrett, and some shallow water. Plus it was lots quieter. *The Debra Kaye* was ideal for the purpose. It wasn't five minutes after that explanation that Barrett found himself with Megan wending through a marsh so thick with saw grass Barrett was obliged with Megan to lift the outboard and pole with a pair of oars to get through. Once past that barrier Megan pushed her snub-nosed craft into what looked to Raines like a canopy of cypress and oak and pine. They entered a run of water, only a few boat width's wide, hip-deep. But it was freshwater, crystal clear, and cold as a well-digger's ass.

"Spring-fed," Megan smiled to Barrett as she navigated upstream. "You'll see the boil up ahead."

"Boil?"

"You'll see."

Barrett watched as a family of soft-shelled turtles splashed into the water.

"You can drink it," Megan urged him. "There's no brine or anything. Go on, have some."

Barrett scooped his hands into the water that slid past Megan's boat.

"How is it?" Megan asked. The top had slid down to completely bare her shoulders and back.

"Sweetest water I ever had in my life!" Barrett was honest in reply.

She blushed as if he'd just complimented a cake out of the oven. "There's the boil."

Barrett looked up. The run of water terminated abruptly into a shallow-banked pit. It was limestone, this pit, quite small but deep, very deep, and as their boat glided toward its center Barrett could see water quite literally boiling up at tremendous pressure from some preternatural depth. Boiling, but ice-cold. Megan's boat rose abruptly as it passed over the top.

"God, is it safe?!"

She only laughed. "Of course it is."

"I've heard of these," Barrett remarked. "Some kind of artesian well?"

"All I know it comes from underground." Megan offered her explanation without contradiction. "You can track it for a ways by the sinkholes, but after that—No one knows."

Barrett looked around. "Doesn't look like the boat will get us much farther."

"Doesn't have to," she smiled. "We're here. Can't you see?"

At first Barrett couldn't see anything. It was near dusk and a camouflage of moss and cypress and pine crowded right up to the spring's rocky rim. But then he saw.

It was an abandoned farmhouse which looked out to the spring from the lip above. Barrett could not imagine at first that anyone could live in the place. Even from the spring he could see where cypress shingles had rotted away to open portions of the roof. A wide porch sagged in disrepair on pine pilings. A chimney seemed in remarkably good shape alongside.

"Beynon's place." Megan wiped perspiration from her forehead. "Or at least—this is where he stayed."

"Looks pretty rundown," Barrett said.

"I don't think he was looking for comfort." Megan killed her outboard and took his hand.

She led him past a kingdom of forgotten things, of porcelain, old trinkets, and deerskins. She led him past a fireplace and a painting withered in its frame, past a hand pump and kitchen to a bronze bed which looked through a shattered ceiling to the sky. A window beside them allowed a sweet, cool breeze to flood the room. Barrett could see a familiar diamond hanging bright and low and unblinking above the horizon.

"Venus," he whispered.

"Evening star," she amended and pulled her halter over her head.

Dust drifted in motes above them on a dusk filtered through moss and cypress. Megan was on top. She straddled him. Held him. Her belly glistened with sweat, familiar muscles finding a new task as she rocked back and forth, back and forth. She moaned, then, tucked work-hard legs behind to come to him, come to him.

Barrett matched her rhythm. He moved with her easily. He was not a young lover. He was not a greedy lover. He did not need to rush. But still, it had been so long, so long! He made himself stay, stay, delaying his own climax to make sure of hers.

She seemed to hang on the moment forever.

They both exploded, finally, and exploded again before night finally fell on the house hidden from Dead Man's Bay.

Something woke Barrett hours later from a deep sleep. Something, someone, was in the house. At first he thought he was dreaming. But a board creaked in the shotgun hall, creaked again. Barrett went cold, scrambled for his trousers. The Smith & Wesson was holstered underneath. He hadn't wanted Megan to see the gun. He hadn't wanted to remind her he was a cop, not while they were in bed together. And then he saw, he thought he saw, a shadow flit on the floor outside the bedroom.

"What is it?" Megan was awake beside him.

"Shhh."

"What you got? A *gun?*"

A quick patter, now, of footsteps down the dog run hall.

"Stay *put!*" And before she could acknowledge the command Barrett was out of the bed and bedroom, sliding down the hall's splintered wall, arms extended, weapon ready, eyes and ears strained to every sound, every sight.

He reached the porch. It was pitch dark outside. Barrett could hear his pulse inside his ears. He could see just about to the end of his nose. That was all.

That's when it came. A long, bone-chilling, harrowing wail. It seemed to Barrett like the Hound from Hell.

"God from Zion!"

"It's just the dog." Megan was beside him.

"Jesus, I thought I told you to *stay put!*"

She was hurt. She had only been trying to help.

"I'm sorry," Barrett felt suddenly embarrassed. He was naked. She had wrapped a sheet modestly around a body which now glowed occasionally with the moon that peered fitfully through a scud of running clouds.

"I'm sorry, Megan, really. I thought someone was in the house."

"It's all right," she said, and when she smiled he knew it really was all right.

They kissed long and deeply. They made love again, right there on the porch. He could track the clouds by the shadows the moon cast on her breasts. And it was only then, only after another long climax together that he thought to ask, "What dog?"

"Red Walker's," she replied simply. "He runs loose. Likes to bay at the moon."

That's where they awoke the next morning, Megan curled in naked slumber on the porch, Barrett playing his hands across her hip.

I shouldn't be with this woman, Bear told himself. But why shouldn't he? How long had it been since he'd been with Laura Anne—ten, eleven months? Would a year make it all right? Would three?

God, I could use a smoke! he thought and realized with a mild shock he'd been a week without that, too.

A cigarette, yes. Something to occupy those so-recently occupied hands. Megan saved him from that temptation, at least. She woke ready for mischief and next thing Barrett knew he was plunging into the frigid stream out front. The water was cold, exhilarating. The urge for penance or tobacco got replaced, at least for the moment, with something else.

"We don't have time," he smiled when she suggested they go back inside.

"I meant to dress!" she protested.

"Sure you did," he teased.

"I did!" Megan insisted.

They dashed back into the house. That brought back unexpected memories. One of the nicest parts of Barrett's domestic life was watching Laura Anne slip out of bed naked to don her pants and bra, her blue jeans or skirts or tops. And now Megan was here, suddenly shy, slipping into a halter and shorts before him.

"You look wonderful," he said suddenly.

She slapped him on the butt. "See you at the boat."

Megan skipped outside. Barrett remained to locate just about everything but his socks.

Where on earth—? Ah. There they are.

Just under the edge of the bed. Barrett's hand dropped

to the wide-planked floor. He fumbled for a sock, missed it. But his fingers came across something else. Paper? Trash? Barrett scooted it out with his sock. "Hello," he muttered aloud.

It was a cigarette package. The wadded cellophane unfolded for his inspection. Camels. Unfiltered.

"You were right, Preacher. The Lord provides a ram!" Barrett tore the pack apart expecting a cigarette. But the pack was empty. Empty! Not a single butt to settle that nicotine fit. Barrett was just about to throw the wadded trash away when he remembered.

Miles Beynon didn't smoke. Brandon Ogilvie did. Brandon smoked Camels. Unfiltered. Barrett dropped his head, upside-down beneath the bed's frame . . . And inhaled as sharply as if he'd been stabbed.

"Barrett?" Megan's voice filtered in as if from a dream.

"*Right there,*" he called hoarsely back.

A litter of trash stretched beneath the bed for Barrett's inverted inspection. Cellophaned trash. Barrett checked a pack. Camels. Unfiltered. He checked another pack. Camels again. Also unfiltered. He checked again and again. Always Camels. Always unfiltered.

"What is it?" Megan asked Barrett when he finally reached the boat.

"Nothing," he assured her. "I'm great."

He kissed her as convincingly as he could.

"We don't want to be too late, do we? People'll talk."

"Let 'em," Megan smiled as she pulled her outboard to life. Within seconds the spring, the turtles, the house, and an evening of amour were behind them.

But Barrett had a feeling a great deal more lay ahead.

15.

Ashes to Ashes

Megan allowed Barrett to skipper the birddog down their hidden tributary to reach open water. The two new lovers then turned north toward Dead Man's Bay on bearings Barrett could only imagine Megan divined from the entrails of goats to run for Dead Man's Bay. A stiff, cold breeze and choppy waves pounded the small boat. Megan quickly donned the jacket and jeans stowed onboard. Barrett had, at Preacher's insistence, borrowed a wool jacket and pullover before leaving the bay.

"Take the helm!" he shouted to Megan and scrambled into the extra clothing.

The pullover fit Bear like socks on a rooster but he was glad for the extra bulk. The jacket was warm, too, and here on the water in a mid-November chill, warm was what you wanted. The forward-mounted Evinrude screamed with wind and water preventing conversation. Barrett was glad that conversation wasn't required. It gave him a chance to think.

Brandon Ogilvie had spent time, probably quite a bit of time, in the abandoned farmhouse at Convict Springs. Made sense that he would. If Beynon were to rendezvous with his old partner, surely both men would want a place that was secluded. Out of the way. Perhaps the house at one time belonged to Brandon. But why hadn't Megan known that? How was it possible she could know that Beynon spent time at the house but have no knowledge of Brandon Ogilvie?

Had Megan set him up? The thought settled like a ache in Barrett's groin. But if Megan did know that Brandon frequented the farmhouse along with Beynon, and if she wanted to conceal that fact, or confuse it, why would Megan risk taking Barrett to the house at all? Was there a chance, finally, that Esther's daughter was simply trying to please Barrett? That she knew only of Beynon, or perhaps—knew nothing at all? Barrett did not have the answers to those questions. He was glad, therefore, to avoid conversation.

It was Megan who saw the fire. They had just skirted the last cypress stick that staked out the shallows along the bay's mouth. Barrett shot past, preoccupied in his own troubled thoughts, when Megan stood suddenly erect in the boat.

"Something's wrong."

Barrett looked up. A plume of ink-black smoke roiled up into the morning sky from Esther's pier.

"Barrett!"

"Hang on."

Barrett gunned the boat toward the pier. The details came clearer, like a negative coming to life in a darkroom. There were figures running back and forth along the pier. They were using buckets, Barrett realized. Buckets! There was no fire department on Dead Man's Bay.

"It's the bar!" Megan was fully panicked now.

"We're almost there," Barrett kicked the rudder so hard he almost tipped the boat.

You could see the fire clearly, now. And hear it, too, wood and resin bursting with smoke and fire that boiled to heaven. But it wasn't the bar. Talmadge Lawson's houseboat was a pyre upon the water. Its sluggish inboard still turned a pair of props like a heartbeat in a blackened corpse.

"Oh, Lord." Megan put her hand to her mouth.

Barrett felt something churning in his stomach.

"Come on," he said.

Esther watched with MacGregor from the pier as a circle of boats converged uselessly around Talmadge's waterborne home. Buckets of water and hand-held extinquishers spit pitifully onto the conflagration.

"Lucky it didn't catch the pier," Esther remarked.

"I wouldn't call it luck." Barrett grated at her side.

"I had nothing to do with this, Mr. Detective." Esther shivered in a housecoat.

"How do you expect me to believe that?"

"A dozen people at least saw it." Esther remained adamant. "Damn fool must have been drunk. Bloody barge drove right into the pier."

"Wait a minute, are you telling me Talmadge was on board?"

"Well, who else would be drivin' his boat?" Esther was back to regarding Barrett as if he were an idiot.

"Did you see the man?" Barrett persisted.

"All I saw was a flash inside. And then a ball of fire."

"I saw the flash," Mac supplied helpfully. "And then we all heard a *boom!* He had a propane stove, y'know."

"Well, there you are. Next thing we've got a fire beside the pier."

"Did you try to get him out?" Barrett asked grimly.

"I'm telling you, man, it lit up like a torch. There was no way."

"No way." A new voice at Barrett's side echoed Esther's assessment.

Ray Boatwright lounged in a bomber jacket and fresh-pressed khakis on the pier.

"When did you get here, Mr. Boatwright?"

"Just now."

"Just when?"

"I saw the smoke from my trailer. Thought maybe somebody'd need some help."

The houseboat leaned far over on its side. Ray slipped off a pair of aviator glasses.

"Looks like I was too late."

"Or too early." Barrett faced off with Boatwright. "Talmadge had his houseboat right down the coast from your trailer, didn't he? Didn't you see him pull out?"

"What if I did? People move houseboats all the time."

"Was it burning?" Barrett grated.

"You got a hard-on for me, Raines?"

"You like to find out?!" Barrett shoved himself into the diver's face, but then—

An explosion rocked the pier with a blizzard of wood and steel and fire. Barrett found himself beside Megan, flat on his face. He grabbed a piling to haul erect. Talmadge's houseboat groaned once, like a woman in labor, before it hissed and steamed to an untimely grave.

Everyone saw the explosion but no one had seen, or would admit to seeing, Talmadge. Barrett wanted some evidence that Lawson had in fact died in the fire and explosion that engulfed his houseboat. "We can try."

Esther seemed doubtful of any attempt to recover Talmadge's body, but with her usual vigor, briskly gathered a group of men and grappling hooks to dredge the sandy bottom around the pier. All they turned up was charred pieces from the pontooned boat. Esther turned then to Ray Boatwright. He demurred—angrily, it seemed to Barrett. Esther remained adamant. An apparent argument ended with Ray fetching his wet suit and scuba gear for a dive.

A rising wind whipped dark, lead-lined clouds into rows like a ribcage over Dead Man's Bay. The water was murky and there were whitecaps showing on the water. It took a lot of experience and a cool head to even attempt a retrieval in these conditions; Barrett found himself wondering what other jobs Esther recruited Boatwright to handle. Ray retrieved Talmadge's scorched remains within an hour. The corpse disintegrated when Esther's fishermen jerked it from the water up to the pier.

So now Bear had a body, pieces of one anyway, but he did not have the authority to order an autopsy. Only the sheriff could do that. Barrett radioed Sheriff Sue requesting that the corpse be examined by someone trained in forensics. "I can call a unit in from Tallahassee," Barrett offered.

"For what—a boating accident?" The sheriff was not impressed.

"I just want to make sure." Barrett felt himself faltering.

"Sure of what? Hell, you got a dozen witnesses saw it happen!"

Barrett found himself in a bind. He didn't have proof Talmadge's death involved foul play. He didn't have anything like a probable cause. What Barrett did have was a dead informer and a gnawing fear that somehow he had contributed to Talmadge's death. Against that were Esther and her brood telling the sheriff that Talmadge Lawson died on his boat in a blaze which was, truth to tell, only a taste of what he'd endure for an eternity in Hell.

Sue declared an autopsy unnecessary.

"What about the death certificate?" Barrett inquired. "You plan on writing that up without even seeing the body?"

"He burned to death," came the sheriff's reply. "I don't have to see toast to write about it."

Barrett was overruled. The villagers held a funeral right away. Esther rigged the coffin. A box meant for icing mullet now bore the mortal remains of Talmadge Lawson. Scrap iron and bricks were added for weight. A jerry-rigged catafalque steadied the crude casket on Jeremy Bantham's boat; Jawbone and Splinter tended the ropes, their faces raw in the wind. Esther Buchanan took a mourner's place alongside. The other fishermen, their families, and children old enough to view the ritual bore witness from their own floating pews. Megan was there with Ben and Sarah. Barrett remained separate from Esther's daughter on MacGregor's boat as Preacher O'Steen payed final respects.

"Ashes to ashes. Dust to dust." O'Steen closed a worn Bible suddenly, as if weary of the comforts offered on its pages.

"Be a lie to say we loved the man we remember this morning." Preacher's voice carried like Moses' to the sea. "He was a thief. He was a Judas. But in God's eyes Talmadge Lawson was no more a thief, no more a Judas, than the rest of us.

"We don't like to think about that, do we? We don't like to remember. Maybe that's why God took Talmadge away. To make us think. To make us remember.

"God bless Talmadge Lawson. God bless us all."

The fishermen, their wives, and children echoed the preacher's amen. Jawbone and Splinter jerked a pair of slip knots free. Talmadge Lawson slid like a sailor into the sea.

Any true Irishman would have been sorely disappointed with the wake that followed Lawson's watery interment. Whether because of a sense of communal guilt or a Protestant reserve, there were only murmurs of conversation in Esther's bar. A murmur, only, even though every living soul on the bay was there. What conversation there was generally centered on why Talmadge had run his houseboat into the pier in the first place.

"Prob'bly tryin' to take the bar down," Jawbone offered as a possible motivation. "Get back at Esther."

"Prolly tryin' to kill hisself." Splinter seemed satisfied with that explanation.

"No," MacGregor disagreed. "He was just drunk."

It was now getting on to eleven and Barrett sat in Esther's bar feeling more the outsider than ever. He added up what he knew. It wasn't much. Miles Beynon visited the bay on more than one occasion. Esther and everyone else lied about it. Could be, as Cricket said, that this isolated community never volunteered information about anyone for any reason. That could be.

But then there was this business with Esther and Ray Boatwright, the mysterious meetings at sea. And there was Megan. Barrett's evening with Esther's daughter intruded on his thoughts, came unbidden and at the least expected moments. She was there now, at the window, making conversation with Sarah, meeting his eye with open invitations. It was not the distance you needed to be a good cop. Barrett forced himself back to the cigarettes—Camels, unfiltered—and he could not escape the feeling that somewhere, somewhere in this very room someone named Brandon Ogilvie was laughing at him over the lip of a Budweiser beer.

Barrett rubbed his wrist where the watch used to be. In less than a week it would be seven years since Miles Beynon and Brandon Ogilvie had robbed that armored car in Miami. The statute of limitations already put the thief who survived out of reach for that crime.

But there was no statute of limitations on murder. Barrett located Ray again. There he was. Still at the bar. Was this man in fact Brandon Ogilvie? Had the man in khakis murdered Barrett's informer and then burned Talmadge's boat to hide the evidence? Ray laughed, now, at some raunchy joke which Esther pantomimed from the bar. An odd couple, there, for sure. What was it the preacher said? ". . . She knows everything." Barrett began to wonder if that might be the literal truth. Why, after all, should Esther have anything to do with Ray Boatwright? What was her business with the former diver? What was in that ammo box which Esther secreted in her icehouse and which Ray dutifully took to the Gulf every three months?

Barrett felt the Smith & Wesson tucked beneath the wool jacket at the small of his back. It was the third Friday of the month. Couple of hours maybe he'd have some answers. Maybe. But for right now an uninvited guest cut Barrett's ruminations short.

Von Stryker lounged in a sweater and twill slacks at Esther's door. A hush fell over the place. Esther cranked her head around.

"Not open to the public. Sorry. We're waking one of our own."

"Actually, I only came to deliver a message." Von Stryker remained at the door.

"It can wait," Esther retorted.

"It's a weather advisory."

He ignored her. "Depression's headed northeast. Heavy sea and winds. They're saying it could reach us this evening."

Barrett wondered briefly if they were headed for a hurricane. Storms in mid-November were not unheard of. But Esther didn't seem concerned.

"Thank you for that trouble," she acknowledged shortly. "We'll keep a listen."

Von Stryker turned as if to leave. "I'm almost certain I saw a great deal of smoke this morning, over the bay. Was that—?"

"Yes, it was," Preacher O'Steen's response was slurred with whiskey. "He was a fisherman. Got caught in the fire, near as we can tell."

"Perhaps the smoke got him," the tall, pale man smiled. "That would be merciful."

"Without question." O'Steen seemed, all of a sudden, sober as a judge.

Von Stryker left the bar. O'Steen kept looking after him, kept his eyes dead on the space the Serb had just vacated.

Barrett eased over to the older man. "Preacher, you all right? Preacher?"

"There's something missing in that man." O'Steen nodded toward the now empty doorway.

"You mean Von Styker?"

"Some piece left out." O'Steen was back to a slur. "Like as if he only had half a life."

Barrett winced. "Yeah, well. I guess there are lots of people like that."

Within a couple of hours Barrett began to think that Talmadge Lawson (God bless his soul, naturally) had been full of shit. The bar was practically empty and scanning the boats anchored outside, Barrett could see no signs that anyone was preparing to leave the bay's safe harbor for a rendezvous at sea.

The weather was definitely turning for the worse. The sky seemed low enough to scrape the tops of the pine trees which bordered the bay. The clouds were bruised and purple but the atmosphere was suffused with a heavy, yellow hue. Lemon-light, Barrett's grandmother used to call it, the color of light before a storm.

Megan began closing shutters on the bar's unscreened windows as gusts of south wind rattled the rafters. Preacher O'Steen hung on beside Esther's ship-to-shore, bleary-eyed and morose. Esther fished up a Hamilton railroad watch that dangled by a knotted piece of twine from a nail on her bar. She wound the mainspring carefully.

"Been a long one," Ray remarked, rising from the plywood counter. Barrett thought Boatwright was about to leave.

"Has indeed," Esther agreed. "I'm dead on my feet."

"Why don't we shut down, Mama?" That suggestion came from Megan.

"Is there anyone needs another drink—Mr. Raines?"

"I'll just finish this one," Barrett replied to Esther's query.

"No point in asking Preacher." Esther took O'Steen's bottle away, ushering O'Steen out the door and steering him in the general direction of his shanty.

"He'll be fine," she muttered to Barrett's unvoiced concern.

Barrett was about to go himself when Ray Boatwright reclaimed his spot at Esther's counter.

"D'you think I have time for one more?"

"Just," Esther replied. "Megan—Home with you, girl. I'll put up."

Megan fastened the final shutter. Barrett tossed back his beer. This was it, then. The bar emptied. Ray left with Esther. The third Friday.

Megan's hand lay suddenly cool on his neck.

"Walk me home?"

Barrett smiled his warmest smile.

"Give me a rain check, okay? I'll see you tomorrow."

Was there the slightest hesitation, then, before Megan replied—

" 'Kay. T'morrah."

16.

Conditions Minimal

It was cold outside. Barrett pulled his loaned jacket tighter, scanned the pier and shore. Megan was nowhere to be seen. Good. No one else about either. Showtime.

Barrett followed the bar's exterior wall until it hitched up with the icehouse. He could see, even from the pier, the eave under which Talmadge spied on Esther and Boatwright. Barrett wasn't about to do that. He edged over to the side of the pier. There was Ray's boat, long and sleek and powerful. And two hulls down, Barrett's whaler waited, fueled and ready.

Barrett dropped into his boat. The wide-bottomed hull rolled with heavy, wind-whipped swells. Barrett slipped a life vest over his jacket. A roll of duct tape secured a flare gun near the whaler's throttle. A squawk told him the radio was working. He tuned in a maritime frequency. A small-craft advisory urged boaters to be alert: "Conditions are minimal." Raines pulled out his 9 mm, checked the clip. Sixteen rounds present and accounted for. He killed the radio and reholstered the weapon at the small of his back. Nothing to do now but wait.

* * *

Many miles across the Gulf of Mexico from Barrett Raines and hours earlier, another man had begun his vigil. Juan Santos was a citizen of Mexico, a small and abused mix of Indian and Spanish descent. You might call him a middleman, a trader. He was actually a stockbroker. He waited at a restaurant not far from Vera Cruz's substantial port from where his cousin's trawler, *Cabrito*, had departed for its quarterly rendezvous.

Juan sucked a cigarette and a San Miguel beer. It was bad weather coming over the Gulf. He could smell it in the air. He had always hated the waiting. At first Juan had not even wanted to be involved in the business. He knew that his cousin's boat ferried the contraband common to Mexican commerce and he wanted nothing, absolutely nothing to do with drugs or druglords or Federales of any sort.

But that was not what this venture was, at all, Ramon explained one Sunday, dressed in white to match the stuccoed concrete from which virtually everything in Vera Cruz was constructed. This was a transaction, his cousin declared beneath a lonely pair of palms. Legitimate business. And something he needed a broker to do. A legitimate broker. With that introduction Ramon hefted a metal box onto the table. It was an ammunition box.

Juan wondered what the hell Ramon was getting him into.

"What exactly do you need, *compa?*"

Ramon opened the box and then, of course, Juan knew.

The operation had gone without a hitch for seven years. Ramon would navigate his trawler on its unvarying schedule to meet the single boat which, four times a year, brought him the ammunition box and its contents. Splitting commission and fees, the business netted the cousins a profit of roughly sixteen thousand American dollars per year, eight thousand each for Juan and Ramon. In the past that had worked out to something like twenty-four thousand pesos annually for each man. Converting pesos to Yankee cash was always a day-to-day adventure but the sixteen thousand American never changed. Plus a *mordida* on the side, of course. Just a little bite. A drug lord might sneeze at such profits, but not Ramon. And certainly not Juan.

It was a gift. A gift from the sea. But Juan Santos never learned the name of the man who owned the box.

"A man I knew when I was working salvage," was all his cousin would say. "A diver."

That was all he would say.

Waiting can be tough, especially when you're in the bottom of a boat rolling in forty-degree temperatures on swells that slap like a boxer. Even with all that, Barrett Raines had to struggle to remain awake. It was now after midnight. The evening before with Megan had given Barrett a decade of sex but robbed a night's worth of sleep. That wouldn't have been such a bad trade under normal circumstances, but right now Barrett needed sleep more than sex. He fought now to stave off a slumber that a week or so earlier would have been welcomed like manna from heaven.

The temperature seemed to be dropping. Barrett shivered. Windchill would be nasty tonight. Made Barrett wish again he'd gotten more rest. He checked the whaler's chronometer. Quarter to one. A few minutes later Barrett's chin hit his chest and he knew if Ray didn't show up soon it was going to be lights out for the boy from Deacon Beach.

Maybe a nap would help. Just a short, sweet sleep. The life vest would make a fine pillow. Barrett slid to the bottom of his whaler and was nodding off when something like a cowbell intruded on the edge of his dreams.

Slap-slap . . . Slap-slap.

Barrett blinked suddenly awake.

Slap-slap.

It wasn't the tide, that was for sure. Barrett closed a numb hand on his 9 mm, rolled to his knees, peeked over the whaler's gunwale.

Ray Boatwright was clambering into his powerboat. A padlock slapped against the ammo box he stowed on board.

Barrett found himself reflecting on the cliche that it was, in fact, a dark and stormy night. Ray launched from the pier without running lights. Barrett followed lightless behind. There was no moon overhead, no pearly glow to illuminate the cypress stakes that marked the way away from and back to the bay. There was nothing close to a star. Barrett hanged on to the silhouette that was Ray's boat. A fitful, greenish glow could be seen occasionally from the Glastron's console. That would be his instrument, Barrett thought. Radios, maybe, or navigation. But it wasn't much, barely a firefly in the gloom, Barrett's only buoy, his only compass, his only way back home. Talmadge would not have approved.

Barrett wasn't worried about being spotted. His whaler was dark against the water and Ray's boat, even in a calm, would drown out any sounds of pursuit. Barrett couldn't risk using the radio, of course. Ray shared the same frequencies. Barrett hoped that the task of navigating to the rendezvous would take all of Ray's attention, not to mention skill, and so far it appeared that assumption was correct. Raines could only suppose that Boatwright was piloting by GPS and Loran. To do otherwise in these conditions was madness which meant, of course, that Barrett, having nothing but a magnetic compass and minimal survival skills, was certifiably insane.

A wave hit the whaler broadside and nearly threw Bear overboard.

"Jesus!"

Barrett knotted a line intended for his anchor about his waist and held on. It was a black night on a black sea. The swells that rose earlier were now replaced by waves frothed with foam like Poseidon's beard. Ray turned his bow straight into the wind to plow through. Barrett jammed his throttle full forward and followed suit. The whaler was not built for these seas. The waves tossed her wide bow almost upright. When she fell, she fell a bone-crunching concussion to the trough which waited ten or fifteen feet below.

"Minimal, my ass!" Barrett screamed to sea gods and meteorologists alike. "It's a fucking gale out here!"

Another wave slammed into Barrett's boat. He rode it high, high into the air. Then the bow dropped and Barrett plummeted in his cradle to another bone-crunching fall. Hurricane season turned the Gulf of Mexico into a monster eager to chew boats to pieces. Watery jaws spread wide now for Barrett's vessel and for Ray's. The wind screamed. The boats screamed. Barrett screamed rage and fear. There was no one to hear.

Barrett didn't give a damn, now, what Boatwright was doing on these waters. He didn't give a damn about Miles Beynon or Brandon Ogilvie. All he wanted now was to keep on Ray's tail. Keep him in sight. Ray was his best bet. Keep close, keep that dim, damp, plunging firefly of light in sight because without it, Barrett knew, he'd never find land. Too late for the radio, now. Suppose someone did hear—What were the odds they could find him in a storm like this? What were the odds they'd even try? A wave broke then to slap Barrett onto his back; his slender line snapped taut.

Hold on! Hold on, you son of a bitch!!

Barrett clawed back to his helm hand over hand, like a waterlogged spider.

"Ray, you bastard!" The words stumbled from novo-
caine lips. It was freezing out here. Barrett shivered
uncontrollably and soaked to the bone. But he had to stay
on Ray's stern. Had to keep up. He did not want to join
the gods and Talmadge Lawson.

Barrett rode the seas like a man on a roller coaster,
knuckles white on the whaler's wheel, eyes straining to
find the firefly ahead. Each crested wave tossed Ray's boat
dimly into view, each trough buried it for what seemed
like forever.

It was during one of those falls, when Barrett was not
sure he'd make it, that Laura Anne came to his thoughts:
She deserved more, much more, than half a life.

Then Barrett hit a new crest and Ray turned on his
lights. They weren't just running lights. They were kleig
lights, halogens. Ray's jet boat lit up like a Christmas tree.

"Thank you, God!" Barrett wrenched his rudder to line
up on Ray's boat. The wave dropped, he rode it down. Up
again and there was Boatwright, pretty as you please.

Barrett latched onto his target, craned over his bow to
keep Ray's stern in sight. He did not see the other, enormous silhouette that bore down as if from nowhere on
Barrett's back.

It was a fishing trawler, forty feet or more, which
ploughed sternward into Barrett's darkened whaler,
ploughed straight and true to rendezvous with Ray's
brightly-lit toy. Barrett was completely oblivious to the
looming collision from behind. His attention riveted full
ahead on the soaring seas and Boatwright. An explosion
popped like a firecracker to wrench the Bear 'round—

"The hell?" Barrett whirled.

A scarlet comet arced overhead.

That's when Barrett saw the trawler.

"*Shit!*"

He wrenched the rudder to starboard. Hard! But it was

probably the sea that saved Barrett, that caught him in a foamy wave and tossed him out of the way.

For a brief moment Bear was level with the deck of the trawler. He saw the startled faces of a Mexican crew. He could almost touch the rigging. The trawler's wake hit with the force of a tsunami. Barrett plummeted once more. The flare burst. Barrett's boat stood exposed with Ray's in stark relief on the water. A machine gun chattered from the trawler's deck.

There'd be no exchange tonight.

Ray gunned his jet boat to run with the wind.

Barrett followed.

It was an uneven contest. Going out, Ray was not concerned with speed, had only used his boat's power to muscle through the seas. Now, though, with Barrett and a growing gale at his back, Ray's twin U.S. Marines gave new meaning to the term "jet boat."

Boatwright flew from crest to crest with Barrett floundering behind. The sea was more dangerous at stern than at bow. Barrett knew that and so did Ray. Neither man's boat was built for the open sea, but Barrett had seen craft like Ray's before, running drugs from Miami to the Bahamas in weather you wouldn't think possible.

Ray had thirty feet of slender length to run before this wind and four hundred horsepower to punch through its seas. Barrett had a boat half as wide as it was long and a hundred mercurial horses. If Ray outran him now, Barrett knew he'd never find land. He suspected that Ray knew it, too.

For a second the two men came face-to-face, Ray turning suddenly to take a bearing for shore, Barrett topping a wave amidships. Ray could see Barrett there, freezing in his denim jacket, fighting the tempest in his tub. Ray gunned his boat again, wind at his back, and Barrett fell forever to the trough which waited below.

The whaler smacked into a pavement of salt water. The windscreen shattered and threw Barrett from the wheel. Barrett knew he had to use the radio, then. It was a miracle or nothing. He had no other choice.

The whaler twisted just slightly, just a tad sideways before a wave that now built almost amidships. The wave rose higher, higher. Barrett watched a wall of water swell as he desperately tried to reach his wheel, to haul his nose into the wind, to meet the monster head-on.

A wall of saltwater hit Barrett broadside and swept him from his whaler like a leaf. He was overboard. The safety line held, cutting like a nylon garrote into Barrett's waist. But a ton of water dragged Barrett beneath the hull of his whaler.

Barrett knew if he hit the boat's hull in this sea it would kill him. And if he stayed beneath he'd drown. His lungs already aching for air, Barrett kicked and pulled and floundered, fighting tons of seawater on a spider's thread. The life vest popped him up, eventually, his lungs and limbs on fire, to surface only four feet from his boat.

"Help me, Jesus, help me, Jesus, Help—!!"

Four feet of safety line stretched like an interstate. A new wave swelled off his beam. Higher. Higher! Barrett rode the monster right back into his boat.

"Thank you, Lord!"

But then his whaler cracked like a rotten stick. Barrett could see the decking split from the hull. A couple more like that and he'd be in pieces. He had to get to the radio. Had to! Barrett crawled up the line to his Motorola.

"*Mayday! Maydaymaydaymayday!*"

A wave slammed like a sledgehammer into the hull. How many more could he take.?

"*Half mile past Whipping Post!*" Barrett prayed now to the ether. "*I'm lost people! I'm breaking up!!*"

The whaler wrenched as if snatched by a giant's hand. Barrett's line snapped tight as a leash.

"*Mayday . . . Mayday . . . May—!!!*"

The boat pitched up sharply to find a new crest. Barrett saw a boat. It wasn't Ray's, this boat. Certainly not a bird-dog, not in this water! Then Barrett recognized the squat, muscular bow and remembered the solitary shrimper he'd seen his first night on Dead Man's Bay.

Barrett ripped the flare gun from its jerry-rigged keeper. He fired a fitful, scarlet plea for help into the air. There was a long moment in which Barrett wasn't sure the flare was seen. But then a green comet scooted up from the shrimper's deck.

"*Thank you!*" Barrett bellowed to heaven.

The shrimper rolled heavily to come alongside. Barrett almost missed the line thrown to his deck. He cut his own safety line, got the shrimper's line wrapped, somehow, around his chest.

"*Pull!*" a voice commanded. He could not. There was nothing left.

But a strong arm could pull and did. A strong arm and a strong grip hauled Barrett up and onto the shrimper's deck like spent squid. That's when Barrett discovered that the arm and the grip belonged to Esther Buchanan.

"*You son of a bitch*!!" He could hear her above the gale.

"Thag . . . Thag you." Barrett could not form the words. He was too tired. Too cold.

"Son of a bitch. *Preacher!*"

O'Steen croaked acknowledgement from the helm.

"*Wind at our back.*"

Barrett emptied his stomach on the deck. Esther collared him with a raw fist.

"What in *Hell* are you doing out here?! *Tell me!*"

"The wuh—" Barrett wanted to tell her. Really, he did. But his tongue was thick and cold and numb.

"*Tell me!!*" Esther bellowed again.

"The work." Barrett got it out.

Esther's face went hard as granite. The thought dimly crossed Barrett's mind, then, that he may have made a mistake. How simple it would be for Esther now to cut the line that hauled him in. Cut it and toss him overboard. That poor government man. Lost at sea.

But Esther's hand left Barrett's throat for his vest. She snapped a second line roughly home.

"You stupid bastard."

Barrett nodded agreement. *Slap-slap.* His eyes rolled white.

Asleep at last.

17.

Impressions

Renoir might have painted such a scene, points of light set so brilliantly and distant. A white launch sparkled at midday beneath an autumn sky swept clear of precipitation. Barrett stirred to life on O'Steen's porch in time to see Ben Folsom escort Sarah on board. She was radiant, her silver hair flowing perennially beneath her wide-brimmed straw sombrero. The sunglasses which protected her clouded eyes made her look, now, like a movie star. Ben was handsome, too, in a Sears & Roebuck suit, white shirt, and a tie rescued from the Depression.

Esther helped Sarah into the unfamiliar launch. Ben followed. Barrett could see Ben and Sarah laugh when Esther guided the older woman to her deerskin rocking chair. Almost ready to go. One last detail.

Ben Folsom presented his wife a gift.

A splash of roses appeared from beneath his humble suit. A splash of roses to set off an ermine ambulance and cerulean sky.

Sarah Lynn accepted the bouquet from her husband. He bent formally from the waist. Their kiss lingered much longer than you might expect from a marriage so long and tested and Barrett realized it was the kind of kiss he'd always wanted for himself, had always imagined having with a wife become graceful with advancing years.

"She's beautiful," Barrett muttered through cracked lips.

Plop. Something dropping from the Preacher's gutting table to the floor of his wide-planked porch brought Barrett from a distant scene to one closer at hand. Preacher's cat teased and chased the saltshaker like a ball of twine practically to Barrett's cot.

"Here, cat." Barrett retrieved the shaker, sprinkled salt on a dampened finger.

The cat attacked the salt lick furiously, its tongue so rough Barrett thought he'd receive a blister. Preacher O'Steen chuckled from one of his two large, unscreened windows.

"So you're back with the living."

"Barely," Barrett grunted and let the kitty go.

"Rough night," Preacher said soberly.

"Rough for you, too, I guess."

"I was scared half to death." O'Steen scooped up his saltshaker.

"Well, I owe you," Barrett tried to sit up. "Christ!"

Every ligament and muscle he owned screamed for Club Med and a masseuse named Ingrid.

"Here." O'Steen intervened gently, helped Barrett to sit erect in his cot.

"Where is Esther?" Barrett managed.

"The bar."

Barrett looked in time to see Esther waving the Folsom's off from the pier. Ben stood erect in the launch, his tie catching the breeze like a banner. Sarah remained seated in her deerskin rocker, her roses bright and scarlet in her lap.

"How long have they been married?" Barrett asked.

"Forty-odd years. Why?"

"Nothing." Barrett turned away. "I'd appreciate it if you'd tell Esther I need to see her. Ray, too."

"Can't see Ray," O'Steen shook his head.

"Hell, I can't." Barrett had decided it was about time he acted like a cop.

"Nobody's seen Ray since last night," the preacher said. "Not him. Nor his boat."

"That a fact?" Barrett didn't bother to hide his sarcasm.

"Esther's organizin' a search right now," the preacher replied as if he hadn't noticed.

The whole community was convened with Esther at her bar. Megan was perched beside the ship-to-shore; the Coast Guard acknowledged her report of a missing vessel. A hushed rumble of speculation and conjecture buzzed back and forth over Esther's plywood counter. Then Barrett Raines limped in.

Conversation stopped like a radio going dead.

"Morning," Esther called a salutation to the door.

"I figure it's time we talked." Barrett refused the familiarity.

"No need for thanks, if that's what you mean," Esther retorted.

Barrett produced his plastic ID, Florida Department of Law Enforcement.

"I want some straight answers. Starting with Ray Boatwright."

"Missing," Esther retorted curtly.

"How 'bout hiding?" Barrett snapped.

"And why would he hide?" Esther spoke for them all, now. Just as she always had.

"Aw, I don't know," Barrett scratched his head. "Wouldn't have something to do with that ammo box, would it? You know, Esther—the one you gave Ray last night. The one you keep in your icehouse! What was in that box, anyway?"

"Wages," she replied simply.

"For who? The Mexican Navy?"

"For Ray. He works on the boats. I pay him something every quarter."

"And then he goes into the Gulf at two in the morning in the middle of a damn hurricane?"

"Only man I saw on that water was you."

"Do me a favor, Esther. Don't piss on my leg and then tell me it's raining."

"What Ray does with his money is his business," her rejoinder was adamantine.

"His money," Bear grated. "But none of yours?"

"None," she denied.

"You're lying," Barrett told her and an ice-cold draught rippled through the gathered fishermen. Barrett spoke up, then, spoke up to them all.

"She's a liar, yes. But then you've all lied, haven't you? Been lying all along."

"About what?" Red Walker tested the water first.

"About Miles Beynon," Barrett laid it out. "About Brandon Ogilvie. And now about Ray Boatwright."

He had called their bluff. Time to pay or play.

"Funny how people just disappear around here, isn't it?" Barrett turned it up a notch. "Beynon, Brandon, Boatwright. Too bad Talmadge begins with a 'T'."

"We had nothing to do with Talmadge," Esther spat out.

"Nothing to do! You hated him—All of you! You must have known he was giving me information. Something about that box. And so you killed him. Isn't that it?"

"No," came Esther's second denial.

"Probably just like you killed Miles Beynon," Barrett suggested.

When the third "No" came Barrett halfway expected to hear the cock crow. No such luck. Barrett would have to earn it the old-fashioned way.

"All right, then. Let's say you're all innocent as lambs. First things first: Who *did* kill Miles Beynon? Maybe Ray Boatwright?"

"That's crazy," Jawbone snarled angrily, "Ray hardly knew—"

Jawbone caught himself too late.

"That's all right, Jaws," Barrett said reassuringly. "You haven't told me anything I don't already know. And we all do know, don't we, that Miles Beynon was here? Right here in this bar, wasn't he? And on more than one occasion!

"And in a way you're right about Ray Boatwright, too. 'Ray' didn't know Miles Beynon at all. But Brandon Ogilvie sure as hell did."

The room stirred, suddenly tense, suddenly electric. Barrett turned to face Esther squarely.

"That's it, isn't it? Ray Boatwright—*is* Brandon Ogilvie?"

All eyes went to Esther. She didn't flinch.

"Ye've got all the answers, haven't ye?"

"It was Brandon who killed Miles Beynon," Barrett kept her eye-to-eye. "It was Brandon who killed Talmadge. And Brandon Ogilvie is paying you people to shut up."

"Esther!"

"Quiet, Mac!" Esther's voice cut through the room like a knife.

"How much do you get, Esther? A boat repaired here. An eye operation there? Or just straight blackmail—February, May, August?"

"Ray didn't kill anyone," Esther said tiredly.

"He tell you that?"

"What if he did?" She sagged like a spent balloon.

"If he did tell you that, *if* he did—you're a fool to believe him."

"You don't know shit from Shinola!" The fire came back in her voice.

"I know a dead man when I see one," Barrett countered. "And if you're covering for a killer that makes you an accessory to murder."

Barrett turned to the rest of them.

"That makes you all accessories. Partners with a killer."

There was no challenge from the floor. Barrett turned, finally, to Megan.

"You're a fisherman, aren't you, Meg? And you played me like a fish. Let me see what you wanted me to see. And when you needed me out of the way why—that wasn't hard to do. Was it?"

She slapped him hard across the mouth.

Barrett tested his teeth with his tongue. "At least we know where we stand."

"Nobody here's a murderer." MacGregor was talking again.

"Let's say for the sake of argument that you aren't." Barrett left Esther to take center stage himself. "Let's say you had nothing to do with Miles or Talmadge or anyone else. But you are hiding something. And whatever that something is, is getting people killed. Now, maybe you don't know everything about Ray Boatwright, or Brandon Ogilvie, or whatever the hell his real name is. Maybe I don't know everything, either. But I can promise you this: I am going to find out."

A score of nervous eyes turned then to Esther.

"Can you give us a minute?" she said finally. "Just to ourselves?"

"I'll be waiting outside," Barrett said and for the first time in a long time he felt like an officer of the law.

Preacher O'Steen shared Barrett's short vigil outside the bar. It was a good day to be alive, Barrett decided, leaning against the cypress-walled bar. O'Steen squinted at the clear, dark-blue sky.

"How long you think they'll be?"

"You know 'em better than I do," Barrett replied.

"Not so sure." O'Steen jammed his hands in his pockets.

"I could sure use a smoke," Barrett declared.

"Lookee here," O'Steen pulled the torn remains of a cigarette from his pocket. "Half's better than nuthin'."

". . . Maybe not," Barrett declined with the barest of hesitations.

O'Steen smiled as he flicked the butt over the side. The bar's door opened, then, and Esther stepped out onto the pier.

"We'll help you find Ray," she said.

"Good." Barrett accepted it as a matter of course. "How about the rest of it?"

"Like you say," Esther replied. "First things first."

Barrett followed Esther inside. A search for Ray Boatwright was organized within minutes around her bar. Megan was designated to remain with the radio. Esther assigned areas for the fishermen to search based on their fishing grounds. "They know their own grounds," she explained to Barrett. "Be a lot faster, a lot more likely to see anything out of the usual."

"How about the Coast Guard?" Barrett asked.

"We called in," Esther answered for her daughter. "They've got an oil rig to worry about and at least a dozen boats missing. So we're mostly on our own."

Esther went back to her men, "You see anything call in to Megan, that straight? Work out from your grounds to the deep water. Agent Raines and I will look for anything's washed up to shore."

Barrett stood with Esther on her birddog cruising close to shore. A lather of foam and debris washed into the jungle of saw grass and cabbage palms which substituted in this region for a beach. There seemed to be even more birds and wildlife about than usual. Barrett wondered if that had something to do with the storm.

Esther scanned the shoreline. No comment came from the woman. Nothing like conversation.

"You don't give him much of a chance, do you?"

"Should never have let him go out," Esther replied, and Barrett understood at last a little of the weight which this woman constantly felt on her shoulders.

"He did break up, are we going to find him?"

"Hard to say," she shook her head.

"How about his trailer?" Barrett said abruptly.

". . . What?"

"Has anybody checked his trailer?" Barrett repeated.

"I don't think anyone's even considered it."

"Well—?"

Esther throttled the mid-mounted engine wide open. Within seconds they were clear of shallow water and flying up the coast.

Barrett saw the flagpole first, Ray's pride and joy. But Barrett knew immediately there was something wrong because the colors of the Confederacy were missing. There was no sign of Dixie on this pole. There was no flag at all, only the erratic clink of a D-ring suspended on a Dacron lanyard against a metal pole.

Ray's powerboat was tied on to a small dock hidden in a maze of saw grass. An Airstream trailer propped above on a foundation of eight-foot pilings. A narrow deck circled the trailer and overlooked the canal and boat in the rear. Esther tied her boat off at the dock. Barrett checked his handgun hoping to hell it was more waterproof than his watch had been.

"Take me to the front," he ordered Esther, and to Barrett's amazement she complied without an ounce of static.

They skirted the deck out back, crossed a maze of palmetto and cypress to reach a stair which climbed to the deck and the Airstream's front door.

"Look!" Esther pointed.

The trailer's screen door sagged open. A wet suit and a pair of fins baked inside its aluminum frame.

"You stay here." Barrett slapped the clip to make sure his weapon's internal safety was disengaged and found the gun shaking in his hands like a goddamned tambourine.

"Are you all right?" Esther hissed.

"Stay here," Barrett said.

"Why?"

"I'm going to arrest him, Esther. He might resist."

"He won't," she said sadly. "I know he won't."

"Just the same." Barrett took a Weaver's grip on his weapon.

"For God's sake, don't use that thing!"

It was almost a plea.

"Unless I have to." His reply stopped well short of reassurance.

The trailer door banged open and shut a couple of times in the fitful breeze that marked Barrett's ten-yard journey to Ray's door. Sweat stung Barrett's eyes as he searched desperately for any sign of a barrel or gun which might be trained on him through the trailer windows.

He sprinted the last twenty feet or so, glued on the edge of the Airstream's smooth, metal skin and challenged as he had been trained long ago to do, at the top of his lungs.

"*Police, open up.*"

A fly buzzed angrily out of the already opened door.

Barrett took a deep breath, exhaled. He lowered to a combat crouch, popped quickly inside. In and out. Nothing. No reaction.

Barrett checked his grip once more.

"Okay," he muttered.

He went in low, arms outstretched. He found a target. The barrel centered on instinct and Barrett had almost triggered his standard two rounds when he realized that Ray Boatwright was dead.

Not just dead. Murdered. Mutilated.

"My God."

His gun wavered and dropped. The one-time diver was crucified onto the wall of his own trailer. Fishline pinioned the man's hand's and feet. Fishing lures with their several barbed hooks hung from Ray's crotch, from his armpits, his eyes, his feet. An electric cord's sheared prods indicated further torture.

"Jesus and Mary!" Esther exclaimed and Barrett nearly blew her head off.

"*Who did it?*" he thundered at Megan's mother.

"My Lord, Ray!" She backed away.

"*Who?*" Barrett pulled her back in, made her look. "*Goddammit, Esther, who did this?*"

"I don't know," Esther said quietly. "I swear on my mother. God in Heaven. I just don't know."

18.

Madame Butterfly

Barrett returned with Esther and a corpse to find her fishermen shifting uneasily at the bar. Esther strode straight in, tossed Ray's wet suit and fins onto the counter.

"Ray's in the boat, what's left of him."

"Esther." It was Mac MacGregor who stepped forward.

"You can put him in the icehouse," Esther went on. "Where's Megan?"

"Esther . . ." Splinter joined MacGregor.

"She's supposed to be on the radio," Esther said irritably.

"Esther, there's something you got to hear," Mac urged shakily.

"Well, what is it?" Esther snapped.

The fishermen stood aside then and Barrett saw, with Esther, the portable Sony cassette player which waited, its shoulder strap still in place, on her bar.

"That's Von Stryker's," Barrett remarked automatically.

No reply. No one would say anything.

"God's name." This time Esther was frightened. "What is it?"

Barrett stepped forward, started the player, and a cultured, sophisticated voice unwound from a strip of magnetic tape.

"Miss Buchanan," the Serb began formally over the cassette. "I have made careful inquiries over the past few weeks, at some inconvenience I might add, for myself and others. You seem to be the only person I can presently identify who can help me locate my property."

"His property?" Barrett felt ice water run suddenly through his veins.

"You owe me half a million British pounds," the cassette continued. "My own interest has not abated in seven years. But I'll be happy to settle, here, for the principal."

Barrett killed the tape. Esther was white as a sheet.

"Is he crazy?" Barrett asked. "Or lying?"

"He's not lying," Esther whispered. "What's he done with Megan?!"

Barrett switched on the player.

"I propose a swap," the monologue continued. "The cash you hold, Ms. Buchanan, all of the cash, for your daughter."

"Oh, my God." Esther collapsed. Splinter caught her. Someone else got a chair.

"Please send the currency with your Negro agent to me," the smooth voice went on. "Mr. Raines must come to me by himself. Alone. I'll be anchored in view of your Whipping Post at six o'clock. That gives you something like two hours. No time to negotiate for your hostage, Mr. Raines. Not nearly enough time to raise help from the mainland. And no time to waste. I will not stall. Some proof of my intention."

A new voice sobbed over the Sony.

"Mama, he's hurting me! He said he'd kill me! *Mamaaaa!!*"

There was a scream, then. Megan's scream. And then Esther's; she rose screaming from her chair and smashed the player to pieces with her fists.

Barrett had never wondered during his week or so on

the bay where Esther slept. A woman so filled with fire and work surely did not sleep, could not sleep, in fact, even if she wanted to. She only had two rooms, a bathroom and another for everything else, inserted above the bar directly over the icehouse. Vents to the icehouse provided a kind of air-conditioning the rest of the community might envy. It also provided the ever-present smell of fish.

Esther's bed was a fold-out couch propped beneath a variety of calendars all out of date and all featuring photographs of Ireland. Barrett saw a four-leafed clover pressed and taped onto "November." He wondered what Esther thought of that talisman, now.

Preacher O'Steen did his best to comfort Esther. The short climb from the icehouse to her perch above had drained Megan's mother of all spark, all chutzpah. Barrett was looking at a woman used to taking charge now suddenly impotent, a prisoner in equal parts of pain and rage and apprehension.

And guilt.

There was a great deal of guilt here, Bear decided. She blames herself for what's happening to Megan. And she probably should.

He cleared his throat.

"In a normal hostage situation you stall." Barrett directed the words to Esther. "You surround the area. You isolate. If this were Tallahassee we'd have helicopters and emergency vehicles and SWAT teams."

"Can you get them?" O'Steen asked.

"Take way too long," Barrett answered. "He knows it and he knows I know it. Another big edge—"

Barrett sat beside Esther.

"I still don't know the whole story. This bastard does."

"He can't kill her, can he? He needs her. Doesn't he? Doesn't he?"

She sobbed then as Rachel, weeping for a child she could not help, could not hold.

"So far he's never killed without a reason," Barrett pointed out.

"Good," O'Steen seized on that. "Then let's not give him a reason."

"Give him what he wants." Esther shoved aside Preacher's offered hand. "He wants money? Give him the money. Fuck the money!"

"Okay. All right." Barrett rose from the couch. "But I won't carry it on me. Not initially, anyway, not till we can make sure she's all right. I'll go out, first. Arrange a swap for later."

"Better come with me, then." Esther ground out a tear with a raw hand.

"For what?"

"For the money," she said. "And everything else."

Esther rose heavily then, passed her calendars and clover to leave her upstairs roost for the icehouse below.

Barrett and Preacher followed Megan's mother past tons of fish and ice before they came to what looked like a cast-iron tomb in the very rear of the icehouse.

"You're kidding me." Barrett leaned forward to inspect the strongbox. "The payroll safe? You've got Von Stryker's cash in the same place you keep fish money?"

"Why not?" she replied. "It belongs to fishermen, now."

She bent, then, to dial the old-fashioned tumblers.

"But I do keep the combination."

"Ray didn't have it?" Barrett prodded a little.

"His name was Brandon," Esther replied. "Brandon Ogilvie. You were right about that, and, no, he didn't have the combination to the safe. He didn't want to have it."

"Did he even tell you where he got the money, Esther?"

She paused. "He said he stole it."

"From an armored car, that's right. Did he tell you it

was blood money? It has to be, you know. Either from drugs or guns or extortion or murder—how else would a man like Von Stryker get a half million British pounds?"

"Brandon didn't know," Preacher O'Steen offered hoarsely. "I'm just about positive about that. If he'd of known, he'd of said something."

"Maybe." Barrett was grim. "Maybe."

Esther returned to her task at the safe. A dial left, right, left again. The door groaned open. A stack of petty cash and coins littered the bottom trays. But up top—Barrett saw an aluminum case, silver and substantial. And stacked beside that modern satchel were British notes. They piled in literal pounds inside the crypt.

"How much?" Barrett's mouth was suddenly dry.

"What we haven't spent," Esther sighed.

"How much is that?"

"Three hundred and seventy-five thousand sterling," she answered.

"That's around, what—?"

"Five hundred seventy-five thousand dollars, roughly."

Barrett faced her squarely. Esther's lower lip trembled. Barrett took the door from her, closed it, and spinned the tumblers.

"That takes care of the money. Now. How about everything else?"

Barrett huddled with Esther downstairs over a Bud which the preacher fetched from the cooler. It was the most unusual interrogation in which Barrett had ever engaged, complicated by the fact that Esther was not only a potential lawbreaker but a victim, the mother of a kidnapped daughter. The daughter, yes! That posed another complication, especially for Barrett. He could not forget Convict Springs. He could not forget the four-poster bed or the moon playing on Megan's hip as she slumbered on the porch. He could not forget any of those things, but he had to forget them if he was going to have any chance at all of getting Esther's daughter back alive.

Take, now, for instance. Esther was talking, finally, but Barrett was only half-listening.

". . . Minute he walked in the bar, I knew sure he was running from something," Esther was saying and it took Barrett a second to realize she was talking about Brandon Ogilvie.

"How'd you find out about the money? Hard to believe Brandon would just open up and tell you."

She shrugged, "He was never Brandon to me, you understand. He said his name was Boatwright. Ray Boatwright."

"Brandon, Boatwright—makes no difference, now. How long did it take you to blackmail him?"

She actually laughed at his deduction.

"No, no. Wasn't like that. I didn't come to him. He came to me."

"He needed your help?" Barrett frowned.

"He was afraid," Esther nodded. "He'd no idea where the money came from. Who it belonged to."

"We still don't," Barrett reminded her. "All we know is Von Stryker's claiming it."

"It is blood money, though, isn't it? Any way you look at it," Esther sighed. "We tried not to look. *He* was always afraid the money was tainted. He worried that some mobster or a legman from some cartel might have claim to the money, would find out, would come to get it back. I tried to tell him it would never happen. Never, I told him! But I don't believe he ever quite believed me. He was terrified of people when he came here, you know. Especially outsiders."

"Why did he trust you?" Barrett asked.

Esther paused just a moment.

"Because he saw me kill my husband."

Barrett's head jerked around as if yanked on a leash.

"Brandon Ogilvie saw you . . . kill your husband?"

"The last man to call me a whore," Esther cradled her beer. "Well. Not counting Talmadge."

"This was after your husband beat you, Esther? After the Whipping Post?"

"Few months after. Brandon's the one found me. Cut me down, else I'd have drowned. He took me to the hospital. Soon's I got my strength, I came back to my husband and first chance I got I gutted the son-of-a-bitch."

She paused again, "Oughtn't you arrest me for that?"

"Probably," Barrett was swimming in a sea of "oughts," "but let's take first things first."

She accepted the reprieve as if it didn't matter.

"Anyway, it wasn't long after that, Red Walker lost his boat. Went down offshore. We didn't know what to do. Then Brandon walks in, pretty as you please, says he'll buy Red a boat. Brand new."

"That's when he told you he'd stolen the money," Barrett surmised.

"He told me," she confirmed. "Nobody else. 'Course, people knew he had money. Most of 'em figured it was drugs."

"So Brandon sort of bankrolled the whole community?" Barrett saw now how Jeremy got his boat fixed. How Sarah could afford her operation.

"People got sick, he'd pay their bills. He made loans, no interest. One of Mac's granddaughters is going to University of Gainesville. Anything she can't get from scholarships or loans—he took care of it."

"In return for silence." Barrett identified the fly in her ointment. "If he was going to pay for boats and college and eye operations, you and everyone else had to put on blinders, isn't that true, Esther? Hear no evil, see no evil.

So this largesse you're describing to me, it didn't exactly come free, did it?"

"Just a place to stay," she smiled wanly. "That's all he ever wanted."

"And you all helped."

"Most of us," Esther affirmed.

"How about Megan?" Barrett asked and immediately wished he hadn't.

Esther turned her face to his. "She doesn't know much. Truly."

"Seems to me she knows enough," Barrett replied roughly.

"No point my trying to convince you otherwise. Is there?"

"One other thing," Barrett slid off his stool. "Those trips out to the Gulf, to the cruiser—those were currency exchanges, weren't they? You had to get dollars for British pounds. But you were afraid to convert too much at once."

"Maybe you *are* a detective." Esther brushed aside a lock of hair. "We use a Mexican broker. We usually give him forty, fifty thousand quid at a time. He converts the pounds to U.S. dollars through a Mexican exchange in return for a generous commission. He cheats us some, but hell, with a half million pounds to draw from—"

"Pays for a lot of mullet," Barrett finished the thought.

"Pays for a lot of everything," Esther replied.

Barrett glanced at the railroad watch.

"May I take this?"

"And welcome," she said. And then, "What's he doing to her? What's he doing to Megan out there?"

"She's alive, Esther. And he needs her alive. That's all that matters. That's all we have to think about."

"Sure." It sounded like a cry. "Of course."

"I'll bring her back. I will."

She didn't reply. She just finished the last of her beer,

tipped the last few drops from an amber bottle. And then, quite deliberately, Esther Buchanan placed her arms onto the plywood counter, lowered her head into their cradle like a schoolgirl at an old-fashioned desk, and cried. A wild mob of Irish hair ranged over her neck and back, but Barrett could see the tears which broke over a swollen face. It was a groan of grief and guilt such as Barrett had never before heard, a lamentation uttered from some deep, woman's place that no man could ever truly understand.

There was Esther, weeping for her child, and would not be consoled.

19.

Endgame

Barrett had to radio in some kind of report to Cricket Bonet; he had to tell his partner *something* about the progress of his investigation on Dead Man's Bay. But Bear had no intention of involving Cricket in the decisions he was about to make. He had gotten Bonet in trouble enough during the past year. He wasn't about to involve the crazy Canuck in a course of action that Barrett knew damn well had the potential for getting somebody killed.

He just hoped that somebody was not Megan Buchanan.

"Raines to Bonet, can you read me, over?"

The static broke.

"For a change, yes, I can. Cricket right here. Over."

"How's it hanging, partner?"

"Boss wants to know when we're off vacation, Barrett. So do I. Over."

"Try tomorrow noon," Barrett said, checking Esther's watch. "But I'll want you out here. Over."

There was a pause before Cricket replied.

"You need backup, partner?"

"Nah," Barrett responded casually. "Just follow-up.

Bring the sheriff, though. Tell him we've got lots of evidence to process. Over."

"I don't like the way you sound, Bear."

"I don't like the way you look," Barrett fired back knowing he couldn't fool Cricket for long. "Just be here, all right? Tomorrow noon. Suwannee River. Over and out."

Barrett switched off Esther's radio. Checked the watch. It was time to go.

A teakettle whistled merrily in the Bayliner's luxuriously appointed galley. A calm hand lifted the kettle from its burner. A fitful whistle and a trail of steam led then from the stove to Esther's daughter.

Megan screamed.

She was bound in tank top and cutoffs to a chair which in turn was secured to the bulkhead. A series of blisters tracked from Megan's legs to her feet. A cord looped around her neck, ran to a cruel anchor around her ankles. Her hands tied behind, Megan had to arch, arch that well-toned back to loosen the noose that was strangling her. But you could not arch your back for long with boiling water poured on your front.

The noose stayed tight as Von Stryker poised the kettle once more over her thighs.

"Nnnooooooo!!"

"Of course not," he smiled pleasantly. "There's no longer any need. Is there?"

He poured the scalding water into a cup of tea. Megan threw back her head, then sobs breaking with fresh fear and humiliation.

Stryker glanced out a well-bolted window. The Whipping Post was just outside. And so was Barrett Raines, easing Esther's boat up to the Bayliner, hands displayed prominently and open.

"Ah. Right on time."

The Serb gathered an assault rifle, an AK-47, and stepped outside.

Seconds later Barrett Raines entered the Bayliner's cabin at the muzzle of Von Stryker's weapon.

"Barrett!" Megan croaked.

Barrett felt a wave of nausea he forced himself to ignore.

"Megan, it's all right. Hang tough, hon. We're getting the man his money."

Barrett turned to face the assassin.

"You maggot."

"Where is my property?" Von Stryker kept the barrel on Barrett's heart.

"Waiting for you," Barrett replied, scanning the cabin for a weapon. There wasn't anything obvious and even if there were, what chance did he have against this character? And would Megan survive the attempt?

"I should kill you both." Von Stryker trained his rifle on Barrett with one hand. His free hand dropped calmly to fetch and light a cigarette, a display of dexterity which was meant, Barrett supposed, to convey confidence.

"You're running up quite a tab," Barrett stalled. "Let's see. There was Miles Beynon. Then Talmadge. And then— Brandon Ogilvie. Or did you know him as Ray Boatwright?"

"That's your question to answer, Detective. Not mine."

"You obviously knew Esther had the money." Barrett nodded as casually as he could manage toward Megan. "Why do this?"

"Time," Von Stryker answered directly. "It would take time to isolate the mother. Time to hold her, to interrogate her. And then, even after I got the combination, what would I do with it? The whole village would be watching her bar, the safe. This way," he smiled at Megan, "Ms. Buchanan brings the property to me. Which leads me again to ask: Where is the money?"

"I want control of the hostage first," Barrett said as coldly as he could.

"I don't have time for elaborate exchanges." Von Stryker's finger tightened on the trigger.

"We can be finished in thirty minutes," Barrett replied. "I'll bring the cash to the Whipping Post. You bring the girl."

"Bring the mother, too," Von Stryker smiled.

"What the hell for?"

"Call it insurance." The killer was backing away, now, to give Barrett an alley to the door.

He passed Megan on the way out.

"We're giving him what he wants," Barrett said, as much for the killer's ears as Megan's. "Then you're coming home. Okay?"

"Okay," Megan managed. She wasn't smiling. But just maybe he'd given her a grain of hope.

"Thirty minutes." Von Stryker set his own digital watch. "If you're not back by then," the killer froze Barrett with those pale, cold eyes, "I promise you will not recognize her."

Barrett returned with a satchel of cash and Megan's mother in a little less than twenty-five minutes. The sun was just beginning to set. Esther leaned far out over the bow of her boat as they approached the Whipping Post. Von Stryker's cruiser was moored on the Gulf side of the dock. A catwalk was lowered from the Bayliner's deck to the dock's rotten planks. Barrett could see a Confederate flag now fluttering from the bridge.

"I see him," Esther pointed to the killer, silhouetted against a scarlet sky.

"Bastard isn't taking chances," Barrett throttled back. "He's moved the boat to put the sun in our eyes."

"*Where's Megan?*" Esther bellowed fearlessly as Barrett throttled back.

"Take it easy," Barrett cautioned and pulled her bird-dog to a tiedown on the bay side of the dock.

That's when Bear noticed his trotline. The tide was rising and had buried his bleach-bottle buoys. They strained like trapped corks beneath the water. Von Stryker smiled over his Uzi.

"You need more tether, Mr. Raines."

"Where's Megan?" Esther bellowed again.

"Over. . . . Over here!"

It came from somewhere on the dock. On the killer's side of the dock. Barrett scrambled with Esther out of the boat.

"*Here!*"

"*You bastard!*" Esther plunged into the water.

Von Stryker had tied her daughter to the pier, the bastard, tied her in a jacket of nylon and fishline to a piling below the dock. The tide was already a briny gag at her throat.

"I have a knife." Barrett displayed the sheathed Rapala. "Let me cut her loose."

"When I have my property," Von Stryker declared. "Not a moment before."

"*Give it to him!*" Esther screamed, but Barrett was already back in the boat. He tossed the leather satchel at the Serb's feet.

"Stay put," Von Stryker ordered.

"Let me cut her loose." Barrett was heaving air like a sprinter.

"Not until I've counted my money." Von Stryker plopped the satchel down, and then, as if he had all the time in the world, peeled open a stack of British currency, thumbed through the notes.

"Never did say exactly how you earned that cash." Barrett risked a question.

"You seem to believe it's my destiny to solve your mysteries, Mr. Raines," the Serb smiled over his property. "It isn't."

"BARRETT!" Megan's strangled voice rose from below the dock, the tide clawing at her mouth.

"Christ, man!" Barrett cursed. "There's three hundred and seventy-five thousand pounds. That's it. That's all there is!"

"You don't suppose the village held some back do you?" Von Stryker offered it speculatively. "A small reserve?"

"*That's all there is!*" Esther's voice came booming from below.

"Well," the killer shrugged. "It has been seven years."

Barrett plunged into the water beside Megan and her mother.

"I have a rifle and a scope." The killer snapped his satchel shut. "If you budge from this spot before I am well clear I shall kill you all."

Barrett yanked his blade free and slashed the mess of cords and lines binding Megan's arms and legs.

The sun finally set on Megan's ordeal. The Serb killer could see it all through his sniper scope. There was the mother, right there in the cross hairs, on the delapidated pier, embracing her daughter. Touching scene. And there was the detective, floundering after the women.

Von Stryker thought for a moment he might kill them all. It would not be an easy shot from this moving platform, though he had made more difficult ones.

But it would violate the rules. Von Stryker had always lived by a simple code of behavior. Duress could only be imposed to extract information. A kill had to take place either for payment, or for preservation. The satchel on the bridge reminded the Serb that he had been paid handsomely. And the detective now in his cross hairs was certainly not the main threat to his preservation.

His finger retired suddenly from the trigger. The Coast Guard was the main threat. Even if he killed Raines and the women there would be someone in the village who would contact the authorities. Raines's partner, perhaps, or some other member of the region's Byzantine bureaucracy would at some point be informed of the day's events.

The Coast Guard would be alerted, perhaps already had been notified. The Bayliner, large and luxurious, would be easy to spot, easy to pick up. That's why Von Stryker had rigged the boat for destruction. One of the advantages of renting, he smiled, it greatly reduced the cost of business. The assassin lowered his rifle and scope. A fresh wake arced gently back toward the Whipping Post. The killer punched coordinates into an inertial navigator, engaged an autopilot. An on-board computer beeped compliance.

The explosives were stowed below along with a modest outboard dingy. His plan was to scuttle the Bayliner in a ball of fire, of course, but the Serb bastard had no intention of being on board. He would be miles away, in local garb, just another fisherman touring the coast after the storm. A second passport would transform geologist Von Stryker to Dr. Eric Bergman, a pediatric surgeon returning to Luxembourg. The originating flight had already been booked in Tampa. From Belgium the good doctor would proceed to Belgrade and then, finally, to Saint Stefan Island, a guarded isthmus resort off the coast of what used to be Yugoslavia. He had a reservation at Saint Stefan. He would be welcome.

One of Von Stryker's favorite operas filtered over the intercom. It was *Madame Butterfly*, of course. One of his more enjoyable trophies. He listened a moment. Mirella Freni's unmistakable soprano gave voice to Madame Butterfly's final moments. The American lieutenant had abandoned her, had left her with a half-breed son. The boy played now with an American flag, an undiscerning witness to his mother's suicide. Lieutenant Pinkerton entered the scene (wasn't there a detective named Pinkerton?), but of course the lieutenant was too late. That was a characteristic of Americans, Von Stryker decided. They always came, when they came at all, too late.

Freni's voice soared, even over the intercom. Such strength. Such control. There was a half-moon rising in a crystal sky; Von Stryker could see Venus hanging low to one side, like a brilliant piece of jewelry from a woman's ear. He breathed deeply of the fresh, salty air which swept past the Bayliner's lofty tower. Time to go below. Time to savor his good fortune, briefly, before he had to blow the boat to bits.

Von Stryker set the Bayliner's twin throttles, collected his satchel and climbed down from the bridge. He was looking forward to the music, to the champagne which chilled even now in his galley's fridge. Most of all he looked forward to holding his money in his hands. More than half a million dollars American. After seven years it was a very sweet victory.

The cabin door swung open. Von Stryker had to lower his head to step below. And then he froze.

A visitor waited inside.

Water pooled beside a pair of diver's fins planted incongruously on the Bayliner's cabin floor. The fins led to a wet suit. Up the wet suit was a rifle barrel and up further still was a face set in stone.

The Serb's hand tightened instinctively on his satchel. "You?!"

A single, almost embarrassed moment of suprise preceded the last seconds of Von Stryker's life.

The rifle exploded like a cannon in the cabin's glove-tight interior. A dumbbell slug tore into the killer's stomach the size of a quarter and came out a grapefruit on the other side.

The man who had killed Miles Beynon, Thelma Johnson, and countless others, the man who had tortured Thelma and Miles and Megan and countless others now captured his own entrails with both hands. He crawled, crawled to retrieve the British notes which scattered like rose petals on the cabin's floor.

"You won't need 'em," a voice filtered dimly into the bastard's brain.

A second slug slammed home into a rifle's chamber.

A second explosion rocked the cabin.

A quarter-sized wound could now be seen on the killer's spine. He was splayed like a butterfly face down on the floor. He could not speak. He just lay there shivering. As if he were very cold.

A fist reached down to strip the satchel from Von Stryker's now-feeble hand.

"See you in hell," someone said. Far away.

The satchel disappeared. Von Stryker tried to protest. Seven years he had worked to recover his property! Seven years spent looking for the thief! Why now (after all this time!) had he been levied the biggest surprise of his life?

He would lose his reservation.

Blood gushed from the killer's mouth. The shivering stopped. A pair of fins plopped past eyes that were pale and blue and blind forever.

20.

Homeward Bound

Cricket Bonet didn't wait for daylight to corral Taylor County's sheriff and get both their asses to Dead Man's Bay. The call had come in from Barrett around seven in the evening.

"Need you to contact the Coast Guard officially, Cricket. Over."

"Go ahead," Cricket was scrambling for a pencil.

"I want this vessel stopped. You can't miss it. A thirty-four-foot Bayliner from Fort Walton, the *Easy Money*. She's a rental registered 'FL89789OK.' May have a Confederate flag flying. Last seen headed west and north from here maybe twenty minutes ago. Over."

"Why we stopping her? Over."

"Arresting her skipper," Barrett replied. "For murder."

"Jesus Christ—Is it Brandon Ogilvie?"

"No. You'll find him in the icehouse."

"The *what?*"

"The icehouse, Cricket. Waiting for you to bag him. Over."

"Murder and body bags? What have you been up to, partner?"

"Just get out here, Cricket. Bring the MCU with you.

And bring the sheriff, too. You can tell him it's not an accident."

Cricket arrived within three hours bringing a pair of boats and the harbormaster, a Mobile Crime Unit and team, local deputies, Sheriff Sue, a partridge, and a goddamned pear tree to find his partner lounging beneath a Coleman lantern.

Cricket threw Raines a briefcase.

"Boss is gonna have some questions, Bear."

"I'll have answers."

"You damn well better. Where's the icehouse?"

"Tacked onto the bar," Barrett nodded over his shoulder. "Just ask Esther. She knows everything."

Cricket hauled himself onto the dock. Taylor County's sheriff was next to disembark.

"This better be good."

"No, Sheriff, you better be good. There's a murder and a missing person out here that you haven't done shit to help us investigate. So if you don't start now—Have I got your attention, Sheriff? 'Cause if you don't start cooperating *right* now I am personally going to see to it the governor puts your ass in a sling."

The boy named Sue was suddenly bankrupt for words which gave the boy from Deacon Beach the second-best feeling he'd ever had in his life.

"See if Cricket needs you." Barrett took his lantern. "I'll catch up."

Megan stretched over white, starched sheets on her mother's foldout couch. Esther had closed the vent on her jerry-rigged air-conditioning from the icehouse. Things had cooled since the storm and, besides, she didn't want Megan worried with the smell. The curtains were pulled now to allow a fresh breeze off the bay. Esther had provided extra comfort with a box fan atop a Coke crate so that the room was almost chilly.

Comfort was easier to provide than treatment for her daughter's wounds. Esther wanted to swathe Megan's burns in butter but Barrett had already told her no, that wasn't the best thing. Use ice water, for now, Barrett recommended. Leave everything open to the air. They'd put Megan on the sheriff's boat when he came in, get her to somebody who knew what the hell they were doing. Esther accepted his prescription without question. Megan saw her mother laboring up the stairs, now, squeezing a lemon into a veritable firkin of iced tea.

"Thank you, Mama." She sat up.

"You have a gentleman, callin'." Esther handed Megan her tea.

Barrett Raines hung in the doorway.

"I believe Agent Bonet needs me." Esther's excuse left Barrett alone with her daughter.

Barrett felt suddenly uneasy, awkward.

"Feeling all right?" he led off. "Stupid question, I guess."

"It's okay." Megan pulled a pillow high over her chest. "Legs hurt some."

"They're still good-looking legs, Megan. They'll heal."

"I know. Thank you."

He stalled.

"I . . . I was pretty damn mad at you, Megan."

"I know."

"I thought you were coming on to me just to mislead me. You know. Keep me from your mama. Away from the money."

"I was at first," she spoke up boldly. "But things changed. Remember Louise's baby? I couldn't have planned that."

"No," Barrett admitted. "How about . . . the other time? The Springs?"

"That was for me." Megan bit her lip before going on. "I wish you could believe that."

He came to the couch, cupped her hand in his hands.

"I can believe it," he said and kissed her once, gently.

"Leaving pretty quick?" Megan knew he had to.

"Pretty quick," Barrett acknowledged. "How about you?"

"No," she shook her head. "I love this place, Bear. It's my whole life."

"Yes, it is," Barrett nodded. "And it's a whole lotta life to love."

He kissed her again, on the forehead this time. He smoothed her short, thick hair, and rose from her jerry-rigged bed.

"It was wonderful making love with you," she said as he was leaving.

He paused beside her screenless window.

"Must have been the evening star."

21.

Here, Kitty, Kitty, Kitty

Cricket and Barrett watched as the FDLE's forensics team conducted an initial examination and description of the man who was for the time being still officially recognized as Ray Boatwright. Ray's mutilated corpse stretched out right alongside a table weighted with other evidence in Ziploc bags, most of it secured from the dead man's trailer. It had taken all night to grid off the trailer and surrounding area. They wouldn't get to the Whipping Post till morning. Ray had been examined inside the icehouse, as close to a morgue as one could have reasonably hoped. A thousand flashbulbs from the Crime Unit's photographer left Barrett with a headache. The initial work finally completed, the diver's body was prepared for transport to Doc Thorpe's Den of Medieval Inquiry.

Sheriff Sue worked a cud of Redman.

"You say the whole village was involved in this thing?"

"More or less," Barrett affirmed. "They took care of Brandon Ogilvie. He took care of them."

"You bringin' charges?" the sheriff spit.

"What for—Obstruction of justice? Seems kind of chickenshit, doesn't it, Sheriff?" Barrett nodded to the body bag. "Compared to this?"

"Just checkin' your druthers," the sheriff replied and Barrett could hear relief in his voice.

"Got something does bother me a little," Barrett said casually.

"Yes, sir." The sheriff seemed open.

Barrett pointed to the table weighted with Ziploc bags.

"There's something missing," Barrett informed the lawman. "A wet suit and fins. I brought 'em in myself."

"It's in some fisherman's boat, now," the sheriff shook his head. "Those damn things are expensive."

"Goddammit, Sheriff, how're we going to find the bastard who killed this man if we piss away the evidence?"

"No need." Cricket Bonet had just left one of Sue's deputies to come striding over.

"What you got?" Barrett could see the bounce in Bonet's step.

"We got lucky," Cricket grinned. "Coast Guard's located Stryker's boat. It's scattered over the whole damn Gulf, Bear. Guard says it looks like an on board explosion."

"They got a body?" Barrett asked.

"No way," Cricket shook his head. "I'm tellin' you, pard, there ain't nuthin' out there but toothpicks. That bastard's feedin' the fish."

"Small justice." Barrett felt suddenly very weary.

"Got that other stuff, too." Cricket whipped out his briefcase. "On the locals—that stuff you wanted? You want it now?"

"Sure. Why not."

"Okay." Cricket moved to place some light over his shoulder. "Here we are. Sarah Lynn Folsom. No insurance coverage at all. Never has had."

"That fits." Barrett gave his partner a thumbs-up.

"Ray Boatwright did, though," Cricket went on. "A group-rate policy. Came through Marine Drilling. Policy was cancelled, though. Too high a risk. Some kind of respiratory problem."

"That fits, too," Barrett nodded. "Guy smoked like a chimney."

"No, he didn't." Cricket was shaking his head.

"I can show you," Barrett said.

"Be glad to take a look." Cricket shuffled through a folder. "But I've got his medicals, right here. I even got the appeal on his policy."

Cricket gave the folder to his partner.

"Ray's problems came from diving, not smoking. Fact is—Ray Boatwright never smoked in his life."

The sun rose over Dead Man's Bay to find Barrett packing his meager overnight on the preacher's back porch. It was time to leave. FDLE's Mobile Unit had finished most of its work. Everything was bagged, photographed, and mapped out. Nothing to do for now but pack and go. Barrett's biggest remaining challenge was to decide if those socks wadded up on the cot belonged to him or to Preacher O'Steen.

There was a gauze of doubt which slowed Barrett's decision, which delayed his departure, a nagging sense that something needed putting to bed. Cricket's revelation regarding Ray Boatwright's smoking habits was an irritant. It didn't mean that Ray wasn't Brandon Ogilvie. All we ever knew about Brandon came from Miles, Barrett was telling himself. Redheads and Camel cigarettes—maybe Miles was supposed to say that to throw us off, to put us off track.

It sure hadn't thrown Von Stryker. Miles Beynon must have admitted under the Serb's torture that his partner had taken a new name and was hiding in Dead Man's Bay. Von Stryker came to the bay knowing, surely, that Ray Boatwright was actually Brandon Ogilvie.

But what Miles didn't know, Barrett guessed, was that Esther Buchanan never trusted Brandon Ogilvie with her massive safe's combination. That being the case, Brandon Ogilvie, also known as Ray Boatwright, could not tell the butcher everything he needed to know to retrieve his property—and for that the diver was tortured to death.

But what about that business with the cigarettes?

Loose ends. Barrett shook himself like a hound. Forget it. There was only so much you could do.

Barrett had about decided the socks he just stuffed into his overnight bag actually belonged to O'Steen when something inside the shanty drew his attention. It was a sound which drew Barrett from the porch into Preacher O'Steen's one remaining room, a scratching sound, irritating, like somebody dragging their nails across a blackboard. Except it wasn't a somebody and it wasn't a blackboard.

It was Preacher's cat clawing the outside of the old man's closet door. Something inside the closet was tempting Preacher's cat, was driving her nuts, in fact. What was it? Catnip? A rat? Barrett decided walking toward the offending closet that curiosity was definitely not confined to cats.

"Here, kitty, kitty, kitty."

The cat practically growled at Barrett's approach.

Barrett was grinning as he reached the closet. A single, rusted hook secured the door; Bear snapped it free. The cat pounced inside to a puddle of water pooled on the floor. Barely a saucer's worth of drippings there in that small puddle, but the kitty licked the leavings voraciously. Barrett knelt to carefully poach a sample.

"Saltwater," he remarked rolling the brine on his tongue.

Saltwater? Hell, it could have come from anywhere. Fishing. Swimming. Anything.

Barrett left the cat to her habits and was returning to that problem with his socks when something stopped him. Raines paused to take a three-sixty around the room. One room, perfectly open. No place to hide anything. The closet was open. There were no chests or drawers. The only thing left was the silk-skirted bed.

The bed.

Barrett dropped his overnight like a lead weight. He moved like a sleepwalker to O'Steen's skirted bed. He ripped a thin blanket free, then the mattress. A rusted set of bedsprings remained.

Barrett yanked the springs off their frame. A swarm of roaches scurried from underneath. But something else remained, a single, solitary something which littered the floor beneath the preacher's bed. Barrett leaned over the bed frame to pick up an old, wadded, cellophane package. It was a cigarette package.

Camels. Unfiltered.

Barrett's search ended where it began. A wrecked hull and a rude church were sanctuary for an altar, Esther Buchanan, and one other. He was a vigorous man, mid-aged. A righteous man and a thief. A clone for Ernest Hemingway.

"That's it, Brandon," Barrett's handgun was trained and steady on Brandon Ogilvie's chest.

The "Preacher" dropped his ancient 30.30 carbine beside a wet suit, a pair of fins, and a stack of British currency.

"I suppose that's Von Stryker's money." Barrett stepped inside.

"It was," Brandon Ogilvie nodded.

"Then it was you killed him?"

"I certainly did." The stubbled face showed no remorse. "I sunk his boat, too. He made that part easy."

"Well, I'll be damned." Barrett looked at Esther. The early morning sun caught her hair, flaming red all the way to her Irish roots.

"So you've jerked me around again."

"Not hard enough apparently," Ogilvie answered for Megan's mother.

"That nice little story about you finding Esther on the Whipping Post. You seeing her kill her husband—that's all crap, isn't it?"

"It's not crap, no. It's true," Ogilvie replied steady as a rock.

"Well, then who the hell was Ray Boatwright?"

"No more than he appeared to be," Ogilvie shrugged. "A black-marketer. A courier. Someone to fetch dollars for pounds once every three months."

"We didn't tell him about Brandon," Esther explained. "Nor any of the rest. Just in case . . ."

"In case he got caught," Barrett finished for her.

"He was like Miles." Ogilvie spread his arms. "Or me. He wasn't the best of men, but—nobody deserves to die like that."

"We're agreed there." Barrett holstered his weapon. "Is there anyone else on the bay who *doesn't* know you're Brandon Ogilvie?"

"Talmadge Lawson didn't know," Ogilvie replied. "Most everyone else, though, they know. They pretty much have to know. Except Megan."

Barrett paused a moment.

"Megan doesn't know you're Brandon Ogilvie?"

"She knows me as Preacher O'Steen. That's all."

"But I found your cigarettes at Convict Springs." Barrett was stubborn. "She had to know you were there with Miles."

"You got it half-right," Ogilvie smiled. "Megan knows I have a house at the Springs. But Miles Beynon never set

foot in the place. I didn't want him to see me, you understand. I didn't want him to know I was Preacher O'Steen,
or exactly where I lived so whenever Miles came to collect
his share of the cash, I'd hide away at the Springs."

"And leave Esther to give Miles his money?"

"That's right," Esther spoke up. "Now, I don't doubt
Miles had suspicions that Brandon was near about. He
didn't know anything about the Spring house, though. Of
that I'm certain."

"But Megan told me Miles used the place," Barrett persisted. "She told me that was where he stayed when he
came fishing. Why would Megan do that? Why lie?"

"Because she wanted you alone." Esther pointed out
what should have been obvious. "And she needed a reason
for you to come."

That was it. He felt relief, for Megan, for himself. And
he was glad, very glad to have tied up those nagging, loose
ends. But he wasn't finished. Justice had not yet been
served.

"You damn near got away with it." Barrett nodded to the
small fortune stacked on the altar.

"Damn near's not good enough," Ogilvie declared.
"What's next for you, Officer Raines?"

"For me?"

"It's all in your hands, isn't it?" Esther clung to Brandon's arm and Barrett wondered how he could not have
seen long ago that these two were lovers.

"You've got the money," Esther went on. "The man.
You've solved your mystery. Now—What'll you do?"

Barrett Raines and Cricket Bonet left Dead Man's Bay
later that morning with the harbormaster, the sheriff, and
a body bag stretched on a bed of ice. A second boat alongside was filled with evidence and FDLE investigators.

"Gotta hand it to you, Barrett," Cricket said once they

were on the water. "You busted this one on your own, you really did."

"Thanks." Barrett accepted the compliment simply. No comeback this time. No sarcasm.

They arrived at Harold's Marina to find an ambulance and Captain Henry Altmiller waiting.

"I send you two out for a simple investigation and next thing I know I'm getting calls from the Coast Guard."

Cricket grinned. "We made the case, Cap'n."

"Where's the money?"

Cricket deferred to his partner. Barrett faced his boss squarely.

"We couldn't recover it, sir. Everything Ogilvie and Beynon stole from that car is gone. It's on the bottom of the Gulf."

Altmiller shrugged. The money wasn't what he wanted most.

"What about Brandon Ogilvie?"

"We've got him," Cricket spoke up.

"Where?" Altmiller asked.

A litter trundled past them headed toward the waiting ambulance. Barrett nodded to the body bag strapped on top.

"Right there, Captain."

A pair of medics helped load the body into the ambulance.

"Are you telling me the Serb killed Brandon Ogilvie?"

"Locals knew him as Ray Boatwright, sir," Cricket filled in helpfully.

"And Stryker did kill him," Barrett confirmed. "Just like the others."

There was a pause while Altmiller thought it over.

"Sooo . . . You lost the money. And you lost the man?"

"Looks that way," Barrett affirmed with his usual cheer.

"Then what the hell are you grinning about?" Altmiller demanded.

"I've been gone seven days, right, Captain? Seven whole days. And I haven't had a single smoke."

Barrett didn't give his captain a chance to reply. He hefted his overnight over a sunburned shoulder, winked to his partner, and headed for their Crown Vic sedan.

Epilogue

Barrett stumbled in exhausted to his empty two-
storey home to find a message waiting on the
machine. It was Laura Anne.

"I want you at the restaurant." Her voice was tin-thin on
the tape. "No excuses. No debates. Just get out here—but
not before eight."

Barrett wondered if she was reconsidering that question of alimony. Nonetheless, Bear made the long drive
out to Pier's End with more peace of mind than he could
remember having had in a long time. No danger of getting there before eight, Barrett didn't use his watch anymore. He rolled the window down, sampled the humidity
in the air, the breeze, checked the sun.

He'd be there around half past.

Eight-thirty was prime-time at Laura Anne's restaurant.
Barrett arrived to find Roy minding the door.

"Laura Anne need to see me, Roy?"

"Yes, sir. She asked if you could meet her on the pier."

The pier? That didn't sound like good news. That
sounded like private talk.

But Barrett strolled out there anyway. Something new,
azaleas lined in boxes along the railing. Oughta bloom

nice this spring. Barrett tested the soil briefly. Too much water. He'd mention it.

There was not a soul on the pier this evening which was very unusual. Normally people would take their drinks and listen to the waves or neck or listen to the vibrant chords of the baby grand which even now offered some concerto to soothe the sea.

It was a blustery evening. Barrett loosened the collar he'd actually remembered to bleach. Only a week had passed but newly worked muscle rippled beneath the dark skin which showed nicely against his perennially white shirt. He'd dropped some weight, too, ten pounds from a frame that wasn't soft to begin with.

It was nice to feel this way, Barrett decided. A little sunburned. A little hungry. It was nice to have broken a case, too. Even nicer to end it the way that he had. Barrett never had really believed that justice was blind. Just nearsighted. He felt a little like Longfellow's blacksmith, "Something attempted, something done . . ." Something like that. Barrett leaned onto the railing.

That's when he saw Laura Anne.

A gust of Gulf wind hiked a gossamer-thin skirt high over well-toned legs which ran straight to a solid half-moon of ass. Cotton-white panties winked briefly. Laura Anne Raines settled her skirt, smiling broadly to Barrett from beneath a floppy, white hat.

"Did I get it right?"

Barrett couldn't reply. He couldn't move. He was stunned. He was frozen. He was ecstatic.

"You look great, Bear."

"You don't know the half of it!"

Barrett's legs seemed weak beneath him. But he kept them moving.

"God, baby!!"

He reached her, finally, threw her floppy hat into the

wind. It soared like a kite off the edge of the pier. Her hair caught the breeze silk-soft and raven black. They kissed, Barrett and Laura Anne, long and hard and the Bear knew he had found his lover, his friend, his wife, and maybe, once more, a whole life as well.